A Trip Towards THE Sunset

A Trip Towards the Sunset

TATIANA GODED

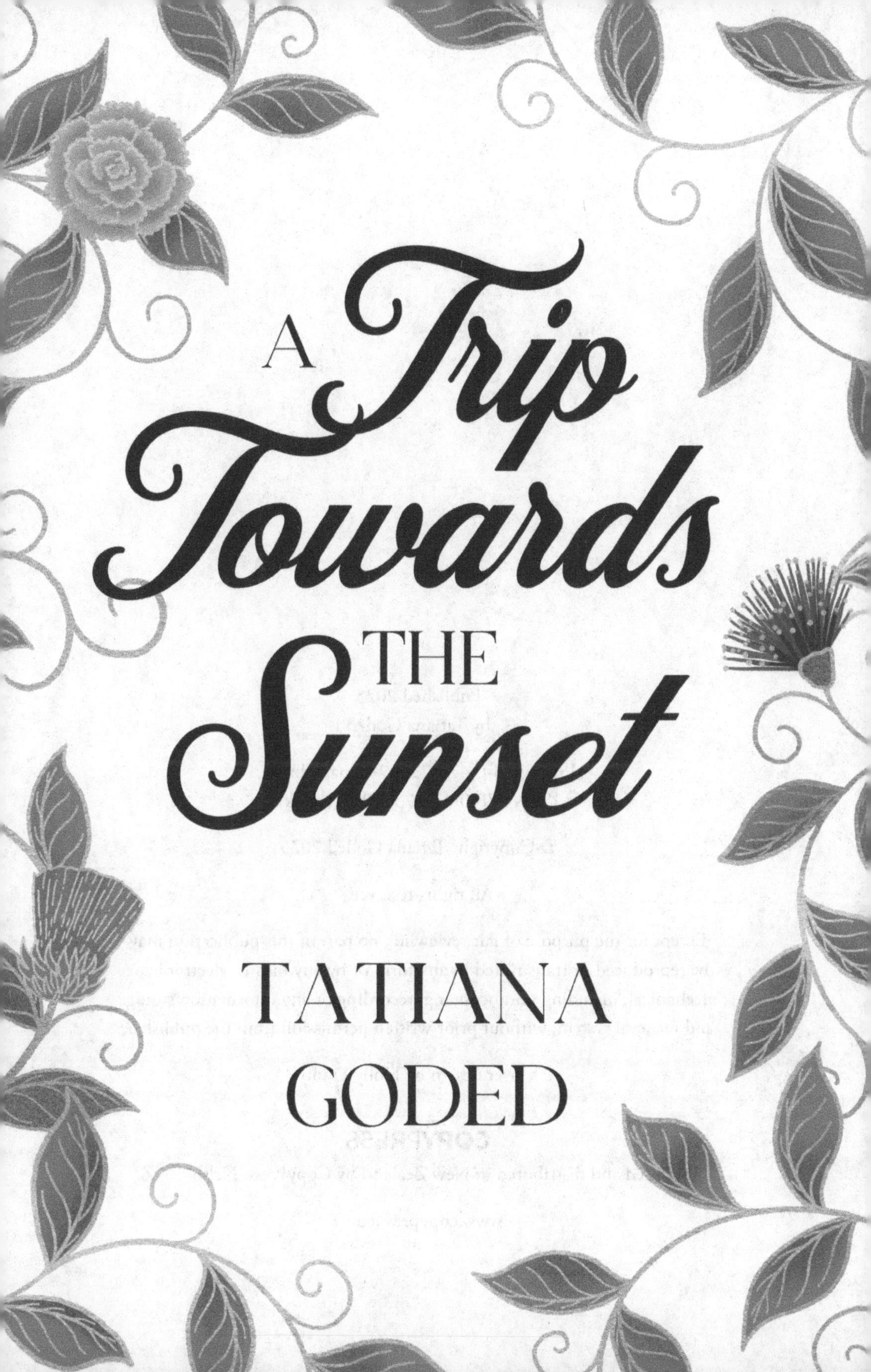

Published 2025
by Tatiana Goded

ISBN 978-0-473-73409-1 (paperback)
ISBN 978-0-473-73410-7 (ebook)

© Copyright Tatiana Goded 2025

Cover design by Holly Dunn

COPYPRESS

Designed and distributed in New Zealand by CopyPress, Nelson, NZ.

www.copypress.co.nz

*To my daughter Katrin, whose kindness, passion and
joy inspires me every day. Your mum will always follow
her dreams without giving up, no matter what others
say, and with the hope that you will always follow your
inner wisdom in every step of your life. I love you!*

*And to the countries in my book:
Spain, my country of birth, which I've learned
to appreciate and miss with time;
New Zealand, the beautiful country
I am proud to call home;
Germany and Austria, very dear to me, where I've
spent many happy holidays in my childhood;
and Scotland, the country of my heart, which, for
some magical reason, always feels like home.*

*This book is for the ones who feel lost in life, the
ones that find the courage to rediscover themselves,
recover their long-forgotten dreams, follow their
inner wisdom and reinvent themselves.*

*It's for the ones who live between two worlds
and don't know where they belong anymore,
eternally feeling in "no-man land".*

*And for the ones who, like me, are part of the two groups.
For them to know that there is light at the other end, and
life can be as bright and full of joy as you allow it to be.*

Foreword

Cora

*Tōtaranui Beach, Abel Tasman National
Park, New Zealand, January 2000*

It was a warm and bright summer morning when Cora walked towards the beach. The campground was quiet, her bare feet barely making sounds in the thick lawn. Wearing a red swimsuit and wrapped in her towel, she passed by a family-sized tent surrounded by bikes and tricycles, strong snoring coming from inside. She crossed the sandy road and there it was: the dark blue sea, calm and inviting. It made her feel at peace, as if everything was good in her life. It was her favourite part of the day, when the beach was almost empty. She could see a woman with a large dog in the distance, a man fishing nearby.

Cora left her towel on the sand and approached the water. Today would be a hot day. The cold water made her shiver. She walked towards the sea, splashing water on her body. Then she started swimming, enjoying every moment. She felt free, as if the knot in her stomach had disappeared. She turned on her back and formed a starfish shape, letting herself be dragged by the sea. She loved to do this as a child; replicating the stars in the sky. With a smile, she closed her eyes and let herself go.

—

Sometime later, Cora noticed other people swimming near her. She got out of the water and sat on the beach, wrapped in her towel. She scooped some sand into her hand. The beach went on forever, the bright orange sand shining in the sun. She had never seen such a beautiful beach. She couldn't believe her life had brought her to such a place, all the way from Spain. She thought of her friend Irene, who loved the sea. She was in Germany now, about to have her first baby. Cora decided she would take a photo later and send it to her. She missed Irene, with her calm company and kind eyes.

Cora and Nick had travelled to Golden Bay a few days previously. They had walked along long golden beaches full of free spirits playing guitars and singing songs. She loved the mix of sea and mountains, beach and bush walks. They had needed some time away from Wellington. In just a few days, this place had conquered her heart.

One day I will come back and live here, she thought, surprised at her own determination. It wasn't only the beauty of the place. The peaceful atmosphere attracted her as well. Even though summers could get quite busy, you could simply avoid certain places: the crowded campground in Pohara, Tākaka's main street in the weekends, the tour trips to Farewell Spit. Despite this, she was surprised when they went to Wharariki Beach. With its endless sand dunes and iconic arches, it was a magical place. She had walked along the beach with Nick, his eternal smile on his face. The beach hadn't felt crowded, despite the number of families and kids there.

She had come to New Zealand a year before, looking for a change. She had found a nice job in a bookshop in Petone, near Wellington. Although it was sometimes busy, especially near Christmas, she loved her job. And then she had met Nick, a Kiwi from Napier, and they had fallen in love. They had travelled around the country. She liked the volcanic area in the middle of the North Island, around the town of Taupō. But the South Island was special. Wild and unspoilt, it was like finding paradise. Coming from the crowded Spanish city of Madrid, she couldn't believe such vast spaces of pure nature could still exist in the world.

But none of them had felt like this magical area on the tip of the South Island.

~

'It's beautiful, isn't it?' A middle-aged woman with long blonde hair and blue eyes was smiling at her. She wore a green swimsuit.

'Yes, it is,' Cora replied.

'May I sit with you?' the woman asked.

'Of course,' Cora said.

'I like to come to the beach early in the morning, when there's nobody around,' the woman said, smiling at Cora. 'By the way, my name's Susan.' She offered her hand, which Cora shook.

'I am Cora. And yes, it is special to be alone, looking at the sea.'

'It makes me feel small,' Susan said. 'Like, for a sacred half an hour, all my problems don't exist.'

'Yes. Like everything is possible again.'

'May I ask where you are from?'

'Madrid, in Spain.'

'That's very far away.'

'Yes, the farthest away that there is.'

'Was it on purpose?' Susan asked, a slight smile on her face.

Cora looked at her. 'That is an interesting question.' She picked up some sand. It sparkled in tones of red, orange and gold. She looked at Susan. 'I was desperate to move somewhere else and start over again. I could have gone somewhere closer to home, I guess. But New Zealand sounded exotic to me, full of adventures, full of new hope. And I also

3

needed to put some distance between me and my previous life and where I grew up. I felt suffocated.' Cora thought how weird it was that she was able to tell all this to a total stranger, but was unable to express her feelings to her family.

'That makes sense,' Susan said. 'And I totally relate to that. I sometimes wish I was far away, living a different life.' She looked at the sea, as if the horizon had all the answers.

'Why don't you do it?'

Susan looked at her. 'Well, you see, I have a husband and four children, plus a demanding job to pay for the mortgage and all the things we're supposed to want to have.' Her face was crumpled. 'And somehow, I didn't want any of it.' She looked at Cora. 'Doesn't this sound awful? I love my children to pieces. It's just that sometimes I wish my life was easier.'

'Yes. It is hard. But I am sure you will find your way. Even as a mother. There is always a way to happiness. And sometimes it starts with easy things.'

'Like what?'

'For example, what things do you like to do?'

Susan's eyes sparkled. 'Dance. I've always loved to do twirls as a little girl, and I'm always watching dancing shows. Ballet. Scottish country dancing. Tap.'

'There you go. Have you looked for dancing lessons near where you live? I am sure you can arrange babysitting. Either your husband, a relative or a friend can stay with your kids for an hour a week.'

Susan's face lit up. Her cheeks turned red and her eyes were bright. 'Yes. I guess I can do that,' she said.

'Mama!' A little boy was running towards them, a bucket and spade in his hands. 'Can you help me build a castle?' he said when he had reached them, his little hand pulling at Susan.

'Yes, darling,' she said. She looked at Cora. 'I need to go now. Thank you so much.'

'My pleasure,' Cora replied.

Susan stood up, dragged by her son. She turned around. 'You have a gift, you know? You see through people.' She ran off, dragged by her son.

Cora looked at them, mother and son running towards a moment of fun. Her friend Irene had always said that about her. How she had a gift for helping people. She missed Irene. Her serene presence. After a year in New Zealand, she still hadn't been able to make good friends.

She had always loved books, ever since her dad had started reading to her at night. As a teenager, she had attempted to write her first mystery book. She and her sister Sofia, five years younger, had spent endless nights making up the plot. Once they were happy with that, they started deciding what they would say in each chapter. It had become increasingly difficult, and they had only managed to write the first three chapters. But the excitement had stayed with her. She knew she needed to do something about it. She had heard about some writing courses online. After a year at the bookshop, she felt there was something else she needed. Something entirely for her.

She looked around. This was becoming her favourite place in New Zealand. There was something she loved about the Kiwis. How they could approach life in such an easy-going way, without all the worries about the future that people had where she grew up. Their independence. And especially, their kindness. How even kids would raise their hand to thank a driver stopping at a pedestrian crossing. How you could have a nice chat with the woman at the counter. She felt as if human interaction still mattered here.

She thought about the question Susan had asked. Had it been on purpose that she had moved so far away? Maybe. Maybe the distance, the cultural differences and the kindness were like a healing balm for her uneasiness and restlessness in Madrid. She had studied history. She had loved it, but the career options were limited. And she needed something else. She had the urge to explore. And one day, sitting at the deck at her parents', her dad had sat with her. 'You are restless, dear girl,' he had said. 'I know the signs. I think it's time for you to explore the vast world, see its beauty, find yourself again.' And that had been it. A month later, at twenty-seven, with a suitcase in her hand, she was saying goodbye to the life she knew.

She looked around. The waves were bigger now, inviting. The sun was warming up her arms. It was time to wake Nick and start their day.

One day I will live here and spend the rest of my life writing, she thought, surprised at her certainty. She took a deep sigh, stood up and turned towards the campground.

CHAPTER 1

Fear of Freedom

Cora

Petone, Lower Hutt, New Zealand, October 2019

Cora was walking barefoot, her shoes in her hands, skipping over the multiple pieces of driftwood left by a tired sea bringing debris from the nearby mouth of the Hutt River.

She loved walking along the beach on her own, dogs and their owners passing by every now and then. On a weekend it would be full of people, children playing in the sand, families having a picnic even on crazy windy days. After having lived in New Zealand for more than two decades, it still surprised her to see the determination and endurance of Kiwis who, no matter what the weather was like, would be out and about. She could still remember watching open-mouthed as a group of what looked like sixty-year-olds ran past her on one of Wellington's stormy September days. She was sure none of them would be sick the next day. Unlike her, who would catch a cold if she got wet or was out in the wind for too long. She envied these resilient and self-sufficient people who were able to enjoy the outdoors no matter what, and to make themselves what they needed without asking for help, from fixing the roof to building a deck.

A woman with short grey hair passed by, smiling at Cora, a golden retriever following, sniffing the driftwood with interest. Cora looked back at them, a smile on her face. She missed dogs. For years her daughter Alex had asked for one. But living in a rental, it was out of the question. Cats might have been accepted. Dogs, never.

Alex's news, despite being expected, had shaken her to the core. Her daughter would finish high school in two months, then move to Dunedin in the next year to study vet nursing at Otago Polytechnic. Cora had known Alex would choose something like that, of course. Her daughter loved animals and had been healing them since she was little, with great gentleness and care. But Cora hadn't been prepared to see her daughter leave. Yes, she had known the empty nest was around the corner, but the truth of it hit her hard. What was she going to do now? She had settled in this town, trying to give stability to Alex while keeping her close to her dad, who lived in Wellington. It had worked for her daughter. She had grown up to be a mature and happy teenager, sure of herself. Cora was so proud of her.

She knew it was time for a big change in her life. Although she still loved her job in the bookshop, she needed something else. Time to go for walks along the beach, to do day tramps, to finish her never-ending novel. And she needed to be closer to nature. Lower Hutt was becoming too crowded for her. Now there was no need for her to stay. She missed the South Island. Wild, largely unpopulated, full of big rivers and snow-capped mountains. Maybe she should book a bach for the Christmas holidays. Maybe Alex would like to come too.

She looked at the sea. Somes Island in the middle of the bay. A quarantine facility when the first European settlers arrived, it was now a nature reserve managed by the Department of Conservation. She had been there many times with Alex, walking around, enjoying the view of the bay, watching the skinks and parakeets, Alex jumping through the war bunkers that (thank goodness) had never been used. To her left, the small suburb of Eastbourne, full of painters and lovely cafés. Next to it, Days Bay, where Alex had learnt how to swim. Next to the wharf where you caught the ferry to Wellington and Somes Island, with shallow waters and small waves, it had been the perfect haven for a small girl. But it had somehow grown too small. She couldn't remember the last time they had been there.

Further away, the iconic lighthouses of Pencarrow Head, one near the water and the other above it on a hill, whose path they had cycled so many times. They always enjoyed the ride there but struggled against the wind on the way back. No matter how nice the weather was, the wind had always been challenging. She remembered the time when Alex was six and they had ended up walking back, pushing their bikes, folded in half to avoid the force of the wind.

The high buildings along Wellington Harbour peaked out from behind Somes Island, the ship-shaped building of Te Papa Museum sticking out. She had loved walking along the waterfront and beyond, even cycling all the way along Evans Bay towards the airport. Too many memories caught her: having an ice cream in Island Bay with Alex, her friend Martha and her son Jonas, when the kids were three and inseparable, before they moved back to Germany. How many friends she'd met over the years who'd come and gone. The majority of the people from overseas had only stayed for a few years then moved back to be closer to their families. And she had felt friendships would evolve, then leave and break her heart a little.

The driftwood had reached the water now. It was difficult to walk past it. Cora looked up. The sun was much higher and there were more people around. It was time to turn around and head home.

———

An hour later, Cora was sitting at her desk, a cup of tea next to her computer. A light rain was tapping on her window. She took a piece of paper and a pen and started writing.

Dear Alex, my girl,

A few days ago you told me that you'll soon move to Dunedin to go to university. It's the right move for you, darling. I am so proud of you! You will find your independence, your truth, fly away from your mum's protective nest and make a life of your own.

I am seeing you taking a step out of the door, smiling and crying at the same time. Pure joy. Sadness at watching the time fly. It was not so long ago that you were eight years old and correcting my English, learning how to sail in a dinghy. Or ten years old and winning the literature contest with Tennyson's Lady of Shalott, after having watched Anne of Green Gables way too often. Or fifteen months old taking your first steps, your dad's face full of pride. It all happened a minute ago.

I am sad, yes. But that is normal. Sad to see you leave while I stay behind, nobody to take care of. There were a few things I would have liked to say to you, and somehow it feels too late. So instead, I am writing these words for you, hoping that one day they will make sense and you will smile at your old and nostalgic mum who only wants the best for you.

Before I leave this world, I would like to have shown you the power of unconditional love, of being filled with profound love beyond all barriers, a pink mantle around you protecting you from any harm.

Before I leave this world, I'd like to see how you make your own choices, no matter what others say, or how crazy they look. I'd like to see you following your instincts, opening your arms to your own truth and goodness.

I'd like to see you spreading your wings and flying towards your sunset, to your own version of the beauty in this world. Don't do anything because you should, or because others expect it from you. Never. Never start anything until you are ready. Take on new challenges, meet new people, travel around the world. But always

come back to your own home, your heart, the only true place of
safety and protection.

I love you, my dear girl. You will always be my girl, no matter
how grown up you are, no matter how far apart we are.
You will always be in my heart.
Mum

She signed the letter, tears pouring down her cheeks. She looked out the window. It had stopped raining. She took her coat, put on her shoes and went for a walk to the track behind her house. The steep, muddy path was deserted. It was quiet and it smelt of freshness and new beginnings. After a while she stopped to see the view. Large warehouses next to the Wellington Harbour in Petone. Hundreds of houses next to each other. How she could have lived there for so long, she just didn't know. She needed more space. She needed nature, space to breathe, to rest and be. An image came to her. Vast golden beaches and snow-capped peaks. Golden Bay. It had always been in her mind, like a dream that might never come true. Maybe it was time for her to go there, rent a bach for a few months and find a small house. She closed her eyes. She could see herself reopening her life coaching business following an unsuccessful start years ago. She would finish that novel. She felt her face warming up with the sun. And then she smiled.

A few days later Cora was walking up the Belmont Trig Track with her friend Angelica. Puffing up the steep slope, she stopped to clean the sweat on her forehead with a cloth. She loved this walk. A middle-aged man on a mountain bike passed them. She was amazed at how he could manage up the hill without needing to stop and push the bike. She definitely would need to do that after the first ten metres.

'The day I can do that, I will have become a heroine,' Angelica said. Wearing short black leggings and a pink t-shirt, she was approaching the walk as if she were conquering Mt Everest.

They had met one day at a café in Petone. Cora had become accustomed to having a hot chocolate mid-morning on Sundays, when Alex was spending the weekend with her father. She liked to just sit and watch people around her. She used to take a small notebook and write whatever came to her mind, most of them short pieces. She loved reading them and remembering her mood from that day.

One day Angelica was sitting at the next table, reading the local magazine with the cultural events in the area. A large family arrived and there was no room for them, so Cora and Angelica agreed to share a table. It was an immediate connection. They found that they both liked going to the movies, and by the end of that day they had arranged to meet again. Since then they had seen each other almost every week: for a coffee, to watch a film, to go for a walk and occasionally for dinner. Angelica was funny and full of light, always finding positive ways to look at life. With a German father and a Kiwi mother, she had a great combination of European and New Zealand points of view. Cora felt understood as a foreigner, and also learnt quite a few things from Angelica about adapting to her new country, including improving her Kiwi pronunciation.

'So, what are your plans now that Alex is heading to university?' Angelica asked. 'Is it time for you to move on?'

Cora looked at her friend, smiling. 'Oh, Angelica. You know me well. Yes. I've felt quite stuck here for a while. I think it's time for me to change scenery. Although, I don't know where to start.' She somehow wasn't ready to tell her about Golden Bay. It still felt surreal. She needed to test it first. Besides, she wanted to keep her dream for herself for a little longer.

'Well, it's a natural move for you. You seem to have been waiting for some time, and now it's your opportunity.'

'Yes. But I'll take it slowly, travel around the South Island for a while until I find out where I would like to be.'

'Yes. That sounds lovely. I should be brave and do something like that too. But I don't have the guts.'

'I think you enjoy your life here and you don't want to get out of your comfort zone,' Cora said. 'You have found a way to live happily here. So why move?'

'Yes, I guess you're right,' Angelica had stopped to drink some water and catch her breath. She turned away from Cora, looking towards the valley below.

'What is it? Are you OK?'

'Yes, I…' Angelica turned around to face her friend. 'I know this is the right step for you, Cora. But I'll miss you.'

'Me too.' Cora embraced her friend, smelling her lavender perfume.

They pulled away, steadied themselves and continued climbing.

'Despite this being the country I was born in, I feel like I'm missing out on something,' Angelica said. 'As if real life is going on somewhere else.'

'Yes. I understand what you mean. When I left Europe I had the feeling that I had left my first version of me over there and started a new Cora here.' She had found this painful. Reconciling the two versions of herself into one whole person was the task of a lifetime. She wondered if she would ever achieve it. 'And when I go back for visits, that Cora comes back. And sometimes she feels more real than this one.'

'Yes. That's somehow how I feel too. Although I'm from here, when I visit Germany it feels like somewhere in the air there is a soulmate walking with me, asking me to be friends. I wonder if other Kiwis with mixed origins feel the same.'

'That would be something for you to find out one day, Angelica.'

'Yes.' Angelica was silent for a while. 'Maybe I need to travel for some time. I always wanted to take six months off work and travel. Finally visit Vietnam. Go to Norway and see the Northern lights. Cross a desert in Africa.'

Cora stopped and looked at her friend with a smile on her face.

'Angelica, if this is what you want, you should go ahead and do it.'

'But…'

'Yes. I know you will have a full list of "buts", with all the logical explanations of why this idea doesn't make sense and how difficult it is. But if there's something I've learnt through the years, it's to follow your inner voice. Whatever it's trying to tell you, listen. Instead of fighting it, just follow it and figure out how you can do it.'

Angelica looked at Cora, a frown on her face.

'I've had this thought hanging around my head for some time, and I've been ignoring it. But now that you're leaving, it seems the right moment for me. I know I can find a path. I have some extra annual leave at the museum, and I'm sure the Director can give me some unpaid leave. Unlike you, I have no dependent family members. So I can just pack a bag and get on a plane.' Her face was lit up now, as if shining from within.

'That's the spirit!'

Angelica was smiling, and sped up the last part of the hill. Cora followed her at a slower pace. As usual, the wind was blowing up the top. They would need to have a quick lunch and turn back before getting too cold. Cora gasped. The whole harbour opened in front of them, Somes Island a constant presence in the middle of the bay. With the high-rise buildings of Wellington on the right, the coast of Eastbourne and the two lighthouses of Pencarrow Head on their left, it looked like two hands opening up to the deep blue sea of the Cook Strait at the far end.

Angelica approached her with sparkles in her eyes. She embraced Cora.

'We've made it,' she said.

'Yes,' Cora replied with a smile.

CHAPTER 2

Encounter in the Mountains

Cora

Nelson Lakes, New Zealand, February 2020

Cora opened her eyes. It was dark. All she could hear was the loud snoring at the end of the room. Warm inside her sleeping bag, she tried to recall the events of the previous day. A wave of deep pain started forming on her chest, like needles pinching her all over. She closed her eyes and took three deep breaths. The wave was still there, but it somehow had stilled, waiting to decide if it should continue at top speed or disappear.

She could now remember the rumble of thunder, and how the Earth had turned white with every lightning strike. She remembered slippery rocks and strange shadows everywhere as she was trying to reach the hut. Her fifteen-kilogram pack had felt like a chain. At one point she even thought she would need to leave all her belongings behind and run to safety. It was getting dark, and she was struggling to keep track of the path. And then her headlight stopped working, leaving her in complete darkness. In a panic, she started to remove her pack. She intended to run. She remembered a flat path ahead from the previous flash of lightning. That should do. And then someone grabbed her arm and pulled her.

'Come on. I know the way.' The male voice was soft and soothing. The two walked, passing rocks, mud pools and grass for what seemed like hours but might have only been minutes. And then she saw it. The yellow candlelight spilling from the hut.

She remembered arriving at the hut (named The Angelus Hut, maybe for a reason) and receiving a round of applause from those already there. The kind ranger gave her a blanket and a cup of hot chocolate. A shirt and a jumper came out of nowhere, together with a pair of warm pants. And there, next to the fire, drinking her hot chocolate, the others related their adventures in getting to the hut. Everyone who had booked had made it. Brave group of Kiwis.

The man who had saved her was in his fifties maybe, grey hair on top of dark, and a warm smile with wrinkles around his eyes. They chatted until midnight. He was warm and funny and welcoming, the kind of man she dreamt of but did not think existed. He had to have a fault or two, she was sure. This kind of man did not exist in the real world.

A faint light came through the window, and she could make out some shapes now. Someone sleeping opposite her on the lower bunk, probably the woman who gave her the jumper. A man above her; her husband. And someone moving above her bunk, maybe her new friend. What was his name? Ah, yes, Tom. She remembered every word of the chat they had had the day before.

'I'm from Dunedin,' Tom had said. 'My wife and I got divorced years ago. I have a daughter, Sylvia, who's studying at uni.' His eyes were bright in the candlelight of the hut. 'I stayed there for her, but now I'm restless. I'm taking some time to decide my next step.'

'I feel like I'm doing the same thing,' Cora said. 'My daughter is also at university, in Dunedin, and I guess I've got empty nest syndrome.'

'Yes, that's hard.'

'Where are you planning to go next?' Cora asked.

'I don't know. I feel like I'm exploring the country for the second time in my life, after many years of merely working as a gardener at the Dunedin Botanical Gardens.' He looked at Cora with caution. 'I love my job. Helping trees grow into mature specimens is so rewarding.'

'I can only imagine. I've never been much of a gardener.'

'You should come to Dunedin in October or November and see the rhododendrons in bloom.'

'I'd love that,' she said with a smile.

Their conversation had brought back memories for Cora of a life lived in peace, without major issues. Of weekends walking along the beach, tramping in the mountains, sitting in the garden with a book in her hands. Those times were long gone, replaced by the burden of being a solo mum. She was suddenly realising she'd never had a perfect life. She had just made it up in her mind, putting a place to every object and every person who had played a role in this major motion picture that was her artificial life. How could she have lived like this for fifteen years? She didn't need a life full of artificial happiness. She needed a real life, with ups and downs, with tears and anger, but also with smiles and peaceful moments, with joy, walks along the beach, eating a sandwich at the top of a peak after a hard day tramping. That was all she really needed. And she didn't have a dog yet. But it was time to get one. She had been longing for one for way too long. She needed a place to call home. And, after too many years on her own, she longed to live with a companion who would be with her and be honest and trustworthy, a person who would never leave her and who would always express his feelings. Unlike Nick, who had rarely said what he felt, even in the early years. She had had enough of silent moments, of keeping it all to herself and releasing it in the most unexpected moments, screaming in anger at her ex about something trivial like not putting away the lawn mower. Long ago she had promised herself that she would never have a relationship in which she wouldn't be able to share her feelings. She hadn't thought about her relationship with Nick for a long time. But now that Alex was at college, she felt lonely. Alex would now come only for visits. She needed to get accustomed to that.

She could hear a zip opening, a shoe thumping on the floor as it fell. With a sigh, Cora slipped out of her sleeping bag and got ready for a new day.

—

Later that afternoon Cora was standing at the end of a pier, open-mouthed. The lake was calm. She could hear the bellbirds in the distance, singing to the setting sun. She turned around and looked at the hut. Simple, accommodating just eight people, it was in one of the most idyllic places she had ever been.

The day had been so much easier than the day before. Tom had walked with her all the way, giving her a sense of peace she hadn't felt in a very long time. They had been silent most of the day, first dealing with an incredibly challenging descent from the hut into the valley, steep and rocky, and then being too tired to talk. It had felt OK. She hadn't felt the need to talk like she did when walking with the people from her tramping club. That used to exhaust her, making her feel empty at the end of the day, missing the peace of nature. This time she felt a profound silence that came from her soul. Her head was quiet, her legs exhausted but happy.

This place reminded her of the European Alps. There was that feeling of being up in the heights that she could only feel in New Zealand in certain places, like Mt Cook Village.

She could hear laughter in the hut; Tom and that young couple sharing a joke, maybe. And then she smelt the food. Her tummy made a grumbling sound. It was time for dinner.

—

A few days later, Cora was walking along the beach in Hokitika, on the West Coast of the South Island. There was a light wind playing with her hair. Despite the calm day, the waves were crashing ferociously against the beach, as if they were angry to have left the deep ocean and demanded to return. Cora stared at the waves, astonished at their force. She had always heard about rogue waves; sudden waves with an immense force that could drag a person from the sand to deep waters. She had never seen one and hoped she never would. But she knew the West Coast was one of the most likely places to see one.

'Are you afraid?' A deep voice came from behind her. Cora looked back. Tom had a wide smile on his face, his deep blue eyes looking intensely at her.

'Yes, I am.' Cora was amazed to notice how soon she had managed to be open to Tom, feeling no need to hide her fears.

'Just keep two to three metres away from where you see the waves ending and you'll be fine. That advice has kept me alive in Dunedin, so I guess it should work here.' He put his arm around her shoulders as they continued their walk along the beach.

The beach was nearly deserted at this early hour. Just a woman walking her dog, a golden retriever happy to be splashing in the water fetching a tennis ball thrown by her owner. Over and over again she would jump full speed into the waves, barking in excitement, swim to the ball and come back and shake herself, splashing water all over.

Tom had a cousin at Fox Glacier, so they were heading that way, taking their time to absorb the beautiful scenery and to get to know each other.

It had been many years since Cora had last been there. It had been a very different experience. Alex was small, and she remembered being overwhelmed by logistics, making sure Alex wouldn't get cold on their walks along the glaciers, and timing their trips around her meal times. Yesterday she had seen a young couple with a baby playing in the sand. They looked happy and relaxed. She envied them. She wished her daughter's childhood had been that easy. And yet, it had also been a time full of lovely memories shared with her girl.

Tom was a quiet person. He was giving Cora space to feel at ease with him, and she loved it. For the first time in her life she didn't feel the need to talk all the time. She had learnt that with Tom they would only talk when it was needed, when it was deep and meaningful. It felt right. It felt safe. It made her feel at ease and content.

'Life in the South Island seems so much more relaxed than in the North,' Cora said.

'It is. I always wondered how people could live with so much stress in Wellington. And no, a friend of mine who lives there doesn't look stressed. It's probably just my perception. Life in Dunedin is quieter and more relaxed, or so it feels to me.'

'One day I'd love to visit Dunedin. I've only passed through, and found it grey and dull. But maybe I just didn't know where to go.'

'Yes, that's quite common with foreigners. It's full of beauty. Wild beaches. Amazing tramps. Good cafés and cultural events.'

'But for now I would like to experience living in the north of the South Island, where it's warm and sunny.'

'That's a nice plan. I guess it makes sense for you now that your daughter is starting her studies.'

'Yes. I need a change of scenery.'

'Where would you go?'

'Golden Bay.' Cora didn't leave space for doubts. It came out of her mouth without her brain having intervened. 'That is my dream.' She looked at him with fierce eyes.

'Then you should follow it,' he said with a smile, wrinkles forming around his eyes.

Cora bent to pick up a golden seashell. She turned it around, amazed at its beauty. 'The truth is, I'm afraid of doing it all by myself. Despite having gained my independence since I split up with Nick, I've always had Alex with me. And now that she has left, I'm scared of going on my own.'

'Yes. That's hard. But you only need to trust yourself.' He stopped and looked at the sea, his eyes far away. After a while, he turned towards her. 'What about we go together for a few days and see if we find a suitable place for you to rent? I haven't been there in a long time, and I'd love to go, swim in the sea and spend a few nice days.'

Cora looked at him, smiling. 'That would be fantastic! It would take away this haunting feeling that I want to do it, but I'm too scared to take the first step.'

'OK. Let's go to Fox Glacier today and then head north in a couple of days.' He smiled at her and touched his belly. 'And now I'm hungry. Shall we have some lunch?' With smiles on their faces, they turned around and headed towards the town.

—

That evening, after a lovely dinner of seafood chowder, they went to their hotel room. Until now they had slept in separate rooms. But this time, without even discussing it, they had booked one room with a king-sized bed, their window looking out over the sea. The wind was picking up, and they had decided not to go for a walk along the beach. The window was gifting them the most beautiful sunset Cora had ever seen. With reds and oranges and some light pinks, the enormous sun was being swallowed by the grand ocean in front of them. Cora stared, tears falling down her cheeks. Tom stood next to her, and in a natural way he held her hand. Then he looked at her with sparkles in his eyes, and he smiled. 'I think this is a great omen,' he said, his intense look questioning. She gave a slight nod. And then he kissed her with infinite tenderness, exploring. She grabbed his shoulders, holding on to this safe haven of a good man who only wanted to live a peaceful life. And with care they started to undress each other, Cora's heart beating fast.

CHAPTER 3

Dichotomy

Irene

Karlsruhe, Germany, December 2005

'Aagh!' Beth's famous war cry reverberated through the living room, every other noise resembling a whisper. The four-year-old ran towards her older sister, who was quietly playing in a corner with her dolls.

'No, Beth, don't spoil your sister's game!' Irene's warning came too late. By the time she had caught her breath to threaten her daughter with no chocolate for afternoon tea, the girl had jumped in the middle of the play, sending shirts and shoes all over the place.

'You're a silly girl! I'm fed up with you!' Irene's oldest, Martha, barely five years old, had developed a deep hatred for her younger sister. She stood up, throwing her Nancy dolls to the four corners of the room. With a reddened face she ran to her bedroom, slamming the door and making her grandmother's painting bump against the wall. Closing her eyes, Irene wondered if that painting of them as a happy family would survive until the girls were at uni.

When Irene turned around, Beth was already playing with her sister's dolls. She was dressing them – or kind of, Irene thought, as she saw a pair of trousers trying to go over a doll's arms.

Irene leant over. 'Beth, darling, this cannot continue. These are Martha's dolls, and you've ruined her play. You have your own dolls here.' She took her daughter to the corner where her dolls were.

'No! I don't like them!' Beth screamed. In slow motion, Irene took Martha's doll from Beth's closed fists and took her daughter to her bedroom. The little girl was using her fists to punch her mum's back, her legs kicking her breasts, sending pain through Irene's body.

'Enough!' Irene put her on the floor. 'Time for you to stay here for a while until I call you.' She closed the bedroom door. Despite her bad behaviour towards her sister, Beth had always obeyed her mother. Bless her. Irene was against punishing them or using the naughty corner, but what could she do? She had no help. Her husband Mark worked until after dinner, arriving tired and silent. They had moved to Karlsruhe, Germany, his home town, before the kids were born, and Irene got pregnant soon after. Without knowing the language, it had been difficult to get accustomed to the people and the different culture. Her only true friend, Marissa, was Italian. Their monthly dinners were like a breath of fresh air, but it felt like ages since the last one.

Irene sat on the sofa, not feeling like clearing up the mess. She had five minutes of peace and she was going to make the most of it. She instinctively crossed her legs in a lotus position, closed her eyes and breathed deeply. Her meditation might only last two minutes, but it would have to be enough.

When am I going to get 'me' time? she asked herself for the hundredth time. *When the kids are at uni*, her inner voice said. *Yeah right*, she answered, as always. *What happened to my long-forgotten dreams? Can I even remember them?* the voice asked. *I used to love to walk in the forest, and at least that's something Germans love to do. Why can't I do just that?*

Marissa used to ask her why she didn't try to go for walks with the girls. 'Beth gets too tired walking on her own, and the forests aren't made for strollers,' she replied. Maybe they were just excuses, or maybe it was too difficult for her to do anything about it.

She opened her eyes, unable to quiet her thoughts. She looked at the photograph on the wall in front of her. Lately she had been looking at it every time she passed. It was a picture of two young girls in their twenties, with shorts and tramping boots. They had heavy backpacks on and were covered in mud up to their knees. They were surrounded by heather, with what looked like a hill in the background. Mist covered most of the peak, and you could see it was drizzling; their hair was soaked. They had huge smiles on their faces.

I still had that dimple on my left cheek, Irene noticed. It had disappeared when she had gained weight, after having Martha. She looked at Cora, taller than her. With long dark hair and hazel eyes, she was beautiful and full of energy. Cora. Her best friend. Irene's lips pursed. Cora had moved to New Zealand years ago. She had come to Irene's wedding, but she had seen her only a few times after that. Cora didn't seem to have any plans to return to Europe.

A loud noise that sounded too much like breaking glass pulled her out of her thoughts. 'Aagh!' Beth was screaming.

'Oh, no!' Irene stood up with a start and rushed towards her daughter's bedroom.

Later that evening Irene was lying on the sofa, an unopened book on the table. Her mind was going round in circles, and she was so exhausted she wasn't sure she could get up and go to bed. Mark had called earlier. He would be late, and had asked her not to wait up. There was a project he needed to finish before Monday and blah, blah, blah. She couldn't remember when she had stopped listening to his excuses. Maybe years ago. He was a good man, and she knew there wasn't any other reason but work. Although, if she was honest with herself, it was probably also the need to be away from the chaos at home. She sighed, letting the air come out in stages.

Irene scanned the bookshelf. She hadn't looked at her favourite books since the girls were born. With some effort, she got up from the sofa and picked one up. *Physical Geology: Earth Revealed.* With tears running down her cheeks, she skimmed through its pages. This book had been so precious in her life. She had wished she could go and explore the world's underground layers. How she had enjoyed those weekend trips at uni! Back then she had pictured herself in the future as a university researcher, taking her students to see amazing formations all over the world, a hammer in her hands. Did that belong to a different person in place and time? She looked around the living room. Despite her efforts to keep it tidy, there was a pile of clothes and toys in a corner, left to be dealt with another day. Nothing to do with the life she had once dreamed of.

She was tired of lonely dinners in front of the TV, of going to bed alone at 11 pm with a book she was too tired to focus on. She had found it difficult to make friends in Germany. Too respectful of her privacy, no one had knocked on her door to ask if she wanted a cup of tea and a few minutes of conversation. Lately she felt like a sergeant to her daughters, always giving orders, trying to make peace, moving them around as if they were soldiers in a perfectly coordinated battle with an unclear outcome.

She wondered if Cora would come back now that she was divorced. Apparently Nick had fallen in love with someone else and had left her and little Alex behind. It would be so easy for her to return now, to be close to her parents and her sister Sofia, who could help with little Alex, now four, a few months older than Beth. She could also find a job in Germany, live nearby. They could watch their girls grow up together. Irene had managed to vaguely mention it to her friend on one of their rare Skype calls. Cora had been upset, asking her what kind of job and life she could find in Germany without any notion of German and no relatives nearby.

You have me, Irene had thought, too scared to say it out loud. *That used to be enough for you.*

A noise took her away from her thoughts: a loud bump on the floor, way too familiar now, followed by a loud scream that shook the walls.

'Mama!' Beth's cries would increase in intensity in seconds. She had fallen out of her bed again.

'Coming!' With a sigh, Irene got up to attend to her daughter.

***

Two weeks later Irene was walking along the streets in Karlsruhe. It was six in the evening and the air was cold and damp. She closed her feather jacket tighter. A group of students passed her, singing Christmas carols. Oof. Thinking about Christmas exhausted her. This year she felt too worn down to make it special, but she knew she needed to make the effort for her girls. What had changed from last year? She wasn't sure. Lately she felt irritable at anything. Especially at Mark. Today she needed to ask a babysitter to come over to take care of the girls. Mark had said something this morning about an important work dinner, but hadn't called to explain further. He knew it was her monthly dinner day with Marissa. Maybe he didn't care.

The trattoria stood in front of her. With warm light coming from the tiny lead windows, it gave her a sense of warmth and safety. She smiled. She so needed this today.

When she entered, she immediately saw Marissa sitting at their usual table at the corner next to the back window, a small table rejected by others but loved by the two women.

'*Cara mia!*' Marissa stood up and gave her a big hug. She had dark curly hair and a huge smile. With a red leather skirt that swayed with her movements and a yellow jacket, she was Irene's idea of a self-confident woman. Just what she needed to feel today.

'Hi, Marissa,' Irene hugged her longer than usual.

'Are you OK?' Marissa's voice was muffled.

'Not really,' Irene said, looking at her while sitting.

'Ok, time for a red wine,' Marissa said, and raised her hand to the waitress.

~

Half an hour later they were enjoying their meals. Tortellini with ragù and tomato sauce for Marissa. Irene had spaghetti carbonara, her very favourite that had become her tradition at the trattoria.

'You know what you need?' Marissa said.

'A start over?'

'No. You need to get away for a few weeks.'

'What? And what about my girls?'

'I can take care of them. They adore me, right? It won't hurt to spend a few weeks with Aunty Marissa.'

'What would you do with them?'

'Spoil them, of course!'

'They are very little…' Irene had a frown on her face.

'And they are very manageable when their mummy is not around. Remember that day you needed to go to that doctor appointment, and they stayed with me?'

Irene remembered that. She was so stressed out about needing to leave her girls. But she shouldn't have worried. When she came back they were peacefully making bracelets with Marissa, a display of crafts on the table.

'Where would I go?' Irene said.

'Oh, so you're halfway there then!'

'Not yet.'

Marissa picked up her glass of wine, her silver bracelets dangling on her wrist. She took a gulp and smiled at Irene.

'To New Zealand, of course.'

'What?'

'Hasn't your friend Cora got divorced recently?'

'Yes.'

'Isn't she having a hard time?'

'Yes.'

'Aren't you, too?'

'Mmm.'

'There you go. So stop thinking too much. I'm calling you tomorrow morning to find out what time your flight is.'

'That simple?'

'Yes. My work owes me a lot of leave. I can take it any time. And what better way to spend it than with my favourite girls and helping my good friend?'

Irene didn't know if she would go to New Zealand. It was too expensive. She would need to be away for at least two weeks. She would feel awful so far away from her daughters. Maybe she should go somewhere else. Travel around Europe, as she and Cora used to do in their twenties. She looked at this magnificent woman in front of her who, since they had met five years ago, had become her sounding board. She smiled and lifted her glass.

'To friendship.'

'To big adventures when you most need them,' Marissa replied.

CHAPTER 4

Longing

Sofia

Madrid, Spain, June 2021

Sofia stared out of the large office window. Madrid stood thirty storeys below her, an ancient and noisy city, vibrant twenty-four hours a day. Tiny cars, most of them probably honking their horns, were humming along the Paseo de la Castellana, eager to be somewhere else. As if wherever they were was not enough. The problem was, people never seemed to find what they wanted, so they needed to keep searching for the precious happiness slipping through their fingers. Could anyone find happiness in such a noise?

'Sofia?' Jennifer asked. 'Are you with me?'

Sofia turned around. For a moment she had forgotten where she was. She recognised the blue sofa, where she sat every Thursday afternoon to talk; about why she was not happy, about her dull life and the search for something else. It was pointless. After three years of therapy she still didn't have a clue what was wrong with her.

Jennifer was looking at her, a warm smile on her face. 'Do you want to leave it for today?'

'Maybe. I don't feel focused.'

'That's OK. Let's stop for now,' Jennifer said, closing her blue notebook. 'Actually, I've been for a while thinking that…' She looked at Sofia. 'Well, I think it might be good for you to have a little break, Sofia. Get out of your routine, get out of the city, be close to the nature that you used to love so much.'

'Not today, Jenny. Seriously.'

'Well, this time I have a plan,' Jennifer said. 'I have some cousins who left their jobs in Madrid some years ago to set up a bed and breakfast up north, in the Picos de Europa. It was difficult at first, but now they're doing well. They've asked me if I know of anyone who could organise a literature workshop. Just some readings of Spanish writers: Machado, Juan Ramon Jiménez, Becker.'

'Mmm,' Sofia said. 'It sounds too much of an effort.'

'It's just for a weekend, Sofia. At the end of July. You don't work then, do you?' Jennifer asked, knowing the answer. The university was quiet in July, slowly closing its doors until September. 'And then I'll be on holiday in August.' Jennifer sighed, as she did when talking about taking a much-needed break. 'In September we can resume our sessions and you can tell me all about it. How about I give you my cousin's details and you contact her to start with? And if you don't like it, just say no, as we've discussed many times.'

Jennifer took a large telephone book from her drawer, similar to the one her mum has had for years. She copied some details onto a small piece of purple paper and gave it to Sofia with a smile. 'You'll love it there,' she said. 'Every time I visit them, I feel like not coming back to the city.'

Sofia took the note and gave Jennifer a hug.

'Thank you, Jenny. You're a good advisor.'

'And therapist, I hope!'

'Yes, that too. I'm just a difficult patient.'

'No you're not. You're searching for something. You've been moving towards it for a long time. You just need to take the first step,' Jennifer said. 'It's there in front of you. You only need to see it.'

Sofia looked into Jennifer's large brown eyes, wishing it were true. Over the years her therapist had become her confidant. Jennifer knew more about her than most of her family did.

Sofia took the lift and waited a few minutes until she reached the underfloor level, where she had parked. Once again she asked herself how anyone could design such a monster building without getting overwhelmed. It only exhausted her.

———

Half an hour later she was going up yet another lift to reach her final destination. Level Seventeen. She came out of the lift and opened the door to her apartment. A dark silence welcomed her, making her feel a familiar punch in the chest: lonely days spent in silence, wishing for something better.

She dropped the keys on the shell next to the door. What was it called? Ah, a pāua shell. It sparkled in silver and blue when exposed to the sun. It had fascinated her when she received it. José had given it to her after returning from New Zealand, saying it would bring her good luck. They had been together for three years. Sometimes she wondered how it had lasted for so long. An adventurous guy, he was always on the move. Diving in the Red Sea, skydiving in New Zealand, rafting in Kenya. She loved his homecomings, when they would spend hours on her balcony with wine and cheese, he recounting his adventures, she wishing she had been there. She imagined herself in a different life, where she was brave and able to take risks, not worrying about the mortgage of her super-expensive apartment or marking exams. She loved looking at his bright face, soaking up all the sunshine from exotic places and the sense of freedom he always brought with him.

If she was being honest, it had lasted because they were always living in different countries – until the day he said he had fallen in love with a girl in Kenya and they were moving together to Nepal. Of course. She had made it easy for him. And with him went the dream of a different life where she would feel happy, brave … worthy.

She opened the fridge. A half-eaten Chinese dish stood lonely in the shelf. She lifted the lid, smelt it with caution and threw it in the bin. When had she got it? She couldn't remember. With a sigh, she called her favourite Indian takeaway.

After a refreshing shower she put on her bath robe and went to the balcony with a glass of her favourite riesling. Even from up here she could hear the never-ending honks along the Paseo de la Castellana. Thank goodness she had double-glazed windows, or she would never be able to sleep. She looked down at the park beneath her building. She missed being in nature. The quiet walks in the forest in the Guadarrama mountains, north of Madrid, where she and Cora used to go with their dad. How was it she hadn't been there in ages? She had been giving herself excuses for too long. The fact was that her friends didn't like the mountains like she did, and she and Cora had drifted apart over the years. Despite Sofia always having been the brave one, ready for adventures, it was Cora who had moved to New Zealand and never returned.

Sofia took a sip of wine. Sweet but not too sweet; just the way she liked it. She sighed with pleasure. Since her two-day hike in the Pyrenees with Cora four years ago, she hadn't been in the great outdoors – unless Retiro Park in the middle of Madrid counted.

She looked through the window glass towards her living room. It was modern and practical, with a large red sofa and a wooden dining table with two chairs. There, in the shadows, she could make out her favourite photo: her and Cora with their dad when she was eight and Cora thirteen, him with his arms around their shoulders, a big smile on his face. They were standing in front of a rock with a metallic cross. The Gratlspitz, in Tirol, Austria. Their first peak. With hiking boots and big backpacks, the girls were proudly smiling at their mum, who was taking the photo.

The doorbell rang. Her butter chicken had arrived. With a sigh, she closed the doors to the balcony and got ready for another lonely meal.

A few days later Sofia was walking through the university campus. The air was warm and the birds were dancing between the pine trees. Wearing a pink sleeveless shirt and a white skirt, she felt beautiful. She wondered how long it had been since she had dressed in something that made her feel nice. She walked towards her favourite spot, a large pine tree with low branches. It gave her much-needed privacy. She took a picnic blanket from her bag, took off her sandals and opened her thermos. The smell of steaming lentil soup filled her nostrils. She smiled. Even though it was warm, she had cooked one of her favourite Spanish dishes. How long had it been since she had last made it? She remembered her friend Maria mentioning once how important it was to have beans or legumes every day. Despite so many Spanish traditional dishes being based on beans, she had got used to easy foods or takeaways.

She closed her eyes and breathed deeply. Today was the last day of term. That morning she had pinned the exam results on the department board, marking the end of her work for another year. And what now? She could go to the outdoor swimming pool every day, maybe take the train to Segovia or Avila. Maybe this year she should take a proper holiday and go somewhere exciting.

She bent over, her chest thumping. Her forehead was suddenly covered in sweat. She put her head down and took three big breaths.

One. Well done. There you are. Two. Three.

'Are you OK?' a distant female voice said.

'Mmm?'

Someone touched her shoulder. 'Professor, are you OK?'

Pursing her lips, Sofia looked up. A young blonde young woman was frowning down at her. Her face was somewhat familiar.

'You look very pale. Shall I help you get up, call an ambulance?'

Sofia smiled. 'That's very kind of you. But I just need to lie down for a bit and I'll be OK.'

'I can help you.'

Gentle arms helped Sofia lie down on the red picnic blanket, her face in the shadow, cooling down.

The young woman sat next to her.

'Do I know you?' Sofia asked, opening one eye.

'Uhm … yes,' the woman said. 'You taught me Spanish literature last year.'

'Oh, I thought you looked familiar. What's your name?'

'Carmen.'

'Ah. The student who loves poetry.'

'Yes. I guess that's me.' She was looking off into the distance, her face white. She reminded Sofia of herself at eighteen.

'You're at a crossroads now, right?' Sofia asked.

Carmen looked at her with her mouth open.

'How do you know that?'

'I felt the same when I finished my master's. I wasn't sure where to go, what to do.'

'How did you make a decision?'

'Well, I pretty much chose what was given to me at the time.'

'What do you mean?'

'I went to see a professor who's now retired. She offered me a position as an assistant professor, and I took it.' Sofia looked up towards the high branches. 'And here I am still.'

'Well, that's a great outcome for you,' the student said. 'You needed a job, and it was given to you.'

Sofia smiled and sat up.

'Are you better now?' asked Carmen.

'Yes, I am. Thank you for your kindness.'

'Of course.'

'Well,' Sofia continued, 'I saw it as a success at the time, and so did my family and friends.'

'Not now?'

'No.'

'Even though you've made a difference in the lives of many students with your passion for Lorca, Machado, Becker?'

'Thank you, Carmen. It means a lot to me. But yes.' Sofia looked towards the faculty, a red brick building far away in the distance. 'Despite that, I now believe it was the most cowardly decision I could have made.'

Carmen stared at her. 'But why?'

'Because it was safe. And the safest option is never the best one. It's only predictable, and that eventually means boring, depressing and life-consuming.' She looked at the young woman. 'You are young and beautiful,' she said, looking at Carmen's slim figure under a yellow dress. 'You can be anyone you want. Don't think you know who you are just yet. Go away. Explore the world. Take a year off. Have experiences, adventures if you like. And when you are done, when you feel like it's time to stop, then you can make a decision.'

'Oh. I'd love to do that,' Carmen said, a sad smile on her lips. 'But what would my family say for losing a whole year? Or what will I write on my CV?'

'Yes, that's a big problem in Spain, and in many European countries. Somehow they believe there should be no gap in your CV, as that would mean you're weak and they won't want to hire you. I'm aware of that. And despite that, it's the best advice I could give you.' She leant forward. 'Some countries have it as a habit. The UK. Germany. Some others have it as a must, where almost everyone goes abroad for a year or so then comes back and goes to uni, gets married, finds a job, or whatever life they decide to go for. They call it an O.E. – an Overseas Experience. And I hope that one day we learn that it is, in fact, the best school. Because it's life lessons that you learn, and nowhere better than in a place of your choice, travelling on your own.'

'I'd love to live in such a place!' Carmen said. 'Where do they do that?'

'In New Zealand.'

'Oh. That looks so far away. They seem to have learnt a few lessons we haven't.' She looked at Sofia. 'How do you know so much about them?'

'Because my sister lives there.'

'Wow! What an adventure!'

'Yes.' Sofia looked at her hands. 'It is. And I wish I had followed her example and moved overseas.'

'Can't you still do that?' Carmen asked. 'Don't they say it's never too late? And you're not that old, anyway.'

Sofia looked at Carmen and smiled. 'Thank you. I guess I could. It's just more difficult when you've settled your life here.'

'Well, I understand that a partner, kids, a mortgage can tie you up. That's hard,' Carmen said. 'But despite that, it can be done. And that's a lesson I learnt recently when I watched *Revolutionary Road*. Despite the tragedy, the story really touched me. It was saying that if you want something you should go for it, no matter what others say. Otherwise you die from inside.'

'That is so true.'

'Carmen!' A group of young women in shorts were approaching. 'We were looking for you!' said one of them, her long dark hair loose over her bare shoulders.

'Yes, coming,' Carmen said. She looked at Sofia. 'Thank you,' she said. She stood up and ran towards her friends.

'Thank you,' Sofia said softly. And looking at the mountains in the distance, she realised she only had one of the three ties that Carmen had mentioned. The mortgage. And that was an easy tie to sort out.

CHAPTER 5

What If

Cora

Golden Bay, New Zealand, July 2020

The sea was restless. Waves were crushing close to Cora, spraying her face with foam. The wind was howling as if it were angry that she had been away for so long. In normal circumstances she wouldn't have come for a walk along the beach. She would have stayed at her peaceful house and looked out from her living room, seated on her comfy, worn-out armchair with a book in her hands and a cup of ginger tea next to her.

But she felt as restless as the sea today. She had been to Nelson that morning then driven back over the Tākaka hill. She couldn't even remember the drive along the winding road. The doctor's words kept coming back to her. *Not much time left. Not much we can do. Is there anyone you'd like to visit in Spain?*

Spain. A word washed out from her vocabulary by the years of waves crashing against the shores since she had moved to New Zealand in her twenties. Spain, a country so far away from her head and heart that for a moment she couldn't think of anyone she could visit back there, or any reason to do so. And did it matter, anyway? She had made it. She had moved to the countryside after so many years daydreaming about it. So much effort moving, so many struggles to deal with. But it had been too late. In her late forties, she had thought she had a lifetime to start over again. Now that the time was right. Now that her daughter Alex was studying and had her own life. Now that she had given Alex as much stability as she could as a single mother long separated from her Kiwi ex-partner. She thought she still had time. To write a novel in peace. To become a life coach. To fall in love.

'Stupid, stupid, stupid!' She screamed at the sea, fists up, challenging the wind to contradict her. Her skirt swayed around her legs, now half-soaked in salty water. A group of seagulls passed by, beating their wings fast to get to the promontory where the colony was, a few metres north of where she stood. One of them almost bumped into her. She didn't care anymore. Rubbing her face, she sat on her favourite trunk, worn down over the years by kids playing fortress in the afternoons and lonely adults sitting in the evenings. She had shared so many hopes with the sea from this tree trunk since she had arrived in Golden Bay a few months before. A half-written novel lay on her desk right now. It was the second one. At least she had managed to finish one – which was currently on the desk of an editor who was probably laughing out loud at her stupid attempt to become a published writer. It was the third publisher she had sent it to. 'Thank you for sending us through your manuscript. However, we consider that your writing style doesn't match our readers and blah blah blah…' They all seemed to say the same thing. She didn't know why she had bothered to try to get it published. She should have just stapled it nicely in a red or blue leather cover, like a PhD thesis, and stored it on her bookshelf with her favourite novels. That would have saved her many bad nights.

A deep, guttural sound took her out of her thoughts. She looked up. Dark clouds were approaching from offshore. A bright light illuminated the sky, followed by roaring thunder. And then it started pouring. Just like that. After all these years, it still took her by surprise how fast the weather could change in New Zealand, with almost no time to react. She ran towards the car, dodging stones and shells on her way. By the time she arrived her skirt was stuck to her like glue. She got in the car and reached for a plastic bag behind her seat, where she kept dry clothes. Her old grey leggings full of holes and her favourite fleece jumper, worn out over the years. She removed all her damp clothes, undies and bra included, and put on her dry ones. What now? She didn't feel like heading home. For a while she just sat there, clinging to the wheel as if it were able to save her from the inevitable, looking at the lightning in front of her. Like the storm, her life was a mess, full of light illuminating the path and then thunder breaking it all to pieces.

A knock on her window made her bump her head against the roof. From under a thick black rain jacket Tom's face appeared, half smiling.

'What the hell are you doing out in this weather?'

She could barely hear his words. He came round to the passenger side, bringing the smell of sea and life with him. He opened the door and got in, water drops flying everywhere.

'Cora, what's going on? I've seen you arriving at the beach, getting soaked to death, and now staring at the storm.' His eyes were bright as starlight but he wore a huge frown.

'It's over now,' Cora said. 'Nothing is worth it anymore.'

'What's not worth it?' he asked, his frown deepening.

Cora's sobs started abruptly, as if a dam had been holding them back for a long time. Tears fell down her cheeks, soaking her favourite jumper.

'Come here,' Tom said, holding her with his characteristic sweet gentleness. 'It's all OK,' he kept saying in her ear, drops falling on her head.

After a long time Cora's eyes had shed all their tears, washing away her hope and dreams, leaving an empty carcass behind. Silence followed. She could only hear Tom's steady heartbeat, every other noise having faded away.

'OK, can you get out and come round to the passenger seat?' Tom asked, looking into her eyes. 'I'll drive you home.'

'But how will you get home if you leave your car here?'

'Well, if you're OK with it, I can stay overnight. We can collect my car tomorrow,' he said with a smile. 'What about I cook that lasagne with leftovers?'

That made her smile. She remembered him last time adding chicken and blue cheese, mixed with berries. It was fascinating to think about what he would include this time.

'That would be nice.' And with that they switched seats and drove home.

~

'This is delicious,' Cora said with a smile, picking up the glass of red wine. Her eyes were still red and her vision somewhat blurry.

'Well, I guess the food has come out OK, hasn't it?' He smiled with one of those broad smiles: open, honest, unforced, without any pressure. His smiles were of genuine pleasure, and she cherished them.

They were seated on the deck, the only remains of the storm being the dripping noise coming from the roof. It was still about one hour till sunset; the light was bright without the afternoon's burning feeling. Soon they would light the candles and simply enjoy each other's company.

'Ok, now it's time for you to tell me what's going on, Cora,' Tom said, carefully placing his wine glass on the table.

'Oh, em…'

'You know there's no pressure. You don't need to say anything if you don't want to. But I'm worried, Cora.'

'You shouldn't worry. It's just…'

'Let me explain,' he said, holding her hand across the table. 'I've seen you looking into the distance way too much in the last few weeks, so I know there's something worrying you. You have two choices now.' His eyes were fixed on her, their dark blue darker now he was focused and worried. 'You can either keep it to yourself and get even more worried and throw everyone close to you out of your world, or you can share it and see if it helps.'

He looked intently at her, his face white. He had his favourite purple shirt and white jeans on. She had only realised now how nicely he had dressed today. (Fortunately, he had brought his clothes in a bag and got changed when they came back from the beach.) To spend a pleasant evening with her. She wished she could stop the course of time, savour that look on his face (a bit less worried would be better) and bottle up this moment on the deck of her beautiful house in front of the Kahurangi Ranges, with the smell of rain on her roses, having a wonderful dinner with the man she had fallen in love with.

It was incredible how clearly she could see things now. She loved him deeply. She had already made the decision to live a life with him; each one in their own place for now, maybe moving in together after some time. One day getting old together, having endless dinners at sunset, feeling free in this wild place at the end of the road, where only adventurous and crazy people stayed, or the ones who wanted a better life, a life where you could choose what you wanted to be and just follow your inner voice.

A tūī passed by, flapping its wings fiercely as if they would not hold its weight.

'I was just thinking about how wonderful it would be to grow old together.'

'I would like that,' he said with a wink, still holding her hand.

'Well, maybe you can come every evening for the rest of your life and have lovely dinners, first with me, one day with Alex.'

'I enjoy Alex's company, you know that. She's a wonderful young woman, like her mother.' He smiled and paused. 'Will you join us some days too, if you're not too busy somewhere else?'

'It's cancer, Tom. Incurable. I might have two months left.'

The silence that followed knocked her soul over.

'That explains some things…' he said slowly.

'The doctor even mentioned that I might want to go back to Spain, kind of to say goodbye.'

'Jesus.'

'Who do I have there?' Her voice was croaky. 'A sister I've barely spoken to since our father died, or even better, a best friend in Germany I haven't even talked to since she got upset with me because I wasn't coming back to Europe.' She pushed her hair backwards, leaning over the table. 'How could I return? That's not home anymore. And after such a huge effort to come here, to the place where I would like to get old, after having given a decent education to my daughter and having her settled at college, I come here, only to die a few months later. What is the purpose, then?' She stood up and bent across the table, her face a few inches from his. Her eyes were burning as if flames from a volcano, trapped and desperate to escape.

As if in a trance, he took her face in his hands and kissed her with all the tenderness and sweetness of a man who wished to make her happy and share every moment left to them. She kissed him back, and they stayed there for a long time, the sun making his hair look golden like a god's.

Slowly, he walked around the table and took her in his arms, hugging her with tenderness. She could see the sun set behind the mountains on the other side of the valley. It was the most beautiful sunset she had ever seen.

CHAPTER 6

The Letter

Irene

Karlsruhe, Germany, August 2021

The letter arrived on a warm, sunny afternoon.

Irene had spent the day in the garden, tending her flower beds. She stood up, wincing, a hand on her lower back. Over the last few years she had developed a real love for gardening. It gave her peace, distracting her busy mind from feeling lonely after the girls had gone to college. In her mid-forties, having been constantly concerned about her health since her early twenties, she longed to find a sense of ease in life; to let it simply unfold and bring her whatever treasures and surprises were still waiting for her.

But she wasn't expecting the revolution that came with the letter from across the ocean.

She washed her hands, sat on the bench and slowly opened the letter. Cora, her dear friend since she was ten, had died of cancer a few days before. It seemed that she had been suffering in silence in the last year. The letter was short. Cora's daughter Alex explained in her neat handwriting that the funeral had already taken place. Cora hadn't wanted anyone to fly all the way to New Zealand. Instead, she had a favour to ask.

Her ashes would be arriving in a week. Cora had asked Irene to take them to Neist Point, the westernmost tip of the Isle of Skye in the Scottish Highlands, the place where they had seen the most beautiful sunsets of their lives. The place the two of them had travelled to in their twenties.

This was a big request. Cora and Irene had drifted apart. They hadn't had any contact for ten years. But Cora was still Irene's closest friend, the one she had always gone to for advice and support. The one who was not part of this world anymore.

After reading the letter Irene made herself a ginger tea and sat in the warm garden. Her flowerbed was forgotten, along with the scones she had baked that morning. Her heart was beating fast. This was not possible. How could she be gone? She had been thinking about her recently. She had picked up the phone a few times, only to hang it up again. What would she say to her, after such a long time? Why hadn't she done it? She used to be so tuned in to her instincts. But they had left her to find someone else who would listen.

She hadn't been to Scotland since that trip with Mark for their tenth wedding anniversary. She had wanted to show him everything she and Cora had done. They had had arguments almost every evening. He hated her talking about Cora all the time. But he seemed to enjoy a few things. He loved the haggis (who knew why) and the porridge. And he made her visit every single castle or ruin they passed. By the end of the trip she was fed up with them. It was not the profound experience that she had shared with Cora twenty years before. She longed for their walks along the Munros filled with heather, that breathtaking view of Ben Nevis from the south when approaching Port William, the wilderness of the east coast north of Inverness. And their chats about life. Their dreams and hopes, their fears and longings.

'Mum, where are you?' Martha's voice brought Irene back to the present. She felt as if she had been far away for hours, digging into her long-forgotten memories.

'I'm here, darling. In the garden.'

'It's getting cold, Mum,' Martha said, always practical. Her beautiful face came into focus now. Nobody would have said she was Irene's daughter, with her long blonde hair and blue eyes. In her early twenties, Martha was already a mum to everyone. To her friends, to whom she was almost a life coach at times, and lately even to her own mother. It was as if Irene was now a fragile old lady in her daughter's eyes.

Martha went to fetch a cardigan then came back and sat on the bench next to Irene.

'Is everything all right?' she asked, knowing already that something was wrong. She had always had that capacity to read her mother's mind.

Irene looked at her. The shadows of the trees had grown longer. She hadn't talked to anyone for hours.

'It's Cora,' she said, swallowing hard. 'She's … she's … she's gone,' she said, struggling to get the words past the lump in her throat. 'She's gone,' she said, and burst into tears.

Martha hugged her, and they stayed there until no tears were left. That afternoon, Irene missed the first sunset in months. It was there, but her eyes were looking somewhere else.

—

One evening several days later Irene was washing the dishes after dinner. Mark, as usual, had gone to watch a match on the TV, leaving her to tidy up. She looked outside. Although it was dark, she could distinguish the bench in the garden where she was spending many afternoons, looking nowhere, wondering where her life was taking her.

She knew she needed to call Sofia. Tell her about taking the ashes to Scotland. She wanted to convince her to come along. It would be a nice trip for them both. Despite the circumstances, she was looking forward to it, to get out of this claustrophobic place that didn't make any sense anymore.

She went to the living room. The TV had the New Zealand rugby team, the All Blacks, playing against Australia. She remembered Cora saying how good they were, that she had seen them live once. Irene went outside.

She walked in the garden for what seemed like hours but must have been minutes. She sat on the bench. The smell of lavender filled the air with its sweetness. The bush had thrived over spring and was almost a tree. *We need to get rid of this*, Mark had said a few weeks ago. *It's getting too big and blocking the path*. In the past, Irene would have done as Mark wanted. A year ago she might have said that there was indeed a path on the other side that he could use, saving the bush. This time she didn't reply. There wasn't any point. After a few minutes she stood up and walked inside.

'I'll be away for the day tomorrow,' she told Mark.

'Mmm?' he replied, his eyes fixed on the screen.

'Nothing,' Irene said, and she went upstairs to their bedroom.

~

The following day, the sun rays through the curtains woke her up. She opened them. The day was bright, her garden flourishing in reds, purples, yellows. She smiled and stretched. She knew where she would go.

While she was having a shower she wondered how she hadn't heard Mark leave earlier. She went downstairs and saw a blanket crumpled on the couch, several empty beer bottles on the coffee table, crumbs of chips on the floor.

With a wrinkled nose, she left it all there and headed to the kitchen. She prepared a bowl of muesli with her favourite yoghurt and honey and ate at the kitchen bench, looking outside. Maybe that lavender bush was there for a purpose, she thought. To remind her that there was always another way, if she could only look at things differently.

A few hours later Irene left the car in the carpark and climbed the steep path. Surrounded by hills, she thought how much she loved Pfalz. A region west of the Rhine, it wasn't frequented by tourists. Hot in summer, it almost felt like Southern Europe, Irene thought as she wiped the sweat from her forehead with a handkerchief. It was an area well-known area for its vineyards, and especially for its Riesling, and it was surrounded by history. After a few minutes climbing, Trifels Castle appeared in front of her, majestically built on top of a hill and surrounded by a deep valley. Irene wasn't sure it had ever been conquered. With several steep towers, it was still mostly complete. Richard the Lionheart, King of England, had been kept prisoner here on his way back from Jerusalem. She closed her eyes. She could see servants in long skirts running around the base, with baskets of laundry or fruit. Servants taking horses to the stables while a nobleman walked through the castle's impressive gate.

Once inside, Irene walked up the spiral stairs. There was a stone bench under a windowsill. It was dark and cool. How many ladies of the court must have sat there sewing, longing to get out of what felt like a prison?

The great hall, with impossibly high ceilings, made her imagine extravagant balls, a fire with a roasted lamb, several long wooden tables full of exquisite food, people laughing while watching the dancers. It was amazing how places kept in them the memories of the past, no matter how long the people had been gone for.

Up another set of stairs, she came out to the big terrace. She could see in the distance the two smaller castles that made up the Trifels. She looked down. Surrounded by trees and greenery there was a big drop to the river. Her stomach jumped a bit. She closed her eyes. She could feel Cora next to her. They had visited so many castles in Scotland,

Spain and Europe. Somehow, every time she visited a castle, she felt Cora next to her. She remembered one day looking from the wall of a castle in the Scottish Highlands, back in her twenties. Cora's eyes were full of tears.

'What if I'm making the major mistake of my life, Irene?' Her face had been contorted with pain and anxiety. 'What am I doing moving to New Zealand to a job in a bookshop on the other side of the world? I know nobody and I won't have the money to come back for a long time. What if I feel lonely there? Will you come and visit me?'

Irene had been very supportive and encouraging. She would find someone she loved there, she had said. She would make her own home. And it would be an experience to tell her grandchildren about when she was old and back in Europe. She remembered hugging Cora and staying there for a long time, two girlfriends in an old castle in a cool summer morning, undisturbed by the hordes of tourists.

Irene had promised to visit her, but she never did. She had met Mark, and it became serious very quickly. A year after the trip to Scotland, she and Mark had married and were about to move to Germany. Martha was born soon after, and a year later, Beth. And with the girls, no family around or a job to pay for her trip, the promise was never fulfilled.

Bummer. She hadn't even imagined that Cora might never come back. Why hadn't she tried? All her family and friends were in Europe. When Nick had left her, why hadn't she returned? And now she was gone forever. Damn it, Cora! Irene was holding on to the cold stone wall, her knuckles white against the dark stone.

'Are you OK?' a young man was looking at her, his face full of worry.

'What?'

'I think you're maybe a bit angry with the wall? You're holding it as if it were to blame for something.'

Irene looked at her hands, white and trembling. 'The poor wall is only to blame for holding memories.' She didn't know why she was suddenly so honest with a stranger. She looked at him. Probably

American from his accent, blonde. Maybe one of the many who came looking for Germanic ancestors.

'Yeah, I know the feeling.'

'You do?'

'Yeah. My house walls bring me memories of the life I wanted to live but never will, because my wife decided to leave me. That's why I'm here now. Pathetically looking for my ancestors. But I like this place. It has all the history we don't have in our country confined in these thick walls.'

'Yeah.'

'And what is your reason, if I may ask?'

'Well…' Irene wasn't sure how much to share. 'This castle reminds me of one I visited in Scotland twenty years ago. I came with my best friend, and we both had so many dreams and plans about how we would live our lives, how I would become a successful geology professor, always in the field finding new rocks. How she would become a famous novelist, how we would both meet again in our eighties and walk the Great Glen Way and retire together.'

'Sounds nice. So, are you planning to visit Scotland with her again?'

'No, er…' She smiled despite herself. She liked him. 'I'm planning to go with my friend's sister. On a trip to release her ashes. She dared to die before me and leave that gap in my heart, the bitch!'

'Oh my. That must have been such a terrible blow for you. You seem to have been really close to her…'

'Yes,' Irene said, looking into the distance. 'I used to be.'

'Not recently?' he asked.

'No. We had a quarrel a few years ago and drifted apart.'

'I see,' the man said, his eyes warm and gentle. 'That makes the grieving even more difficult, when you haven't said everything you wanted to say.'

'Yes,' she said, looking up at him. She always thought Americans were superficial people only interested in their careers, in having a big house and conquering the world. But this man was genuinely interested in her feelings; he wasn't just being polite.

'May I ask what happened?'

Irene looked up to the sky, her face bright in the midday sun.

'I'm not sure. We had accumulated unspoken conversations. I was upset at her for not having returned from New Zealand, for not being closer. And even more, I dared judge her for not having tried hard enough to save her marriage, when it was he who left her. I was so unfair to her.'

'You missed her,' he said, his hands on the stone wall.

'Yes. I did. But it was more than that. I was feeling lonely and was upset that she hadn't found the courage to start over again in Europe, near me and her family. Her mum was getting old. Her dad had died the year before. She had divorced a decade before that. What was keeping her there?'

The young man stretched. 'Well, I didn't know your friend or her circumstances. But sometimes, when you're in a different place for so long, you simply don't belong to your country anymore. You become a citizen of nowhere and everywhere at the same time.'

'Those are wise words that seem to come from personal experience,' Irene said.

'Well, not personal. It's what has happened to my sister.' He looked at her, a sad smile on his face. 'She moved to southern France fifteen years ago. She first went for a year. I think she needed to find herself, discover who she was away from home.' He looked down to the valley, a frown on his face. 'And then one day she called to say she was staying there for a while. She had found a job in a shop and had started some studies at La Sorbonne. A year later she found a Frenchman whom she eventually married, and some years ago my parents and I stopped asking her when she would come back.'

'Is she happy?'

'Yes, I think she is. She has the life she always wanted. She goes to the opera often, and travels around Europe.' He looked at Irene. 'But she is lonely. I spent a few days with her last week, and she feels lost. She says she will always be a stranger in France, and she doesn't belong to the States anymore. She says she feels like she's in no man's land. And it makes me very sad to think that I cannot help her. No matter where she lives, she'll always be an outsider.'

'Oh. I'd never thought about it that way.' Irene was quiet for a while. Maybe she hadn't been supportive of Cora. Maybe Cora needed her as an anchor in Europe, a place to go where she could be herself, to feel connected with her youth. And Irene hadn't allowed her that in the last four years. She had behaved like a little girl. And now she would never be able to tell her how sorry she felt.

And before she could realise what she was doing, Irene was sobbing on the shoulders of a complete stranger, her hair swaying in the light breeze, the green valley below them.

CHAPTER 7

Sweet Delights

Sofia

Madrid, Spain, June 2021

Sofia walked around the centre of Madrid. It was late afternoon, and still quite warm. She could feel drops of sweat falling down her neck. She passed by a mother holding two small kids with candy floss in their hands, their mouths pink, smiles on their faces.

Maria had told her about a Muslim café that used to be a bath back in the Middle Ages. She saw the street sign: Calle Atocha. And there it stood, in a small corner she'd never noticed before, very close to the Plaza Mayor, Madrid's main square. There was a second door next to the café. *Baños Turcos*, it said. Turkish baths. What a surprise to find in the centre of Madrid. She should come and visit them some day. The door of the café had a beautifully crafted iron sign with a teapot. She went in and was immediately transported back several centuries. Small iron tables covered in coloured table cloths filled the room. There was an arch at the back, opening to another space. A sign indicated they offered *danza del vientre* (belly dancing) on Saturdays.

'Sofia!' Maria was at a table in a corner, waving at her with a smile.

She was wearing a shimmery green silk dress crisscrossed with gold, draped down to her ankles.

'*Hola, guapa!*' Sofia said, giving her a kiss on each cheek followed by a warm hug. 'You look beautiful!'

'Thank you! I searched in my wardrobe for something special, and I found this. I probably haven't worn it in fifteen years.'

They sat down. Sofia looked at the menu, searching for a tea. 'Wow! There are so many choices! I feel a bit lost. Any suggestions?'

'Well, you don't like caffeine, right? I strongly suggest the lavender tea. I never get tired of it.'

Maria was suntanned, indicating that she had already been on holiday, as she and her family used to do in June: always to La Manga, in Murcia, to the same small cottage next to the sea. But below that broad smile of hers were wrinkles that Sofia hadn't noticed before.

'You look tired,' said Sofia.

'Yes, well, life, the kids, school, juggling work, Madrid's traffic…' Maria waved her hand.

'Maria,' said Sofia, putting her hand on top of her friend's. 'We've been friends for a long time. What's wrong?'

Maria gave a big sigh, looking away. Her smile disappeared. 'We're not doing well, Carlos and me. I think we're on the verge of divorce.'

'*Que desean?*' A waitress with long blonde hair and a red dress approached them. She looked so young and free, her hair loose with red ribbon laced through it.

'Could we have a pot of lavender tea to share and a selection of Morocco desserts, please?' Maria asked, taking her hand away from Sofia's.

'Sure. Good choice!' The waitress left with a smile.

'She probably thinks we're lovers,' said Sofia.

Maria laughed. 'That would be something, wouldn't it? Shall I show you how big Monica and Roberto are now?' she asked, searching for pictures on her mobile.

'Not now, Maria. Maybe later.'

'I can't fool you, eh?' she said with a sad smile, closing her mobile case.

'No. We haven't seen each other for … what? Eight months?'

'Yes, last time was at Roberto's fifth birthday, back in October.'

'I'm sorry. I could make excuses. The classes, my therapy sessions, visiting mum… But none of them would make sense. The truth is, I could have made time for us. This won't happen again, I promise. From now on we'll meet once a month, OK? Next time I choose!'

'Good idea! I've missed you, Sofia. You seem to have been in a bubble for too long, and I have too.'

'Does he have a lover?'

Maria smiled broadly. 'Oh, that would be so much easier, Sofia,' she said, tucking her hair behind her ears as she did every time she was saying something important. Sofia remembered her doing that at school, when she was a young girl full of energy. 'No, I don't think so. Love has just disappeared from our lives. We've been years without much time for us. Babysitters are too expensive, too tired in the evenings to even have a chat, draining each other's energy with conversations about the kids, money, projects around the house… And then one day I realised he hadn't said "I love you" in months, maybe years,' she said with a sigh. 'I can't even remember him saying once that I looked nice. I think love simply disappeared. Our dating years have been replaced by family time but no cuddles.'

'Oh, Maria. I'm so sorry to hear that. Carlos and you loved each other so deeply from the start.'

'Yes, that was before the children. They don't tell you that if you're not careful to protect couple time, it simply goes with the wind.'

'What about your time? Do you have any spare time for yourself, to reconnect with who you are?'

'Rarely. And I wouldn't even know what to do. Having tea with you is already a luxury.'

'No, it's not enough. What about painting classes? You used to love it when we were at high school.'

'Do you think they would even accept a forty-year-old nearly-divorced woman who has totally lost her way in life?'

'Yes, they would if they were smart enough. It's not all about twenty-year-olds with their whole lives ahead of them.'

'OK, enough about me,' she said, waving her hand to switch topics. 'What about you? How are things going for you? Anyone new? It's been a while since José.'

'Oh, you know me. There's no time for men.'

'There you are, ladies.' The waitress arrived holding a silver tray profusely decorated, with a large silver teapot, two cups and a plate of food.

'That looks amazing!' Sofia took in the small delicacies in fine filo pastry covered with honey. Some of them had dates or walnuts, as she soon discovered.

'Mmm!' Maria said, a pastry in her mouth. 'I could live off these for the rest of my life.'

'How is it that I never knew about this place?' Sofia said. She was feeling guilty for how much she had been hating Madrid lately. Sometimes she thought it wasn't so much the city itself, but the lost opportunities, like seeing Maria more often, or going to the mountains for a hike.

'Well,' Maria said, a second gooey dessert in her hand, 'I think you just disconnected from life after José left. Or to be more precise, you disconnected even more.' She swallowed, closing her eyes with pure pleasure. She opened them again. 'It's time for you to move on, Sofia. You can't go on hiding in that sterile apartment of yours, living a dull life, working crazy hours at uni. If there's something I've realised lately, it's how quickly time passes; time that won't come back.'

'Yes, I know. The problem is that I don't know where to start.'

'It doesn't need to be a huge step. Just a little one to get you going. Like me. I've talked to a lawyer, and after a few days I think I'll go ahead with the divorce.'

'Oh, sweetie!'

'Yes.' Maria looked away, trying to hide her tears. 'But you know what?' She looked at Sofia now, her lips trembling. 'I've also discovered that there is so much life ahead, so much future beyond Carlos. When all this is over I think I'll take a couple of months off work, leave the kids with Mum and travel. Thinking about that makes me keep going.'

'Where would you go?'

'To Angkor Wat,' she said with a smile.

Of course. Her favourite place in the world. Sofia remembered a library book that Maria would borrow over and over again at primary school.

'Wow, Maria,' Sofia said, tears in her eyes. 'That is a dream come true.' She took her friend's hand again. 'Promise me that no matter what, you'll take that trip. If you need money, I'll lend it to you.'

'Yeah, money might be an issue after all this. We'll see.'

'I'm serious, Maria. It's time for you to do this.'

'Yes, it is. To disconnect from my little world and connect again with myself and the outer world.'

'Yes.'

'Anything else, ladies?'

Sofia and Maria released their hands.

'No, thank you,' Maria said. And they both burst into laughter.

~

Half an hour later they were walking along the Plaza Mayor, holding each other's arms like they used to do in their teens. It had started to cool down, and families with small children were filling up the streets. If she ever left Madrid, Sofia thought, she would miss the way that the city came to life when the sun went down.

'You haven't told me if you have any plans,' Maria said.

'Well, not quite. My therapist thinks I should go to some kind of literature workshop a friend of hers has organised for a weekend.'

'That sounds interesting. And something different. Where is it?'

'In Picos de Europa, in an Airbnb hidden up in the mountains.'

Maria stopped, her mouth wide open.

'You should go,' she said. She took her friend's face with both hands, making her look at her. 'You should go.'

'What?'

'I dreamt of you the other night. That's why I called you. You were hiking in some beautiful mountains; it looked like the north of Spain to me. You looked happy.'

Sofia smiled. 'I love that you're still having those dreams.' She had always believed in her friend's premonitory dreams. And something within her had been telling her lately that she should accept her therapist's offer.

'Promise me you'll accept,' Maria said, starting to walk again.

'I will, Maria. Something tells me it's the right thing to do. And your dream just confirms it.'

'Good. And now, what about having an ice cream and going for a walk through the Sabatini Gardens?' Maria said. The entrance to the gardens was in front of them, with an enormous set of stairs with carved iron handrails leading down towards an area full of flowers and old statues. They used to love going there when they were young.

'Are you able to fit in an ice cream after those heavy desserts?'

'Of course I can! If there's anything I've gained lately, it's an appetite for the food I like. And I don't bother anymore about my weight!' She gently touched her stomach with a smile.

'Ok, let's go then!' Sofia replied.

—

Two days later Sofia was walking around Retiro Park in the middle of the city. She loved going there when she needed some time to think. It was ten in the morning and already warm, and Sofia's neck was sweaty. She headed towards one of the cafés near the lake. She picked up a cold water bottle and headed to the small temple. She knew the squirrels loved to be around that area, climbing the pine trees, waiting for people to come with nuts. She sat on the grass facing the glass house that was now an art museum. The pond around it made it cooler than other areas. She lay down and sighed with relief. She felt a bit freer here than in other places in the city.

How she missed the mountains, and walking for hours in the countryside, nothing around but her and nature. But she didn't want to go on her own. She missed Cora terribly when she thought about the mountains and the hikes they'd done together in their twenties, when she was starting to shut down and Cora was opening up to the world before crossing it to the furthermost possible point. After that they would organise hikes together when Cora came for a visit, which had been less often over the last ten years. Her sister belonged to New Zealand now, and was no longer part of this landscape. And somehow Sofia was still waiting for her older sister to go to the mountains with her. It was time for her to move on and make some changes in her life. She had been waiting for someone to fix her life, to make decisions for her. Since José had left her she couldn't fantasise she was going on adventures anymore (even though they had been his and not hers). Who was she trying to kid? She was forty-four years old now, for God's sake! If she didn't make a move now it would be too late.

A crowd was forming close to her. She stood up and went to have a look. A squirrel was high up in a tree, eating a nut. Somehow it had managed to come down the tree trunk, grab the nut from a small boy on the ground and climb up again. Sofia loved those creatures. This one was red with a large thick tail, and seemed to be smiling down at them, happily enjoying its reward.

A group of five-year-olds with two adults (teachers, probably) was heading towards her, the kids screaming in delight. OK, time to head home now. Peace was over. With a sigh, Sofia turned around and headed towards the underground.

CHAPTER 8

Making Plans

Cora

Madrid, Spain, July 1998

Cora was sitting on the seventh peak of the Siete Picos, in the mountains north of Madrid. Her legs hanging over a cliff, she felt free. Madrid could be seen in the distance, on the plains, a dark cloud above it. It was a hot day. It had taken her a while to find her way up the seven peaks from where the funicular had dropped her off at the Puerto de Navacerrada. She loved the trip up the mountain, the sense of freedom and adventure, and being surrounded by people who, like her, adored the 'Sierra'. Families with day backpacks, climbers with heavy rucksacks and sleeping bags, a group of veteran men in worn-out tramping gear remembering old times. These days the funicular was the only train with windows you could open to be one with nature while it slowly moved up its way through pine forests.

It was very dry; a simple match could light everything on fire. Cora shivered remembering when the other side of the mountain had been on fire a few years ago. She still remembered the smell from afar, a sense of hopelessness filling her.

She was almost out of water, but she knew there was a fountain somewhere down the track. She would find it on her way back to Cercedilla and fill up her bottle.

Things had not been going well for a while. She was restless. She had finished her degree in history, and she should have started looking for a job and thinking about settling down. *Like everyone else*, she thought. A job. A house. A partner, then husband. Two cars. A family. Expensive holidays every year to make them feel alive for a few days, then a return to their dull life. She could see that path so clearly in her head. No. She didn't want that. But what was the alternative?

For now she had organised a trip to the Scottish Highlands for the following month with her friend Irene. Six weeks visiting castles and hiking in the isolated north of Scotland. She really needed that. But she knew it was only a distraction, and soon she would need to make a decision. Even her dear dad, who had never put any pressure on her, had started to ask. 'What would you like to do now, *mi niña*?' She wished she had an answer. Especially for Dad, who had always believed in her. She felt as if she was disappointing him by not having settled down yet. Especially compared to her little sister, Sofia, who was now an assistant literature professor at the Complutense University of Madrid, who had just paid off her first car and was looking for an apartment in the city centre. Of all places. After all the hikes in the mountains (Madrid, Gredos, the Pyrenees, even the Alps). Cora just couldn't understand why Sofia wanted to live in the city. Her sister used to be such an adventurous little girl. She was never afraid of anything. Unlike Cora, who always needed their dad's encouragement, as everything felt like a huge step for her: climbing up a big rock, going up a ladder to go down a slide in a fortress in the forest. Sofia would just do it without thinking. Until she suddenly changed the last year in high school. She was scared of everything, then started following the rules: degree, job, car, house. Cora wouldn't be surprised if a nice guy just appeared in Sofia's life and there was a wedding. And she would be left behind. The older of the two, without a partner, job or life security.

She needed something else. And lately she felt as if Madrid, despite its enormity, was not enough for her. She needed more. More space to be silent, without the noise and busyness of the city. Space to be herself without being judged. Time to find out who she really wanted to be.

She heard someone approaching. And then she saw them. Four young people her age coming towards the peak where she was standing. Two guys and two girls. The guys had good hiking boots. The girls had beach sandals and were complaining of the heat. Two guys who loved the mountains and were dragging their city girlfriends along with them. Typical. She wondered what their marriages would be like. She had no doubts that both couples would get married and have children. It could go two ways. The guys might stop hiking after their wives complained of not enough family time and leaving all the housework to them. Or they would continue hiking, eventually get divorced and find new partners who loved the mountains like them. Cora hoped it was the second. Well, in an ideal world the men would decide to break up with those city girls and avoid all that trouble and traumatised kids. But that wouldn't happen, because their mothers would love those nice-looking girls for their sons, as if they could put them in their display cabinets next to their Swarovski figurines. Cora really needed to get out of there. Especially now, after they sat too close to her and started talking about how beautiful Madrid looked, the women commenting on the shopping they would do the next day. She felt like vomiting. She took her belongings, exchanged a pitying look with the two guys and headed down to look for that fountain.

———

Two hours later Cora was sitting at an outdoor café in Navacerrada town, enjoying the breeze on her face and a Trinaranjus.

'Having a nice time?'

Cora opened her eyes. A suntanned woman around her age with a long brown ponytail was smiling at her.

'Very much. Especially after the heat up Siete Picos!'

'I bet. I love how it's always cool in Navacerrada.' Irene came to embrace her. 'Nice to see you again, dear friend.'

'Yes,' said Cora, hugging Irene. 'It's been a while.'

'What would you like?' A young woman with a long blonde braid was standing waiting.

'I'll get a *clara con limon*, please,' Irene said, then sat opposite Cora. 'Ready for the big adventure?'

'So looking forward to it! It's all planned now.'

'With some room for adventure, I hope!'

'Yes!'

'Are you sure?' Irene asked, tilting her head. 'You don't usually leave room for the unexpected, Cora.' Irene's face was serious now. 'And we both need that on this trip.'

'Yes, I definitely do.' Cora looked at her friend. 'What about you? I haven't heard from you for a while. How is life treating you?'

The waitress came with the beer, a chorizo *tapa* and a basket of chips.

'Good, I suppose,' said Irene, taking some chips. 'I have a position as a geology assistant at the university now. It's keeping me busy.'

'That's great, Irene! You've fought for a long time to get something more permanent. I'm happy for you.' Cora took a toothpick and stabbed a chorizo sausage. 'What does it involve?'

'Well, I still teach some lessons, theory and laboratory. But what I enjoy most are the field trips,' Irene said with a smile.

'Wow! That was your dream!'

'Yes, it was. I'm now preparing a month-long trip to the Catalonian Pyrenees, which will keep me busy before we go to Scotland.' Irene was smiling.

'You look happy.'

'I am.' Irene looked away.

'And?'

'And … well … I've met someone.'

'Oh!'

'Yes. Who would have thought? His name is Mark. He is nice and sweet, and we enjoy being together.'

'Do you do outdoor adventures with him?'

'Er, no.' Irene looked down. 'Not that. He's scared of everything. Spiders, even wasps. So we go to the cinema, for walks around Madrid, that sort of thing.'

'Oh.'

'Look, Cora. The ideal man doesn't exist. You only get the "good enough" ones.'

'Is that what he is? Good enough? That's not ideal, Irene. What is his profession?'

Irene looked down and whispered, 'He's an economist, working for a company on Castellana Street.'

'Irene. Look at me. Are you saying you'll be marrying a yuppie? For God's sake!'

'He is not a yuppie!' Irene started to stand up. 'Who do you think you are, judging me? You should get to know him first before saying a word about him.'

'I'm sorry, Irene. You're right.' Cora's face was white, her breath quite loud. 'We used to be able to be open with each other, Irene. That's all.'

Irene sat down again. 'In my family, I've heard only good things about Mark, from my mother, sister, neighbours… You've been missing in my life for a while, Cora.'

'Yes, I know. I've been…'

'What's wrong?'

'I need a change, Irene. I'm restless. Madrid is just not enough for me anymore. I need to be somewhere else for a while.'

'Where would you go?'

'I don't know.' Cora sighed. 'Maybe there's no place for me in the world.'

'Maybe the Earth is too small for you. Will Mars work?'

'Don't be silly.'

'Yeah, sorry. Any plan?'

'No. Nothing past the Highlands.'

'Well, who knows? Maybe it will help you take the next step.'

'Yes, I hope so. And what about you?'

'Well. I need some time to think. Mark has proposed.'

'Oh.'

'Yes. And I'm not sure I'm ready for it. Now that my career is taking off. Because Mark hopes his work will ask him to move to Germany, in Karlsruhe, next year.'

'That's a big change.'

'Yes. It is.' Irene looked beyond the café, her mind somewhere else.

Cora moved forward, grabbing her drink. 'Well, let's raise a toast. For our trip. Let it bring clarity to our minds and memories for a lifetime.'

Irene looked at Cora and smiled. 'To our trip!'

~

A few days later Cora was walking with her sister Sofia in the pine forest in Las Rozas, on the outskirts of Madrid, where Cora was now living. It was a poor substitute for their walks in the mountains, but it was a good walk for a Sunday morning, when they didn't want to go on a long tramp. It was early morning. It would become way too hot by midday. A place where locals would go for a run or walk their dogs, it was unusual. A few old bunkers from the Spanish Civil War were spread throughout the forest, the trenches built by the soldiers still visible. A significant battle had been fought there. Cora remembered her grandfather coming to visit it, his deep eyes scanning the place, trying to keep his feelings in check, as he had been part of that battle. It had made Cora put things into perspective. Now it was like a live museum resting in peace.

'So, are you heading to Scotland soon with Irene?' Sofia asked, walking with brusque movements.

'Yes, I am.' Cora saw her sister was annoyed. But she had learnt to stay away from that anger, keeping herself in a safe place behind the fence built by Sofia.

'I see. I hope you have a lovely time.'

'Thank you. You and I could have organised something similar, you know.'

'Yes. Well, I mean, no. I'm too busy with lectures now. I'm a busy person.' Sofia looked at Cora, a frown on her face.

'Yes. You're a busy and successful teacher. And you also love hiking and travelling. Or at least, you used to love to travel when we went with Mum and Dad.'

'Yes, but that was in the past. Now I have too much to do here. And besides, I have a boyfriend now.'

'Well, you could go with him too.'

Sofia's partner Pedro regularly went on long weekends with his own group of friends, which sometimes included partners. Cora had always wondered why Sofia didn't join them. She used to be such a fearless girl. Until suddenly, in her teenage years, she had closed herself off to life and became the grumpy and serious woman she was today. They would still go hiking together every now and then, but Cora had the feeling that her sister had found a deep cave to hide in, and she couldn't reach her anymore. After having tried for many years Cora had given up, focusing instead on not being the target of her anger.

'No. Pedro doesn't like the places I like, and I'm not going by myself. I'm happy here,' Sofia said.

Cora didn't dare reply. She didn't agree. Sofia looked grumpier by the minute.

Cora had talked to their dad many times about this. 'Let her find her way back to the light,' he used to say. 'It will happen, sooner or later. When an event in her life takes her out of her comfort zone and makes her confront her wolf.'

Cora loved the way their dad looked at things. A gentle man with a bright philosophy on life, he was the one who taught them to love nature and explore the world. And now that she was about to do just that with Irene, Cora felt terribly sad for Sofia. Somehow it felt like they had reached a crossroads where she and her sister would take different paths: Sofia to stillness and security, Cora to movement and the unknown.

Sofia stopped walking, wiping the sweat from her forehead.

'You know what?' she said, her voice getting louder. 'I've realised there's a lecture I need to prepare urgently. I also have a talk on Tuesday that's not ready, and I need to rehearse before Pedro comes back from his hike in the Pyrenees. So I'd better go.' Looking distant, Sofia gave Cora a brief kiss on the cheek and ran towards her car.

Cora stood still, looking at her sister running away from her. She felt terribly lonely. She wondered if one day they would manage to close the gap between them. With a sigh, Cora continued her usual circuit in the hot sun, with the trees, the pigeons and the occasional person and dog as her sole companions.

CHAPTER 9

Light at the End of the Tunnel

Sofia

On the train from Madrid to Santander, Spain, July 2021

The train rattled, waking Sofia up. She looked out the window. She could see the Castilla-Leon plains as far as her eyes could reach. There was a castle in ruins on a hill far away. When she was little, she used to imagine herself living in one of those castles in Medieval times, walking along long corridors with think granite walls, with assistants to dress her and comb her hair. She imagined she was a young princess waiting for her prince to arrive, sitting on one of those stone benches next to a window, reading a book or doing some cross-stitching.

The door opened.

'Would you like a drink?' asked a waitress in a white apron.

'No, *gracias*,' Sofia said.

There was a woman in front of her. She looked out the window, sighed and went back to sleep. With a long brown corduroy dress and a white blouse, she reminded Sofia of her mum. She wished her relationship with her mum had been better; warmer and closer, like with her dad. Any glimpse of closeness they might have shared in the past was gone when her dad died. They had been growing apart even more recently, and she didn't know if she wanted to do anything about it.

The train turned right, bringing bright rays of sun through the window. Sofia hoped it would be cooler outside. Unfortunately, she knew the heat of Castille. She was glad she was going all the way to Santander, where the air would be cooler. She had booked a room in a small hotel close enough to the beach that she could go for a swim. Despite the strong currents, she loved to swim in the Cantabric ocean. Sardinero Beach was one of her favourites. Endless and sandy with the exotic Magdalena Palace on one side, it made her wish she lived in a smaller town with more air and space to be herself.

The train stopped, and minutes later a man in his late forties entered her compartment. He had dark brown hair and deep blue eyes and wore a grey summer suit. He lifted a large brown bag onto the upper shelf and sat next to her. With a smile, he held out his hand to shake her hand.

'*Buenos dias, señora*,' he said, with a strong British accent.

'*Buenos dias*,' Sofia said, shaking his hand, feeling amused at the formality of it all.

'My name is Peter. I come from England, so my Spanish is not that good. Do you speak English?'

'Yes, I do.'

'Great,' he sighed in relief. 'I'm on my way to a little Airbnb in Picos de Europa, and I'm not sure I know how to get there. Are you by any chance stopping in Santander?' His face was eager, his blue eyes surrounded by thin wrinkles. He looked relaxed and approachable.

'Yes. I'm going all the way to Santander, and can help you there. I'm actually heading to an Airbnb up in the mountains too.'

'Is it called El Retiro?' he asked, pronouncing the Spanish single 'r' in the gentle English way.

'Well, yes, it is!'

'Isn't that a wonderful coincidence! I'm planning to meet some old friends from New Zealand there and go hiking in the area. I've been told it's such a lovely place.' His smile broadened. 'I finally get to walk the famous Ruta del Cares.'

'Well, I'm sure you will enjoy it. It's a special place.' Her memories flew to when she was four years old. *Come on, mi niña, come with Papi! Don't be scared of looking down to the river.*

'Why are you going there?' he asked.

She noticed his almond-shaped eyes, full of warmth. But there was a darkness inside them that reminded her of her own miserable life.

'Well, I need a break from the city. I live in Madrid. It turns out that the owner is a relative of a friend, and she asked me to provide some literature evenings. I'm a literature professor at the Complutense University of Madrid.'

'*Caminante, no hay camino. Se hace camino al andar,*' he said with a strong accent, reciting the famous words of Machado: Walker, there is no road; you make your own path as you walk.

'Exactly.'

'What is your name?'

'Oh, my apologies. I am Sofia.'

'Nice to meet you, Sofia. Are you OK if we travel together from now on? You can be my guide, and I promise to be good company,' he said.

She smiled back. Her heart felt lighter now. She hadn't connected with someone in this way for a long time.

For the next few hours they chatted about their lives as if they had known each other for years. There was something vulnerable about Peter, as if there was a space that he didn't want to share. He mentioned that he hadn't travelled in three years. The ring on his right hand made her think there was a story to tell, but she didn't want to be too nosy. She wanted to give him space to talk about it if the time arose. She had not felt so at ease with anyone in a long time.

———

Santander had not changed since Sofia had been there years before.

Full of bright light wherever you looked, with the sea on one side and a few hills on the other, it seemed to always be in holiday mode. Peter and Sofia walked together to her hotel. They got changed and went to the beach.

'Wow! The Magdalena Palace does not have any reason to envy our pompous castles in London!' he said. 'And my niece would definitely adore knowing that it's pink!' he said, taking a photo.

It was late afternoon, and the beach was almost empty. Sofia took off her shirt and skirt, revealing a blue swimsuit with gold trim. She walked towards the water. It was cold, but she welcomed it with a smile. She couldn't stand the bath-temperature warmth of the Mediterranean.

She heard a sudden splash behind her.

'There you are,' Peter said with a smile, swimming towards her. 'What about swimming out a bit further? I'd rather do it with someone else,' he smiled, 'in case I drown.' They chased each other, swimming and splashing around. Sofia noticed how fast he swam, and how unfit she was.

Later they sat in silence on the beach, wrapped in their towels. She enjoyed not feeling the need to speak. It was such a luxury for a literature professor always with words on her mind.

There was a light breeze playing with her hair. It was cool; so different from the heat in Madrid.

'Mary loved the sea. She would have liked this beach,' Peter said with a sad smile. He stared at the water, avoiding looking at her. His face was in shadows but she could sense a sadness in his whole body.

He turned to her. 'She died of breast cancer three years ago. It's the first time I've managed to share that with someone outside my circle of relatives and friends. I haven't travelled since she passed away. This is a big step for me.'

'I'm so sorry to hear that. It must be so hard. My dad died five years ago, and I still talk to him at times.'

'Yeah. I know the feeling,' he said. 'And I've been buried in my work for too long. One day I woke up and discovered I was getting some grey hairs, but still had quite some life ahead of me. I decided to take three months off work and travel. No big plans. This is the only thing I had in my schedule.' He embraced himself with the towel, protecting his vulnerable core.

'I need a change in my life.' Her words came out by themselves, without her being aware of them. It was her soul speaking. 'Madrid is making me drown. I need space, mountains, forests.'

'Don't you have them near Madrid?'

'Yes, but I don't go anymore. Too many memories hiking with my dad.'

'Yes. We limit ourselves to things that make us happy short-term. And that doesn't help.'

'No.'

'Does work help? Or does it feel like a prison?'

'God. I've never been asked this.'

'I'm sorry. I've gone too far.'

'No.' She grabbed his forearm as he tried to move away from her. It felt warm and welcoming. 'Please. This is the sincerest conversation I've had in ages. I welcome your question,' she said with a broad smile. She looked at the sea, her cheek warm in the sun.

'Work is not what it used to be. At uni I studied something I was passionate about. I used to recite so many authors: Becker, Machado, Shakespeare… With my group of friends, we even organised competitions where we tested each other to see who could recite the most poems without a mistake.' She looked at the waves, strong, determined. Everything that she wished to be and was not. Then she looked at him. He was staring at her, smiling, encouraging. 'But now I only see that I'm analysing what others have done. There is nothing genuinely mine in the work that I do. Just studying the genius of others. And I wonder where I fit in all this. It is hard to compare yourself with Shakespeare or Cervantes.'

'Well, I can't help with that,' he said, looking into her eyes. 'I'm sure you're not like Cervantes. He lived in a different world. And he probably didn't have those beautiful eyes,' he smiled. 'Have you ever written poetry?'

'I did in my youth, but I lost interest; or even worse, I lost inspiration.'

'Well, inspiration comes with the states of your soul,' he said. 'And it's hard to be inspired if you are sad, depressed and imprisoned.'

'Yes.'

'And talking about inspiration, what about getting inspired with a good dinner?'

'That's perfect. I know a wonderful seafood restaurant nearby.'

'Great Spanish seafood from the Cantabric sea? That sounds lovely.'

And with a last look at the bright sea, they collected their things and walked towards the restaurant.

⁓

'This is delicious.' Peter left the remains of his lobster on the plate, rinsed his fingers in the small bowl with water and lemon, then cleaned his hands in the serviette and picked up his glass of Albariño wine, smiling at her.

'You look almost local now.'

'I think I could stay here for a while, yes.' He frowned. 'What about you? Do you like the north of Spain?'

'I always did, yes. However… well, I need a change of scenery. Travel around the world. Maybe go to New Zealand.'

'Why New Zealand?'

'Well, my sister Cora has lived there for more than twenty years. And I've never had the guts to go and see her. I always made stupid excuses. I think I was scared of seeing her brilliant life, comparing it to mine and then feeling miserable.'

'I'm sure your life has not been that miserable, and that hers is not so perfect. Have you been in contact with her much lately?'

'Actually, no. Since she moved to a place in the countryside somewhere in the South Island, she seems to have drifted away. We only have occasional phone calls every month or so.' She missed Cora so much, and somehow felt guilty for not staying more in touch.

'How is she?'

'Courageous, strong. She left the safety of a permanent job to do life coaching when her daughter moved to college. But yes, her life has not been great. She divorced from her husband fifteen years ago and has raised Alex all on her own.'

'Wow. I'd love to meet her one day. She sounds like quite a character.'

Those words raised the hairs on Sofia's neck. She looked up and saw a woman coming into the restaurant. She looked just like Cora, with long black hair, brown eyes and a red flamenco-style dress. Everyone stared at her. And then, the lady locked her eyes with Sofia. They were sad eyes, full of infinite misery. A shiver went down Sofia's spine.

'Are you OK, Sofia?' Peter's voice sounded very far away now. Sofia checked her mobile. Later she would remember all this in slow motion. There was an email from Alex, Cora's daughter, saying that she was coming to Madrid in a week. And a text message from Irene, Cora's best friend, from Germany.

I need to talk to you. When is a good moment to call? I have some bad news to tell you, I'm afraid.

She hadn't seen since her since Sofia's dad's funeral years ago. And then she knew. It was Cora. She had been feeling strange in the last few days, as if something important in her life was missing, without managing to figure out what it was. Irene's message put all the pieces together. Sofia knew her sister was gone.

'Cora is dead.' She heard a voice that sounded vaguely like her own. Then she fell off her chair and the world turned black.

CHAPTER 10

Falling Apart

Cora

Lower Hutt, New Zealand, July 2005

Cora sat in her garden, motionless, a letter on her lap. The sun was shining on her face, warm and welcoming. Last week she had been sitting in the same spot, legs folded, meditating, a smile on her face. She had been thinking about how wonderful life was, how at peace she felt. Her daughter Alex was four now, a happy and adventurous girl. She loved her work in the bookshop. They owned a lovely house near the bush, with ferns extending their leaves in all directions, and a small creek at the back. She and Nick were relatively happy and had settled into a routine: one day a week each of them would have a day to do whatever they liked. She would go tramping in the mountains or have a coffee with her friend Angelica. He usually went mountain biking, choosing a more challenging track each week.

She had read the letter three times and still couldn't fully understand it. A few words were floating in her head, and she was struggling to make the connection between them. *I've been unhappy for a while. You must agree that things have been difficult since Alex was born. I need space. I've found someone else. We want to get married.*

He had left the letter on the low boy where they used to leave nice notes to each other. *Gone for a run. Love you,* or *At playcentre with Alex. Will be back for afternoon tea.* Cora was expecting it to say he had gone to have a beer with his friends, as had been the case for the last six months. She had pictured Rob and Mark, his university friends, laughing out loud at a funny story about Alex. But it hadn't been his friends, after all. Instead, she visualised a young blonde student with a short skirt and chewing bubble gum, leaning at his office desk at the faculty. Him looking up to smell her perfume. Damn it!

She looked up. The bright blue sky was still there, promising a warm winter day. She had the day off work. Mondays were not very busy at the bookshop, and she used to go for walks and sometimes have lunch at a café in Petone with Angelica, whose baby clothing shop was close by. Angelica would leave her assistant in charge for an hour.

But today she didn't feel like much. A big lump was forming on her throat. Too many questions were spinning in her head. What now? Would she need to go back to Spain? Who would keep the house? How was she going to manage with a little girl all by herself? Tears dropped down her cheeks, burning them. She held her knees up and leant her head against them, rocking herself back and forth. And then, a deep guttural sound came from inside her tummy, muddled by her posture. Uncontrollable, it grew louder and louder, full of anger, making the kererū in the kōwhai tree fly away to a more peaceful perch. Cora looked up, wondering where the noise was coming from. A scream of agony and hopelessness. Until she noticed her sore throat and realised it was her soul.

Cora woke up and found herself on the lawn, damp and cold, now in the shadow of the big ponga tree. She had worn herself out and fallen asleep. She stayed there, looking up at life from below. It looked different; easy. A tūī was singing nearby, its beautiful sound resonating in her chest. She closed her eyes, sinking into the bird's song. Tears fell down her cheeks, a waterfall around her eyes, dampening her jumper, now full of dirt.

With a final deep sound, the tūī stopped and flew away. Cora opened her eyes. This was the new world she would need to live in from now on. She looked at her watch. It was time to grab something to eat and then go to daycare to pick up Alex. She would take her to the stream for a walk. They could throw some stones and look at the afternoon sun until Cora figured out her first step. She looked at the house. In just a few hours it had transformed from her dream house to simply a roof to protect her from the cold. It was not her home anymore. She pulled herself up and went inside.

A few days later Cora was having lunch with Angelica in a café in Petone, opposite the bookshop where she worked. She used to enjoy those days, walking along the vibrant streets full of second-hand clothing and furniture shops, an Indian spice shop and even a Dutch shop full of European cheeses. Then they would exchange anecdotes while having lunch.

Today Cora was quiet, her scrambled eggs getting cold in front of her. She had called Angelica the day after she had received Nick's letter. She was screaming, in tears, Angelica trying to understand what had happened. After calling her for a few days in a row Angelica had managed to spend the day with Cora. The café was getting full now, closer to midday. A family of four next to them was making too much noise.

'When my parents got divorced I was numb for months,' Angelica said. 'I wouldn't talk to anyone. My friends didn't interest me anymore.'

'What happened?'

'Well, time passed,' Angelica smiled, 'and one day I realised life was still going on, and that I wanted to keep going after all.'

'That's it?'

'Yes. It was that simple and that complex.'

'Oh.'

'I know this hurts like crazy now, Cora. And that everything looks black and impossible. But you will find your way, you will see the light and you will have a life after this. There will be joy and smiles in the future, I promise. You just need to digest all this and take one step at a time. No more. No less.'

Cora held her friend's hand. 'Thank you,' she said with a half-smile.

'I'm here if you need me. Always.'

Cora squeezed Angelica's hand. 'Shall we go for a walk along the beach?'

'Good idea.'

There were only a couple of people at the beach. A cool breeze swept Cora's face. They dodged big trunks swept down by the Hutt River and left on the beach, like passengers waiting for a trip across the ocean. A small boy was collecting items from the sea. With a long black piece of wood in his hand, he ran to his mother seated nearby. Cora smiled. It made her think that having Alex was the best thing in her life. Her daughter was the reason she would wake up every morning, make breakfast and think about basic things like what food to buy or what meal to prepare. After the first weekend at home without Nick she had realised she needed something to do, and she needed some exercise too.

'Has Nick come to collect his belongings yet?'

'Just a few things. He's planning to come with a van this weekend and take the rest. I've managed to take his clothes out of the wardrobe, so I think that's a big step.'

'It is.' Angelica smiled. 'I'm proud of you.'

Cora felt tears falling down her cheeks.

'What about the house? Have you talked about what you would like to do?'

'By text, I told him I needed time to make a decision. He said he was OK to keep paying the mortgage together and give us some time.'

'Good. That's a good sign that he's happy to work together, at least. What about Alex?'

'He's already told me that he'd like to spend one day each weekend with her. I think it's reasonable. And I'd like to take the time to go tramping and shake it all off for a few hours.'

'That's a great idea. And with time we can think about making plans together. You could leave Alex with him for a whole weekend and we could travel.'

'Oh.' She hadn't thought about that possibility. 'That would be nice.'

'I've always wanted to spend a weekend in Napier. We could have a look at the wonderful Art Deco buildings. Walk along the long beach. Treat ourselves to some nice dinners. Maybe rent bikes.'

'Ah. I always wanted to do that. But Nick had other plans.'

Angelica stopped and held Cora's arm. 'Well, it's now time you make your own decisions. And let me tell you that you will discover a new sense of freedom that you couldn't ever imagine you would have.'

'How do you know all this?'

'Well, I … I was married once.'

'What? You never told me!'

'No. I don't usually talk about it.'

'What happened?'

Angelica had stopped to look at the sea, and her eyes seemed to be fixed on a faraway spot.

'I got pregnant and lost the baby. I basically broke down, and pushed Paul away from me.'

'Oh, Angelica. I am so sorry.'

'Me too.' She smiled at Cora. 'He was a nice guy. He's now happily married with two children. And I'm a single woman free to do what I like.'

Cora hugged Angelica, wondering how she had managed to find such a special friend, full of fun and drama. This explained somehow why her beautiful friend was not interested in men. She felt Angelica was still hurt, her heart aching for her baby.

'You know what?' Cora said, releasing her friend. 'Let's take off our shoes and get in the water.'

'What? It's freezing!'

'Yes. We might catch colds tomorrow. This will be our baptism: me into a new life of freedom, you into a life of acceptance of the past and openness to the future.'

And without thinking twice Cora took off her shoes and socks, pulled up her jeans and went into the shallow water. The soil was muddy and the water brown from the rain the previous night. She looked up towards Somes Island, a sentinel in the middle of Wellington Harbour. She had never been there. A work colleague had told her you could see parakeets and skinks, sometimes even a tuatara. Maybe she should take Alex on the short ferry ride and spend the day there.

Angelica was next to her, silent. 'This is crazy. I might be sick tomorrow. But I love it!' And with a croaking voice she burst into laughter, hugging Cora.

Cora hugged her back, a deep feeling of peace finding its way inside her heart.

<hr>

A few days later Cora was sitting on a picnic blanket on the grass at Avalon Park. They loved to come on warm days and enjoy the sun, go on the little train on the weekend or use the playground. With sandpits, a structure with canals and water pipes and a flying fox, it catered for kids of all ages.

'Mummy, look!' Alex run towards her mother, a red flower in her hand.

Cora took it from her daughter. It was a beautiful dried flower, long red stems forming a fan.

'A pōhutukawa flower!'

'Yes. Well done, Mummy! That's what Maria said at daycare today.'

Alex adored her teacher Maria. A gentle woman who kept peace in the class of four-year-old children by being strict but fair, she had helped Alex become a confident girl.

'Darling, time to have afternoon tea.'

'Yum!'

Alex sat on the blanket and Cora took off her shoes.

'Now, what would you like to have?'

'Grapes!'

'Good girl for thinking about fruit first. Yes, we have some here.' Cora looked in her bag and came up with a container full of them.

'Yeah!' Alex screamed in delight, picking one up and eating it, the red juice falling down her chin.

A few minutes later Cora packed up and looked at her daughter.

'Darling, there's something Mummy needs to tell you.'

'Is it about Daddy?'

'Yes, darling. How did you know?'

'Maria said maybe Mummy needed to talk to me about Daddy, and I should listen carefully.'

Cora couldn't hide a smile.

'Yes, Maria's right. It's about Daddy.' She moved to fit her legs beneath her, breathed in and continued. 'Daddy will be living somewhere else from now on.'

Alex made a pout, her face full of wrinkles. 'Does he not like us?'

'No, darling. Daddy loves you very much, and he will always do so. But Daddy and Mummy can't live together anymore. You'll visit Daddy lots, and get to spend a whole weekend with him every now and then.'

'And you? I want to be with you both!'

'I know, darling. But it's better this way. This way Mummy and Daddy won't be arguing, and you'll have fun with Daddy. He'll take you to nice places.'

'Like where?'

'Oh, different places. Maybe to Te Papa Museum in Wellington, or to the movies, or to the beach on holidays.'

'Will he take me on holidays? Just Papa and me?'

'Yes, that's right. Would you like that?'

'Yes!' Alex was beaming, the sun shining on her small face.

'Good. Do you have any questions you'd like to ask, sweetie?'

'Er, no.' Alex was looking towards a girl with an ice-cream.

'Well, if you have any questions, you can come and ask me, OK?'

'Yes, Mummy.'

'And now, let's pack this away and have an ice-cream.'

'Yeah!' Alex stood up and started to put all the containers in the bag.

'You're being very helpful, sweetie.'

'Thank you, Mummy.'

When they were done Cora took her little girl's hand and they walked together towards the ice-cream truck.

Half an hour later Cora was sitting on a bench watching Alex ride along the bike track for children on her bike with trainer wheels. With Give Way signs, pedestrian crossings and a couple of railway crossings for the small train, it was designed to teach children how to handle traffic and follow the road rules.

Cora looked at her mobile. She so wished she could talk to Irene now. But it was night in Europe. The time difference sucked.

Alex was pedalling fast, her face under the helmet shining with a big smile. She had got so confident on her bike lately. She was growing up so fast. Even though Cora hadn't yet had the nerve to talk to her daughter about Nick's departure, she had the feeling that Alex had already sensed what was going on. She shook her head in amazement at her girl's sensitivity and acceptance. She wondered if she would have more questions one day, and marvelled at the resilience of children, who could go through so much and still see the bright side of life.

'Admiring your girl?' An old woman was standing beside her. 'May I sit next to you?'

'Of course.' Cora moved down the bench to leave some space. The woman had a white bun and wore a faded blue dress down to her ankles. She looked at Alex.

'She looks like a bright girl, and a happy one too.'

'Yes, she is,' Cora said. 'Nobody would guess that I've just told her that her mum and dad won't be living together anymore.'

'I'm sorry to hear that,' said the woman. 'It must be so hard for you.'

Cora looked into the distance, feeling a knot in her throat. 'Yes.'

'Don't worry too much about her. She'll let you know when she needs more answers. Children are so resilient at this age.'

'Thank you. But I still wonder how much we're harming her.'

'Was there any chance of fixing things?'

'No, there wasn't.'

'Then it's better this way. I myself stayed too many years with a drunk husband, just for the sake of the children. And that harmed them deeply. The quarrels at night, the screams and tears.' The woman looked beyond the bike track. 'Now my oldest is going through the same as his dad. And I wonder if I could have avoided it by leaving when the kids were small, when my son could have avoided copying his habits.'

'That's so hard. What a terrible choice to make.'

'Well, I had no choice back then. Or I thought I didn't. There were a few women who got divorced. Most of them ended up alone; no other women would get close to them, as if divorce was contagious. Such stupid thoughts. But so many of our children could have been better off with a single mum.'

'Yes, I guess you're right. But I still feel guilty, depriving her of having a family.'

The woman looked at Cora. 'You are her family now. You just need to fill in the gap. And as time passes you will find ways to do that. Remember you are strong and powerful, and women have ways men don't understand. You will manage, you will survive the first years, and one day you will find yourself on the other side of grief as a stronger woman, full of hopes and dreams, happy to make your own decisions without depending on anyone else.'

A few minutes later the woman squeezed her arm and stood up. 'All the very best, dear.'

'Thank you.'

The woman walked away, her shoulders back. Cora watched her, wondering how life had brought this lady to her when she most needed it. She realised that since she had moved to New Zealand she had started to share personal things with total strangers. She would never have done this in Spain. Somehow, being away from her family and most of her friends made her feel more open to strangers. And often, her effort to open up had paid off, making her realise how much wisdom she was gathering from these conversations.

'Look, Mummy!' Alex screamed.

Cora looked at her. Alex was riding with the legs off the pedals, as if spreading her wings to fly.

CHAPTER 11

The Trip

Irene, Germany and Sofia, Spain, end of August 2021

Sofia was lying on her old sofa. Trinaranjus bottles lay everywhere: on the coffee table, on the floor. The drink was advertised as a kind of orange/lemon juice, but with less than seventeen percent juice it couldn't be healthy, Cora used to say. But Sofia just adored this very Spanish drink. And it was her right to drink whatever she felt like, even more so if it annoyed Cora. *Used to annoy Cora*, her brain reminded her.

Cora was dead.

Nobody would have guessed that two days ago this living room had looked very different. Sofia had hosted a memorial party for her sister. A few of Cora's and her old school friends came, sharing stories about when Cora was in her teens, what a model student she was, how nobody would have guessed that she would end up living on the other side of the world. That was Maria Dolores, Cora's friend from kindergarten. With a few too many kilos and about ten kids (all running around her apartment and making everything messy and dirty), she seemed to be jealous of Cora's adventurous life. Well, none of them knew that Cora had forgotten about her family. The last time Sofia had seen her sister was the year after their dad's funeral, four years ago, when she came on a quick visit. Cora had spent most of her holiday with Irene in Germany. Sofia barely had an afternoon of quality conversation with her. She hadn't been able to process her grief over their dad's sudden death. She remembered how she had complained to Cora about needing to take care of their mum on her own. It hadn't been pleasant.

Damn it! She was making a scene out of all this, feeling like a victim. It was way too hot, so she got up to fetch the air conditioner controller and close the curtains. The sun was drenching the windows on the balcony. It had to be *forty-five degrees outside*. Other years she would have gone to the swimming pool with her friend Maria, shared some jokes and read a book, followed by dinner in the centre of town, in one of those lovely cafes with outdoor tables in Chueca or along Fuencarral Street.

Her niece Alex had been there too. She stayed for two days before leaving Spain to travel around Central Europe. She wanted to go tramping in the Alps, she said. She was twenty years old now, a mature young woman who knew what she wanted from life. She was studying to become a vet nurse at a technical college in a town called Dunedin in New Zealand's South Island. Sofia could still see the face of the shy sixteen-year-old girl who had come with her mother last time. But apart from the face, she looked different. Slender, with that sense of self-sufficiency. Sofia would have enjoyed her company had it not been for the circumstances.

Alex had told her that Cora had died after an illness she had only known about for a few months. She had decided not to tell her family. They would have worried, asked her to come to Europe, or even worse, gone to New Zealand to take care of her, and she didn't want that. Cora even hid it from Alex for the first months.

'My mum was courageous,' Alex said in her defence. 'But it hurts me that when she finally had the life she had always wanted, it was all over.' Apparently life in the countryside, where she had moved when Alex went to study, had been good to Cora. She had started helping out in a community garden, reading to older people … she had even met Tom, 'a wonderful man from Dunedin who adored Mum.'

Well, good on her, Sofia thought. Why hadn't her older sister told her any of this? Sofia was trying to remember their last conversation. She still couldn't place it in time; she couldn't even remember if Cora had described her new life to her. But definitely they had talked over Christmas. What about? She scratched her head. *Ah yes. It was about José having left me and gone to Nepal with his new girlfriend.* Cora had been trying to support her, encouraging her to go hiking in the Alps for a few days. Yes, Cora had been sweet and supportive, and Sofia had been a selfish woman. She had not asked Cora about her life. But there was no excuse for Cora not having told her that she was sick. After all, she was her little sister!

Sofia's mother had refused to go to the party at her apartment. Sofia knew her mum was OK because the grocery bags she dropped at her place every three days had disappeared by the time Sofia had got back in her car.

The phone rang. As if in slow motion, Sofia got up from the sofa, picked up the phone and sat at the dining table, adopting a different position for her sore back.

'Hola?'

'Hola Sofia, soy Irene.'

Oh, no, this is too much to deal with, Sofia thought.

'Hi Irene. How are you?' Sofia couldn't remember the last time she had seen Cora's best friend, who was based in Germany. She used to pay her a visit when she was going to see her own family. But over the last few years Sofia had had other plans when Irene called. She vaguely remembered her at her father's funeral in 2017, holding her two daughters' hands.

'I'm not dealing well with all this, Sofia. I'm sorry for your loss.'

'Yeah, that's what it is.'

'Somehow I feel that she's not really gone; like she still just lives twenty thousand kilometres away from us and all this is a bad dream.'

'Yeah.'

'Alex has told me that she visited you. How did you find her?'

'She's tall, mature and sweet.' Sofia sighed. Irene had a wonderful way of calming her down.

'Sofia, there's something I need to tell you.'

'More important than the fact that my sister has died?'

'Well, it's related to that. Alex sent me a letter from Cora that she wrote before she died,' Sofia could hear Irene sighing. 'She gave me some instructions about what to do with her ashes.'

'Her ashes? I didn't know she was cremated!' In a state of panic, Sofia tried to go back over all the conversations with Alex. Had she missed an important point?

'I think she must have changed her mind over time. And it's a practical decision when you live so far away and want to be taken to Europe.'

'Where are her ashes, then?'

'I have them. Alex brought them to me in Germany.'

'What? Instead of bringing them to her mother and sister? But … why?'

'I suspect she thought that was easier, as you both might not have been happy with her decision.'

'Take them to Gredos, our adored mountains in Avila. Or maybe to the Peñalara peak outside Madrid?'

'No, Sofia. She didn't want her ashes in Spain.'

'What? But why? She was Spanish, for God's sake!'

'I wonder how Spanish she felt after having lived twenty-three years overseas. Maybe she had changed?'

Sofia stood up, opened the curtains and frowned at the sun outside. How did it dare to shine on a day like today?

'OK, can you tell me then where my dear sister decided her ashes should go?'

'To Neist Point, a lovely cape on the west coast of the Isle of Skye.'

'Skye? And where the hell is that?'

'In Scotland, Sofia. Cora wanted to be buried in Scotland. In a lovely place we went together in our twenties before she moved to New Zealand.'

'And why did she want her ashes in Scotland, a place she hadn't been to in twenty years?' *Twenty years away doesn't mean it didn't have meaning for her*, Sofia's common sense was trying to tell her. But Sofia did not want to listen. 'Does she want her ashes to be shat out by those stupid black-headed sheep, by any chance? Or even better, by those fat Highland cows?'

'Look, Sofia. I know this is very upsetting for you. And no, I don't know exactly why Scotland, although our trip was very special for both of us. I know how this must be hurting you and your mum. But the fact is that Cora's last wish was for me to take her ashes to Scotland, and I'm going to do it. It's the least I can do.' She stopped for a few seconds. 'So … I wanted to ask you if you would like to come with me. We would travel to a few places along the way. I've decided to fly to Paris and take a car from there. Use it as a road trip and try to reconnect with things. Take a break, you know.'

Silence followed. Sofia couldn't even hear the noisy boys from two floors down.

'I don't know, Irene. It's a nice offer, but I need to digest all this. It's too much for me at the moment.'

'Yes, I understand that, and I was expecting it. I'm leaving on the fourteenth of September, two weeks from now. What about I call you again in ten days?'

'Yes, that sounds reasonable. Thank you. And now if you don't mind, I need to go.'

'Sure, Sofia. All the best.'

'Yes, all the best to you too.' Sofia dropped the phone on the sofa and went to throw up in the toilet.

Nine days later Sofia was still undecided. She had gone for walks, even ventured a trip to the Sierra, the mountains to the northwest of Madrid. She hadn't been there in ages. She found it depressing to go there on her own, to see how full it was of hiking groups destroying the peace she so desperately needed. What would she gain from that trip to Scotland? She would probably argue with Irene, that perfect woman who had all she lacked: a nice family, a husband who adored her, a lovely house in a nice rural area near Karlsruhe. And she would get even more annoyed with Cora, who had never shared her love for Scotland and now even demanded her ashes to be scattered there. Would she now need to travel to the end of the world to talk to her sister? Bah!

Back in her apartment, she opened her work emails on her laptop. So many emails about coming back to class, exams she needed to handle and an email from that student who always had two pages of questions. Exasperated, she closed the laptop. She wasn't ready for this just now. It depressed her to know that the same problems were waiting for her in the new school year.

She went to the balcony and sat on an outdoor chair worn by the sun and rain. It was warm, but there was a little breeze that helped her breathe. This city depressed her. Her mind was going back to that day with Peter in Santander and her longing for something else. The literature evenings had been nice. Everyone had enjoyed them – except for her. She had been disconnected from herself since that moment at the restaurant. The phone call to Irene had confirmed what she already knew: Cora was gone. And since that day she had felt like she was on autopilot.

After a while looking at the perfect blue sky from her perfect apartment, Sofia stood up, went inside and made a phone call. About ten minutes later she went to the kitchen and made herself a cup of tea. Her colleague Ana had been very supportive. She would be in charge of her students, give them her exams and cover the class for the first semester. She would send an email to Elena, the head of the department, later. She would take that sabbatical that Elena had been suggesting for ages.

With a cup of tea in her hand, she picked up the phone again.

'*Guten tag.*'

'Hi, Irene. It's Sofia.'

'Oh, Sofia, good to hear from you. I was planning to call you tomorrow.'

'Yes, I know, but I have an answer now.'

'And?'

'I'm coming.'

CHAPTER 12

Feelings of Independence

Cora and Alex

Mt Ruapehu, New Zealand, July 2010

The forest was peaceful. Cora could hear tūī here and there, announcing their presence to anyone passing by. Cora and her daughter Alex had been walking for more than an hour. Despite the sign saying the walk would take that long, Cora still couldn't see the end of the track. She didn't mind at all. She could keep walking that track for hours, listening to her own footsteps and those of her daughter, with the constant roar of the river nearby, full of melted snow from the mountain.

'Look, Mummy!' Alex called, pointing at the branch of a small rimu tree.

They both stopped to listen to the song of a tiny pīwakawaka. Spinning around to show its beautiful white and black plumes, the fantail lifted off to twirl in an elegant dance, then returned to the branch.

'It's trying to catch the mosquitoes,' Alex said.

'How do you know?'

'From school, Mummy.' She sounded frustrated at having to explain to her mum how native birds behaved. Cora sighed. That was the consequence of living in a country she wasn't born in but her daughter was. She would always be the one learning instead of teaching.

After a last twirl, the fantail flew away.

They continued walking up the hill.

'Mummy,' Alex said, taking her time as she did when she was trying to express something important that worried her, 'why is it that you're the only one who makes me wear gumboots when it's barely raining? All the other kids wear normal shoes, and they're fine.'

'Does it make you feel embarrassed?'

'Well, to be honest … yes,' she said. 'I feel a bit like a baby because nobody else wears them.' Her face starting to crumple.

'Oh, darling, I'm so sorry,' Cora said, embracing her small daughter. 'It's difficult to explain, because you were born here. People here seem to be very easy-going, and less worried about their kids getting wet feet and catching a cold. I guess it's because they're rarely sick.'

'Well, I don't get sick very often either!'

'Yes. That's true. Despite your Spanish blood, you are rarely sick! Aren't you a lucky girl?'

'Then why don't you just let me be like the other kids, Mummy?'

'Umm. I guess you have a point there.' *After so many years in New Zealand, I really should start to worry less about everything and be more relaxed,* Cora thought. She looked up and saw a sign saying it was only ten minutes to the carpark. 'OK, let's do something: you can wear shoes just like the other kids for the next term, and if I see you're doing well, you can stop taking gumboots to school. Does that sound good to you?'

'Yeah! Thank you, Mummy!' Alex ran towards her mum and gave her a hug, a huge grin on her face.

'Shall we go home now and have lunch, darling? It's a beautiful day. I bet we can have it outside.'

'Yes!'

Back at the rental bach, Cora looked towards the mountain and gasped. After three days without a glimpse of the volcano, Mt Ruapehu suddenly appeared in its full splendour. Bright with recent snow, the wide cone with a peak on its eastern side appeared above the clouds.

'Look, Mummy! I think we'll have more snow tomorrow!' Alex said with a huge grin on her face full of freckles.

'Yes, tomorrow we can try going up to Whakapapa ski field and rent a snow sled. What do you think?' Cora asked.

'Yes!' Alex was jumping up and down, screaming with pleasure. The neighbours next door looked on, a frown on their faces. Cora sighed. They would never understand that those screams of excitement were part of the way Spanish people expressed their joy.

'Ok, let's do that if the weather holds until then. Now it's time to have lunch.' With that, she served the salad and salmon on the small wooden table on the deck.

The following day it snowed steadily, covering the mountain in white. Cora and Alex spent the day inside, playing games and watching films, happy together. Cora felt calmer than she had for years. After Nick had left her for another woman five years before, her life had crumbled. She had found a small rental in Lower Hutt and had hidden inside its walls for as long as she could, refusing dinner invitations from friends. Alex had been grumpy and difficult. When things were not going well she would scream at Cora, saying that she wanted to live with her dad. Cora had hated those moments. Until one week things got easier, and the week after even easier, and then they had settled into the routine of being just the two of them, with Alex visiting her dad every second weekend. This was one of the first trips they had done on their own, after struggling to save the money for a bit of luxury in the snow.

Cora didn't know what the future would look like. She knew she needed a change but she didn't know in what direction. And so, she did what she always did: stayed still until the clouds cleared. But she knew deep inside that those clouds might never go away. Going somewhere else was the most obvious choice. Start over. Meet new people. But she felt faint just thinking about taking Alex's school and friends from her life. She couldn't do that to Alex. She was determined to find a solution that didn't mean breaking her daughter's heart again.

Looking out the window, cosy in the little bach, she felt at ease. It felt good to go on holiday, to make her own decisions without another adult giving their opinion. She was free to go left or right, up or down.

The next day was sunny and bright. Cora could hear the constant dripping from the roof. She opened the curtains. Mt Ruapehu was white and welcoming. It was time to go to the snow.

'Mummy, look at me!' Alex passed by her at top speed, beaming in delight, her hands firmly holding the reins of the sled.

'Wow!' Cora smiled. Seeing Alex so happy and relaxed took a huge weight off her shoulders. She hadn't seen her daughter so joyful for a long time.

The ski field was packed, full of families with children making snowmen, parents teaching their little ones how to ski and teenagers trying the steepest slopes on their snowboards. One day she might try snowboarding. Maybe next year, if Alex was eager to take a ski course. That would give Alex self-confidence and her a bit of a break. It was hard to be a solo mum and deal with your own needs as well. Cora found this the most challenging. With no family around, even going to a movie by herself involved days of planning. Sometimes she didn't even bother.

'Mummy, let's make a snowman!' Alex was running uphill towards her, a huge smile on her face.

'Sure, darling.'

They walked down to the end of the ski area for kids, where mounds of ice marked the end of the safe area. Beyond was the slope for the experienced skiers, who were passing at top speed, their faces red with determination.

'This is a good spot. Let's look for soft snow and build the body.'

Half an hour later Cora took a photo of Alex embracing a small snowman wearing her snow hat and scarf and a stick for a nose.

'This is the best snowman ever!' Alex was now jumping around it.

'Yes, it is.' Cora smiled. She felt complete today, as if nothing else was missing. 'Let's go to the café and have a hot chocolate.'

The café was nearly empty, with a few families here and there and an elderly couple near the window looking at the view. Cora and Alex sat next to them with their hot chocolates. Alex wouldn't stop talking about the day.

A few minutes later Alex was quietly drawing in a notebook. Cora looked around. She overheard the elderly couple's conversation. It was around moving to a quieter space and having time to just live. She might have looked at them, as the woman stopped talking and smiled at her.

'You must be looking for some quiet too, I assume?'

'Er, yes. I'm sorry for listening to your conversation. I think I'm quite tired after today.'

'Yes, I can believe that.'

'Look, Mummy! It's snowing!'

Thick snowflakes were falling like in a slow-motion movie.

'Wow!' Cora said.

The man stood up and offered to take Alex closer to the window to look at the falling snow. Alex was so excited.

'May I?' the woman asked, standing next to Cora.

'Please.' Cora moved her chair to make room, and the woman sat down.

'I assume you are a single mother?'

'Er, yes. How did you know?'

'Well, to start with, there are seldom single parents with children on the ski field, and it's even more uncommon for that parent to be the mother,' the woman said with a smile and a wink. 'And then … well, I think I can recognise them. It reminds me of myself a few years ago.'

'Oh.'

'Yes, I was a single mum of two six-year-old twins, and remained that way for ten years.' She looked out the window. 'How I managed to survive, I have no idea.'

Then the woman looked at her, her dark blue eyes serious. 'It's the hardest job you'll ever have. All the responsibility on your shoulders: the income, the house, the children, and last but not least, taking care of yourself, which is the hardest thing of all.'

'Yes.'

'But let me tell you something.' The woman reached her hand across the table. 'Once you've gone through it, you realise in amazement how strong you have become, and how there is nothing that could stop you. That is the moment to pursue your own dreams.'

'Did you manage to do that?'

'Yes, I did. I took painting lessons at the age of fifty and have been painting since. Now we're looking at moving to a quiet area where I can keep painting and Robert can enjoy daily walks and recover from ongoing stress.'

'Where are you planning to go?'

'Golden Bay. There's no other place for us. Full of artists, lovely beaches to walk along and swim. Being at the end of the road appeals to me. My twins are adults now, so my role as a mother is almost over. Although, my role as a grandmother will begin soon.' She winked at Cora. 'But that's a different story.'

'Wow. I admire you. And Golden Bay is my dream place. Years ago I told myself I would move there one day. But now it seems impossible.'

'Well, something tells me we will see each other there in the future.' The woman stood up, patted Cora's shoulder and whispered: 'You will get through it. Just trust yourself. And keep your dreams close.' With a smile, she went to where her husband and Alex stood, joining in the excitement of watching the snowflakes fly in all directions.

Cora sipped the last of her hot chocolate, a deep frown on her face. There were some days when she wondered how she would make it through the day without causing trauma to her daughter with her impatience. Days when she felt like the worst possible mum. But then other days she held her daughter tightly and felt like the most blessed person in the world, completely fulfilled.

With a smile she stood up and went to join the group at the window.

CHAPTER 13

Jumping in the Air

Tom

Dunedin, New Zealand, August 2011

Portobello Road, long and winding, lay before him. The wind was rustling the bushes. A storm was approaching. Tom pushed down on the accelerator. He needed to get to the tip of the peninsula before the lightning. A car zoomed passed him in the other direction.

He passed the sign for the yellow-eyed penguin colony. He changed gears as if he were battling with a bear, the gear box complaining.

Samantha had done it again. In a few sentences she had ruined his day and mood. This time it was something about going to see her family in Queenstown 'for once' over Labour Weekend. For once. He had spent twenty-five years of his life enduring Samantha's dad and brother. Always criticising him about how he earned his living as a gardener at the Botanical Gardens.

'You should look for a proper job now, Tom,' they would say as soon as they saw him. Then followed a list of 'better' jobs for him, from accountant to lawyer. Bah! They had a large property in the north of the city, a big section he had turned into his own green paradise and a lovely fifteen-year-old daughter he adored. Tom needed no more in life. If only Samantha wasn't so unhappy and angry every weekend. If they didn't have any plans (visiting friends, violin rehearsals for Sylvia), he would spend most of the day in his garden, creating something. Last spring he had started a new veggie garden in the upper part of the garden. He had realised how much sun it received even in winter, and was tidying it up to start planting something in early spring. He would try strawberries again, and courgettes.

But Samantha had appeared at midday and sat on a bench on the deck. She stared at him for almost half an hour before getting up with a long sigh and rushing to the kitchen to cook some lunch. He didn't feel like coming back in. What was it this time? Not enough cuddles? Not enough time to talk? A bit of both it seemed, after he decided to come in. And he had forgotten they were having guests in the evening and needed to clean up the house. The Forbes. Again. An evening of drinking wine in silence while listening to their nonsense.

So after having set aside his weekend gardening plans to vacuum the whole bloody house and then patiently host the neighbours, the storm arrived the next day. He hadn't been polite or engaging enough. He had just sat and drunk, uninterested. Well, enough was enough. He took his coat and banged the door, rushing towards his old car.

The car swayed towards the cliff, bumped by a wind gust. *One more like that and I might not make it*, he thought. A sigh of relief followed. At least that way he would get some peace.

After the next bend he saw it: the visitors' centre for the albatross colony. The largest albatross in the world, the Northern royal albatross, was something special. He loved seeing the parent arriving and the chick welcoming it after months of being apart. God, he loved reunions. When he was in his twenties and studying in Auckland, he used to go to the airport when he felt depressed. He would look up when the next international flight would arrive and arrive half an hour earlier. He would go to the arrival gate at the airport. He loved seeing the people waiting, their eager faces, the flower bouquets, small girls with their best dresses waiting for a parent or grandparent, the nervous teenager waiting for a girl or boyfriend, the old couple waiting for a son or daughter who lived overseas. And he would watch every hug, every kiss, every smile. He would then go home, cuddle up with a blanket and a book and have a big cry. For himself and his loneliness. For the hope that there was still love around. He only needed to find it. When he met Samantha he thought he had found love. But there he was twenty years later, knowing that it hadn't been the love he had dreamed of.

A car passed by him and parked, and a family got out. Tom watched the four of them. Stressed out mum needing a break. Big dad too proud of himself, showing off to his children. Girl with long straight hair, almost a teenager, wanting to impress dad with her knowledge. Ten-year-old boy wanting to be somewhere else. He had seen too many of these families in his life. They would come to the botanical gardens to relax, but they didn't really look at the garden, the trees, the birds. Tom imagined a typical scene with the dad arguing with one of the children, who would then go to the mum, who was just trying to get five minutes of peace but needed to mediate. Tom used to wonder why being together as a family was better than taking some time to be alone or with friends. They didn't seem to enjoy each other's company any more. But maybe he was just seeing the sad families, and not focusing on the loving mums and dads and adorable children. Maybe he just needed a break, go somewhere else.

He loved his job. It gave him a sense of self-respect and plenty of silence and peace. And God knew how much he had needed that lately. He would spend hours focused on what he was doing, making sure his plants were happy. Each day he had a few tasks: plant new flowers, prune some bushes, check the birds in the aviary had enough to eat. When he was done he would go back to the plants and trees he had tended in the previous few days, making sure they were doing well, growing roots, enjoying the spot he had carefully chosen for them. It gave him a wonderful sense of pride to see them thrive. That clematis paniculate had found the rimu tree to climb on. In a couple of years it would adorn the rimu in bright white flowers. The baby rhododendron will soon catch up with its teenage siblings and find the light next to the mature ones, who would protect and nurture it until it was strong enough to on its own.

Mornings were best. There were few people around, and none in a hurry: an elderly couple, hand in hand, who came often; a student maybe skipping a class, a young mother with her baby. He would see them choosing a bench in the sun and sitting for hours, playing, talking, watching nature unfold. It was so different over the weekends. Years ago he had asked to do weekdays, even if it meant longer hours. Now he would rarely be asked to work on a weekend to substitute for a sick colleague or one on holiday.

Tending the garden was his way of healing, of disconnecting from the stress at home. Few people could say their work saved them from life problems; it was usually the opposite. But somehow he needed a change. And he bloody knew what to do. But he was afraid. Of the storm. Of things going the wrong way. Of regrets. Of destroying his daughter's life when she most needed her parents. *Not this way*, a voice inside said. No, Sylvia didn't need yelling parents, or silent dinners, or TV with the volume too high to avoid listening to her mum crying. She needed peace, a safe environment, a strong and sturdy dad to help her through her teenage years. She needed him to be present and loving. And alone. He knew what he had to do; he just needed to find the right words. No matter what he said, Samantha would make a drama out of it. He knew that. He should get ready for it. And talk to his friend John to see if that spare room was still available. He would stay in Dunedin until Sylvia went to uni. And then he would go from there.

He got out of the car. He didn't want to go to the visitor centre, hear all the tourists oohing and aahing over the albatross chicks. He held those memories from his childhood, with fewer tourists around and more time to ask questions. Instead, he headed towards the coast. The wind was howling. It was a bit fresh but not too bad, unusual for the tip of the peninsula. A few albatrosses were flying further north, effortlessly. Tom closed his eyes and opened his arms. He imagined opening his wings and letting himself be taken by the wind. No worries, no regrets.

A strong *whoosh* sounded above his head. He opened his eyes. An albatross had just passed above him. He flew north then circled, returning. This time Tom had his eyes open. The albatross looked him in the eye and headed towards him. Hypnotised, Tom stood still. With wings spread wide, the bird turned sideways and passed him about two metres away, turning in a big circle and heading back north.

Tom was breathless, holding the veranda. He had even smelt the bird. Fish, sea salt. Freedom. And the power of letting go. He stayed there for a long time, facing the sea.

'Look!' the family from before had finished their visit and were heading his way, pointing towards a seagull colony on the cliff.

Tom looked at the sea again. The sky was pink and purple now. He closed his eyes for a few minutes. And with a smile he opened them again, turned around and headed back to his car.

⌒

A month later, Tom woke up in his small room. His friend John had invited him to stay for a while. It felt strange, but somehow it was the right thing for him. The break-up with Samantha hadn't been easy. He had the feeling that she had clung to him for years for safety and security, and felt lost now. He couldn't believe he was showing empathy for a woman who had thrown a frying pan at him when he said he was moving out. But she had looked calmer the other day when he went to pick up his last belongings.

He had no idea what the next step was. Staying around for a while, while Sylvia finished high school. Looking for a house to share with someone, maybe a post-doc from the university or something; definitely not an eighteen year-old student who would fill the house with empty bottles and loud music. He was too old for that now.

The sun was creeping through the thin curtain. It would be a sunny day. He would soon get up and head towards the beach. His friend lived in Warrington, a small town north of Dunedin with one of the safest beaches for kids. Shallow and protected from the open sea, it would be crowded in summer. But now in spring it was a nice place for a morning jog, a midday walk, an evening stroll.

Sylvia had come for a visit the day before. He had been surprised by her maturity. 'You're doing the right thing, Papa, and I'm proud of you,' she had said a brave smile on her face.

'Thank you, sweetie,' he had replied. His eyes had filled with unshed tears, the heaviness in his shoulders feeling more bearable. He would still keep his close bond with Sylvia, no matter the cost. Because his daughter was a treasure to him. 'You know you can come to me any time you need, sweetheart. Do you know this?' he had asked.

She had nodded her head, a wrinkled face full of emotions. 'I'll be fine, Papa. I won't let Mum's craziness invade me'.

Tom had been unable to ask what she meant. Better to let it go. His daughter would tell him if it was becoming too much. That was all he needed now: the love of his daughter and her trust.

He got up, put on some shorts, running shoes and a t-shirt and closed the front door with a soft sound. Their neighbours were already awake, gardening. He said hello to the old lady tending the roses and went down the street towards the sea.

The breeze was freezing, but he loved it that way. He couldn't stand too much heat. He passed a couple of regular runners. The woman in her thirties, looking as if she released her stress by running each morning with all her being; the man in his fifties trying to reduce his big tummy. They nodded at each other in recognition and continued running.

When his temples were drenched with sweat, he stopped. He took off his shoes and entered the water. It felt so good; his tired feet were getting a break, relaxing in the water.

I will survive, he said to himself. *I'll be OK for some time. And one day, I'll move on.*

CHAPTER 14

The Castle

Irene and Sofia

Stirling Castle, Scotland, September 2021

The impressive stone walls stood before Irene and Sofia. Big and strong on a hill overlooking the town and the Forth River, it was Sofia's childhood's perfect castle, full of dreams of princesses and dragons. She had read that it had been sieged a few times. Did any of them succeed? What machine, what amount of human effort could break through those walls? She couldn't imagine. Thank goodness she hadn't lived in those times.

'Oh my God.' Sofia was gobsmacked, her long hair swirling in the summer breeze. 'I wish I had been living here, looking through that lovely stained glass window towards the meadows, listening to the far-away cry of Robert the Bruce in Bannockburn when he knocked down the English army.' Sofia looked at Irene, a shy smile on her face. 'Sorry, I tend to get carried away near castles.'

'Yes, I can see that. Come on, let's go inside and see the thrones. Years ago, you could sit on them and take a photo.'

'Well, that's something!' Sofia rushed up the ramp, past a group of tourists following a woman with a red umbrella.

They entered the ballroom. A noisy crowd was just leaving, restoring a much-needed sense of peace. Sofia walked towards the thrones. She touched their arms with reverence. She had been quite smiley lately, especially after talking to Peter, who called her every evening. She looked at Irene. Despite the mission they were both on, Irene looked better than when she had last seen her two years ago, during her last visit to her parents in Madrid. She had looked lonely and worn down, as if something was missing in her life, despite her two wonderful daughters and husband.

She still needed some time to accept Cora's wishes of taking her ashes to Scotland. Her lips would purse in tension every time their mission was mentioned. But she obviously was delighting in looking at the thrones, and that made Sofia happy. Maybe coming to Scotland had been the right decision.

'Can you take a photo of me now, Irene?' Sofia asked.

'Sure.' Irene took a few photos of a smiley Sofia from different angles. With her short red skirt and her hiking sandals, she looked nothing like a medieval lady.

'All done. You can explore the other buildings, too. The whole complex is huge.'

'Oh, I'd love to get lost in the castle corridors!' Sofia almost ran out of the hall.

Irene didn't follow her. She had seen the castle already, and just needed some silence. She walked up some stairs leading to the walls of the castle, and disappeared.

⁓

The castle was so impressive. It surprised Sofia, despite her determination not to get caught up by Irene's crazy love for Scotland, and apparently Cora's too. Edinburgh was noisy, full of tourists and bagpipes in every corner. She just wanted to scream at all of them and make them disappear. What Cora had seen in this mixture of tartan, bagpipes, strident noise and overly simplistic history, she just didn't understand. And yes, she admitted that she liked Edinburgh, with ancient buildings that spoke of an exciting past, an amazing castle in an extinguished volcano and all the heritage buildings along the Royal Mile. Despite all, she had admired the architecture and the sense of pride that emanated from every point along the Royal Mile. But it was still a big city. It surprised her to realise how much she loathed cities, how she craved the fresh air. And how her life had been bottled up in her small apartment; a constricted life in a city that didn't let her breathe.

But this castle was something. She could imagine herself living amongst these walls in medieval times. When she sat on the throne, a sudden memory came back to her. She must have been five years old and Cora ten. They had been to the Alcazar in Segovia, northwest of Madrid, an impressive stronghold of the Catholic Kings, full of rounded towers, said to have inspired the famous Neuschwanstein castle in Bavaria. She and Cora had gone up the spiral stairway to the tower. Looking down at the view of the vast kingdom, they had felt like princesses. In the great hall, the two girls had admired the throne. She remembered her father dreamily telling the two of them about life in medieval times, fierce and passionate at the same time. She remembered looking down from a huge window to the rocks below, and how their dad had told them a story about a royal nanny who had been rocking a baby prince to sleep one day by that very window and had accidentally dropped him. Horrified, she had thrown herself out the window as well. Sofia shivered now, looking down a similar drop at Stirling.

Sofia and Cora had played princesses for many years after the visit to the Alcazar. They had had imaginary maids serving them, dressing them, combing their hair. They had danced in lovely balls with dresses down to their toes full of glitter and silk. She remembered spending more time preparing the balls than actually playing. The preparation had been as important (sometimes even more) than the play itself. Attention to detail mattered back then. When had she forgotten about those dreams? *Maybe the day Manuel raped me and destroyed my innocence*, a voice in her head told her. Maybe that was the day she became the shadow of who she had been. Maybe that day was the turning point that had made her stay behind with their parents while Cora left to live an adventurous life in a faraway land. The thought surprised her. She had forgotten about Manuel, about the incident that had cursed her to a dull life. Cora always knew there had been something, but never asked her, probably waiting for her to open up when she was ready. But Sofia had never felt ready to open up to Cora or anyone else about what had happened that day. Now she realised she had been bottling up that tragic moment and letting it infect her whole life, like the red smoke bombs that soldiers used to throw to confuse their enemy. Sofia had been living in that dirty smoke since that day, letting her life be tinted red, while others lived a life in a clean and safe air.

She was walking along one of the long stone corridors. It was cold, her skirt not covering enough her legs. She had felt so alive wearing a skirt from her twenties. Now she felt ridiculous. She felt the goosebumps on her legs. A group of tourists passed her, pushing her aside. One of them, a man with a long brown beard, stopped in front of a window looking towards the river, took a quick photo and disappeared. Sofia could imagine him going back home and showing the pictures to his friends, taking more time to explain each picture than savouring it in person. She despised rushed trips. She always had. And now she almost despised everyone who went on them. She'd rather savour one single castle for three hours and remember how it felt to be there, what it smelt of, how she could imagine living there, than going to all the tourist attractions in a country and not remembering any of them. She was so lucky to be on this trip with Irene, she thought for a moment, before remembering the reason for coming here.

A young couple with hiking boots passed by. It made Sofia think of the hikes she'd done with her sister. She remembered how Cora had organised the trips in the Alps every time she had visited, leaving her daughter Alex with their parents. Her sister had put a lot of effort into making sure they had quality time together as sisters. She hadn't realised that until now. But that had been in the early years, when Alex was a little girl. Before Cora and Nick had split up. By then, Sofia rarely went to the mountains. She had reduced her time in the outdoors to the rare hiking days with Cora. There were no more of those now. How she hated Cora for that. *How dare you leave me alone, Cora, without giving me any notice. How dare you.*

'Are you okay?' A woman was looking intently at her. With dark blue eyes, blonde hair and a long blue dress, she could have been part of the castle. Sofia was sitting on a stone bench looking out the window, tears in her eyes. How she had arrived there, she couldn't remember.

'Uh, yes,' she said, drying her eyes.

The woman sat beside her and looked towards the window. She had a frown on her face. Her lips started to tremble.

'This place reminds me so much of all we could have had, of a life where we could have been princesses, passionately loved by princes who would come on splendid horses to conquer our hearts,' the woman said.

'Yes.'

The woman was now looking into Sofia's eyes, tears running freely down her cheeks.

'But life is a bit more complex than that. There are regrets too, and even if we find the modern version of a prince, they never come in shining armour to conquer your heart.'

'No.'

'This place reminds me of all I could have achieved and didn't. All the bad choices I have made. And all the lost chances, too.'

'Yes.' Sofia sighed. 'And even back then, the prince in shining armour would probably come so rarely that the princess no doubt forgot his face and idealised his personality.'

'That's true,' the woman said with a smile that formed wrinkles around her eyes. 'Maybe back then was not that great after all.'

'No, maybe not.'

The woman stood up, touched Sofia's shoulder and left. After a few minutes Sofia got up and went out to warm up in the sun. She was getting hungry. It was time to look for Irene and find a place to have some lunch.

CHAPTER 15

The Rift

Cora visiting Irene

Heidelberg, Germany, July 2017

Cora stood by the castle entrance, looking up at the unassailable building. Huge, made of pink stone, it was built to resist any invasion. She wondered how many years it had taken to build and how many men had been needed. She could probably find out. In her twenties she would have bought a book about the Heidelberg castle and read it thoroughly, then gone room by room reading every single sign. But she had changed. Now she was content with just looking around and getting a feel for the place.

'What do you think?' Irene asked, hooking her arm through Cora's.

'I think wow! But also, what a waste of money and men's back health.'

Irene's laughter resonated on the large walls surrounding the fortress.

Cora looked at her dear friend. Her usual long dark hair was gone, replaced by a boyish cut, which now had a few white hairs. With new wrinkles around her eyes, she looked worn out. Martha and Beth, her two daughters, were now in their teens, the same as Alex, and were keen to spend the weekend with their friends, so had stayed home. Alex was spending a few weeks with her dad in Wellington. So for once it was just the two of them, free to explore, to forget about meal schedules and to reconnect with each other.

'Well, it's probably one of the most impressive castles I've been to. The view from the top was breathtaking. But I think I've had enough history for today,' Cora said.

'Yeah. Me too. What about having a cool drink somewhere? It's quite warm already.'

'Good idea.' They turned around and left the castle for the rest of the tourists, now arriving by the hundreds.

—

Half an hour later they were seated outside a café with views to the immense Neckar River.

'Do you remember when we went swimming in the lake below Peñalara?' Irene asked, holding a glass of Coke. The lake at the foot of the highest peak in the mountains near Madrid was famous for its cold temperatures and swimming competitions.

'That was damn cold!' Cora said.

'Yes, it was. But remember how sweaty we were after going up Peñalara in summer. There are no trees there, remember? Just bush and bare land.'

'Those were happy times for us, weren't they? A peak each weekend. No responsibilities. Just keeping each other company.'

'Yes. And no men around us. Remember how we used to laugh at our school friends getting so hung up on one boy or another? Like Anna, who got married just after finishing school and had three children by the age of twenty-two.'

'My goodness! What a mistake, not to live your life before having children.'

'Yes,' Irene said, gazing at the sparkling waters of the river below.

'I've been thinking a lot lately about how my life would have been if I hadn't had children.'

Cora looked at her friend, a frown on her face. 'Do you have any regrets?'

'I love my girls with all my heart. But lately I feel empty inside. I'm not needed anymore, and all my dreams were left behind.'

'It's not too late to follow your dreams, Irene. To start new projects that make you happy and fulfilled. We're not in wheelchairs,' Cora said. 'In fact, now I'm in my mid-forties, I feel like I can do anything I want. I don't care anymore about what others think. I just want to live my life the best I can and make the most of each day.'

'You're right, I guess. I just don't know where to start,' Irene said with a sigh.

'What about contacting someone from Karlsruhe University? I'm sure the Geology department could do with some help.'

'I'm very rusty, Cora. I haven't opened a geology book for years. They wouldn't know what to do with me.'

'Well, you won't know until you try. But most of all, you need something to boost your confidence. You're a very valuable person, Irene. You used to be top of the class. And you're kind and focused and have a good manner with teenagers. They would love you.'

Irene smiled and looked at her friend. 'Oh, Cora. I've missed you so much.'

'Me too,' Cora said with a smile.

'I wish we lived closer.' Irene didn't want to tell Cora how she had missed her when her daughters were small, how she had envisioned them walking through parks with their strollers, sharing the wonders of motherhood.

'Yes,' Cora said sighing. 'But now I don't belong here, Irene. It's been too many years overseas, and Europe is rejecting me.'

'That's not true. You could come for a few months and see how it goes.'

Cora was silent. She didn't want to tell her friend that she and Alex had lived for a year in Germany five years ago. It hadn't worked, and they had gone back to New Zealand knowing their time in Europe was over. She hadn't told Irene or her family about it. She wanted to avoid the expectations and disappointments that surely would have followed.

'Well, I'd like to have a look at a few shops here. They have such lovely things. Would you like to come with me?' Irene stood up and turned around.

'Sure. Let's do that. 'I'm always keen to brush up on European fashion.' Cora stood up too, a lump in her throat. She hated keeping a secret from her oldest friend.

—

A few days later Irene and Cora were having tea in Irene's garden. Closing her eyes, Cora smelt the sweet fragrance that reminded her of home. After all, she realised, Europe did have some specific smells that reminded her of her childhood. Fresh geraniums, pine trees after the rain, old wood from mansions centuries old.

'You've made a paradise out of this garden, Irene,' Cora whispered.

Irene smiled. 'Well, it's my refuge, where I come and think when things aren't working, where I pour out my frustrations. Over the years the garden has benefited from my salty tears, I guess.'

'Oh, Irene…' Cora touched her friend's arm.

'It's OK.' Irene was wiping her tears. 'It's good to share this with you.' She looked at Cora, a half-smile on her face. 'Who else would I share it with?'

'Haven't you made friends here, after all these years?'

'Well, I have a friend or two. But none like you. And the distance hasn't changed that. But at the same time … well, the distance, both geographical and in time, has taken its toll, Cora.'

'I know.'

'Somehow this isn't enough anymore. And it's not only about my profession. I'd like to spend more time with you. Go on a trip together again. Not just wait for our monthly catch up.'

'I understand that, Irene. But it's too late for me to come back. There's no space for me here anymore.'

'How do you know? You haven't tried!'

'And what? Spend thousands of dollars, come here, realise this is not what I want anymore, then go home again? Quite a few people I know have done that.'

'Do you want to make decisions based on the experience of others?' Irene's face had turned red, her fists tightly clenched around her cup of tea. 'Because it might not be yours.'

'No, it might not. But I know I don't belong here anymore, Irene. Surely you must understand that?'

'How do you know?'

'Stop, Irene. Or we'll hurt each other. How about you come and spend some time with me? Your girls are grown-ups now. They'll survive.'

'How? With what money? And besides, my life is here.'

'Yeah. And mine's there. So there's no solution but for me to leave my life over there and come back?'

'No. Of course not.'

Cora stepped closer to Irene. 'What is it?'

Irene stood up from the bench and reached for her rose bush. 'Things with Mark are not going well.'

'I know. They haven't for a long time,' Cora said. 'Have you tried couples therapy?'

'I suggested it. But we only went once and then he refused.'

'That's hard. What did he say?'

'That it wasn't solving anything. That we don't have a relationship issue. That it's me being restless and angry all the time.'

'How cowardly to think it's all your fault.' She looked at Irene. 'What are you going to do?'

Irene looked at her, her mouth open.

'What do you mean, what am I going to do? Keep going for the sake of my children, of course!'

'Mm. That isn't always the best option.'

'What do you mean? Do we all need to be divorced like you?'

Cora looked at Irene. She had closed fists and her face was white. 'That's not fair.'

'Well, maybe some people try harder to keep their relationship!'

'What?' Cora's face was red. She stood up, her face close to Irene's. 'Nick left me for another woman!'

'Maybe you hadn't put enough effort into your relationship!'

'How dare you!' Cora was screaming now.

'You didn't try hard enough, Cora.'

'Do you mean you need to suffer for years?'

'If you need to, yes.'

Cora breathed three times, the words fighting to get out. But she knew they would only cause pain and not be of any help. 'Right,' she sighed. 'I need some time.' She stood up, carefully placing her cup on the table. She grabbed her jacket and looked at Irene.

'I'll find a hotel for the night, and I'll come tomorrow morning to pack my bags and leave. I need some time to myself.' Tightening her lips, she turned and went around the back gate to the streets of a city she barely knew.

———

A couple of weeks later Cora was walking along the Main River in Frankfurt, killing time before heading to the airport to catch her flight back to New Zealand. Following the visit with Irene, she had spent a few days in Spain with her mother and sister. It hadn't gone much better than with Irene. Her mother had simply shut down after the death of Cora's father. She had barely talked to Cora, unable to look at her in the eye, and hadn't even asked about Alex.

It hadn't been much better with Sofia. They had fought about how Sofia had taken care of their mother on her own. Sofia had complained about not having had much help from Cora, who had asked many times how she could help without receiving any reply.

It was a warm sunny day, and there were a few families with small children walking along the path, a little boy with a tricycle, a girl on roller skates. Cora felt a lump in her throat. She was returning to the other side of the world without any idea where home really was. She didn't feel welcome in Europe anymore. What used to be her home had shut its doors on her. The disconnect between her and her little sister and best friend were too hard to bear. Now she was going back with a broken heart. She was looking forward to being back in her refuge, where she could be numb from a pain too far away to feel real. Was her life going to be like this from now on? She loved working at the little bookshop in Petone, organising evening talks with writers or poets, attending to the regular customers. Feeling at peace, especially on weekday mornings when only a few people would be in the shop, silently looking at books, the feeling of worship of the written word in the air. But somehow it wasn't enough. She needed more. More in her heart and soul.

There was a café with tables and chairs outside overlooking the river, with umbrellas offering good shade. Cora sat at one of the tables and ordered some food. A lovely salad arrived, with tomatoes, lettuce, carrots, beetroot and a delicious vinaigrette dressing.

She was feeling tired in her bones lately, worn out by a feeling of time speeding up and her not being able to keep up. Alex was growing. At sixteen, she was a self-assured young woman, happy to hang out with her friends. She had already gone on a trip with her friend Carla and their family. She was becoming independent, and Cora was not taking that very well. In a couple of years she would go to university and Cora would be there on her own, wondering how life had passed by so fast and what she had made out of it. She needed to find a path towards self-fulfilment. But most of all, she needed to find peace within. A way to silence all the voices in her head: a mixture of her own, Sofia's, Irene's and her mother's, saying how selfish she was to live so far away.

The *bananensplit* arrived. Chocolate, strawberry and vanilla scoops, with banana and lots of whipped cream. It reminded her of her childhood, going to Germany with her parents, having ice cream every day. She took the first mouthful. The sweetness of the chocolate eased her soul. She closed her eyes, and with a smile told herself that it would all be OK. She had a good life, a wonderful daughter and the promise of a fulfilling future.

CHAPTER 16

At the Feet of the Hero

Irene and Sofia

Balquhidder, Scotland, September 2021

The valley was perfectly silent. Irene could even hear Sofia breathing on the other side of the tomb. The sun was low but it was still warm. Irene could see a few houses scattered around, several abandoned ones. She closed her eyes. This was the perfect countryside scenery she had been longing for. Green as far as she could see. Old rounded Scottish hills in the distance. A gentle breeze caressing her cheeks. Not a car to be heard. No city noises constantly thumping in her ears. A murder of crows flew by, squawking as if annoyed that two human beings had dared disturb their peace. She couldn't blame them.

She felt at peace. They had come looking for Rob Roy's grave; that Scottish hero from the Walter Scott novel, who, like Robin Hood, had taken money from the rich to give to the poor. From a humble origin he had become the national hero. He had a lovely restful place here, at the cemetery of a sixteenth-century church ruin, she thought, looking at the few abandoned tombs. But she knew Scottish never forgot, no matter how many generations had passed. She remembered having seen a vase of carefully chosen roses on a tomb from the eighteenth century. Surrounded by people from his time, unaware of the terrible pain that his people would suffer in the following two centuries, Rob Roy had the rest that he deserved. She wished she would one day have that sense of peace.

'Look, Irene.' Sofia's lovely Spanish accent reached her. They were trying to speak English to each other on this trip. Sofia was pointing at something, but Irene couldn't go to her now. Too many memories came to her of when she had been here with Cora, with all their lives ahead of them, so many possibilities open to the world.

She had been unsure about coming on this trip. It hadn't been easy. Irene liked to keep her thoughts to herself, and Sofia needed to talk about Cora. She hadn't been prepared for that. It was too soon. Just the mention of her dear friend brought a huge lump to her throat, as if she was at the end of a boxing fight in which she was the loser, gasping for air. She had been trying to avoid looking too deeply into that, distracting herself along the way. First in Brittany, where Cora and Sofia had spent a summer as teenagers. Sofia had been quiet at times, then enthusiastically talking non-stop. Then they had crossed the British Channel the old way, on the ferry. Sofia said that was the way she had crossed with Cora and their parents years ago, and she would not take that suffocating tunnel and add money to the coffers of the UK and France for that. Following a brief two days in London they had travelled north to Thornton, Yorkshire, the birthplace of the Brontë sisters. Irene had suggested it when she remembered Cora saying how she would love to see the wild moors where Emily had imagined Heathcliff walking away in the storm, Cathy searching for him. Irene and Sofia had loved it: the old stone house still standing against time and weather, the heather growing everywhere … so much like in the Scottish Highlands.

Irene put her hand in the pocket of her rain jacket, and there she felt it. The letter from Cora. The one that Alex had given her, alongside one for Sofia. She raised her head now, looking for Sofia. She was nowhere to be seen. She might have gone down the road a bit to explore the peaceful landscape.

Immersed in her thoughts, Irene had been walking through a meadow looking towards the valley. An old stone bench stood in front of her. She sat on it with the letter in her hands. The envelope was becoming yellow from her touch and a bit of rain. It only said *Irene* in Cora's beautiful round handwriting. She had probably used the pen that Irene had given her when she turned eighteen, to make sure she would write in the future.

'Never give up writing,' she had told her friend. *Did she ever write a novel?* Irene wondered. She might never know. How much time wasted being angry with her friend. Looking at the beautiful scenery and taking a deep breath, she opened the letter.

Mi querida Irene,

This is probably one of the most difficult 'writings' of my life. I wouldn't have imagined that I would be writing a farewell letter to you in my forties. More in my eighties, with false teeth and a warm pink bath robe, with my old husband sitting in the sun outside our house, wherever that would have been.

But no, life has decided that the time is now for me to say goodbye to the life I have only started to learn how to live with joy and optimism. It is hard. I almost left it too late to do what I always wanted: live in the countryside away from civilisation, living an easy life, with time to smell the roses, to go for a walk along the beach, to be myself without judgement, without criticisms, with all the goods and bads of who I truly am.

I managed, Irene. I managed to come to this beautiful place in the South Island of New Zealand, Golden Bay. A place I fell in love with the first time I came with Nick, our lives ahead of us, feeling the adventure of exploring a new country with a man I thought I would share my life with. And it was love at first sight. Its never-ending ranges, its golden sandy beaches where it is safe to swim (almost impossible to find here, they are either sandy and wild like crazy, or rocky), its sense of freedom and fulfilment. But then I went back to Wellington, to being increasingly unhappy over the years, to having all my time taken up by a (wonderful) daughter and work, to a traumatic separation, and to decisions made because they were the best for my daughter: the best education for her, not taking her away from her friends, keeping her close to her dad, securing my financial status with a permanent job … all the wrong excuses to live a half-life. But only now I realise that.

I waited too long, Irene, and now it's too late.

One of the things I regret most is having let our friendship fall away over a stupid argument that is blurred in my head now. I know it was around me not coming often enough, or spending enough time with you, as I needed to divide my time between different countries in each trip to Europe. The trips were only every three to four years as I couldn't afford them more often. And only for five weeks, as I didn't have any more leave to take. I could have taken some leave without pay. I could have asked to work from overseas for some months. But I didn't. My trips ended up being exhausting, and leaving everyone I saw feeling as if the visits were never long enough. My mother. My dad. Sofia. You. And me too.

You once asked me why I hadn't gone back to Europe. You said I hadn't tried hard enough. You said it was as if I had rejected that part of my life. You said the real truth was that I didn't want to come back. I have been thinking a lot over the years about those words and asking myself those questions. I still don't know if I have an answer for them, my dear friend. Since I moved to New Zealand my soul has been divided into two. The Cora I left behind, whose life continued briefly for five weeks at a time every three years and was left in standby mode in between, and the Cora I created here. Many times I have wondered if they are the same person, if there was a way to 'glue' them together and make one single me. But I never managed to do that. They obstinately wanted to be two independent women. And I let it happen.

I never found a true path to return to, Irene. I tried. But life in Europe was too strict, too rigid, too difficult, and somehow a wall had been drawn in front of my face, not letting me come back.

I tried to come back, Irene. I really tried. I even took one year off work and accepted a job in a small library in the South of Germany. Alex was around ten years old. And we didn't fit in there. At school the other girls left Alex out, not letting her be part of the group. And it was incredibly lonely, feeling forgotten by the world. Nobody knew, not even Sofia. I went back to New Zealand with my tail between my legs, knowing that the door was closed for me.

I have finally fallen in love, Irene. Tom is a Kiwi from Dunedin who has been looking for a place to settle and be free to be himself. He is funny, he is easy-going and makes me do adventurous things, like learning how to kayak (we have done the Abel Tasman by kayak, amazing!), or jump into a pool from fifteen metres high. He accepts me as I am and has helped me accept that I am who I am, and I need to make the most of my time. We have been together for fourteen lovely months. I wish there were fourteen years more.

How is your life going, dear friend? I bet Martha and Beth are at uni now, or almost there. Driving you crazy with teenage hormones, I guess. When Alex was fifteen I missed you so much. I wished we had shared mothering experiences and how to deal with a girl who refused to wash her hair or tidy her room. Who would have said, given that I didn't know that well how to handle her back then, that she would turn into such a beautiful, smart and peaceful girl. She knows exactly where she wants to go. She loves horses and is studying in Dunedin to become a vet assistant. And she is planning to come to Golden Bay and be in charge of the horse veterinary clinic, helping the current vet who is in her sixties and adores her. I am so proud of her. Most of her childhood she has spent with me, paying regular visits to her dad. I have learnt how to be a family of two where I was the only adult and many times not the one making decisions (Mum, I don't want to go tramping today again, it's boring!), but I am so happy I made it, Irene. I managed to raise my lovely girl to be a mature and confident woman. And my heart sinks thinking I won't see her grow up and become the wonderful vet assistant she longs to be. Make her own decisions. I wonder if she will ever move to Europe (my mother instinct says she will), or if she will create a family one day (probably in her late thirties, after having had a fulfilling youth); if she will always accept herself as she is. Leaving her the hole of my absence in her life is the worst thing I am dealing with lately. It makes me get up in the middle of the night wanting to scream as loud as I can. I end up running in the garden until I feel exhausted. I then sit on my long chair and see the sky turn pink before it turns light blue. That is where Tom has been finding me every morning lately.

My gut tells me that you abandoned yourself when you became a mum. That is what I witnessed after your children were born. You were the perfect mother, Irene. I was envious at the start. You seemed to know how everything should be, how to deal with every problem, how to handle it all. But deep inside, you had abandoned a career as a geologist at the university, something that you loved. And you stopped painting — 'the love of your life', as you used to describe it, remember? You told me at the foot of Rob Roy's tomb in Scotland. I never forgot that moment, when I suddenly realised that you already knew what you wanted in life, and I still didn't. I felt proud and jealous of you at the same time.

Irene, there is no time to waste. Your children will not need you that much anymore (well, they will always need you, but in a different way). You have probably experienced the empty nest syndrome like I did. It's tough. It makes you feel useless and question who you are. But it's also the perfect opportunity to recover past dreams, projects that you left behind, buried under soiled nappies and walks to the playground, family holidays and to-do lists. Don't waste your time, Irene. Rediscover who you really are, who you always wanted to be. You don't need to enter a midlife crisis. You only need to listen to that twenty-year-old girl, beautiful and honest, who came with me to explore the Scottish Highlands and laughed at each one of my jokes. Go back there, feel the scent of the heather, touch the wonderful thick thistles for me. But most of all, make a commitment to yourself. And never, never give up.

I love you, my dear friend, and I will always be side by side with you, laughing with you at your own mistakes, and smiling at your successes.

Cora

CHAPTER 17

Encounter in the Forest

Cora, Northland, New Zealand, February 2017

Cora looked up. The four kauri trees extended in an infinite path towards the light. She was closer than she had ever been to such big trees. They were sharing their journey in a loving connection whereby branches intertwined in a life dance.

She felt as if she was one of them, her friend Irene next to her, walking through life hand in hand. She missed her. Moving to New Zealand had brought her a deep sense of loneliness that she couldn't get rid of, even after almost twenty years. She would be visiting her in Germany in a few months' time. She was looking forward to it. Now that Alex's and Irene's daughters were old enough, they could spend some time on their own like in the old days.

She was alone in the forest. She could hear the fantails twittering, a bellbird in the distance. She walked around the trees using the wooden platform designed to keep them safe, preventing people from stepping on their roots and spreading the deadly kauri dieback disease. The previous day she had seen Tāne Mahuta, the Lord of the Forest, the most ancient kauri in New Zealand. Sick, it still stood majestic caring for its younger siblings.

The third tree could be Sofia, her sister, who was withdrawing from her every day. She leant on one of them. It vibrated somehow, transmitting its warm energy to her. Cora closed her eyes. How much had these immense beings seen? How much had they witnessed in silence? At least she was sure of something: they would never feel alone like Tāne Mahuta. They were eternally together, and they would remain that way till the end. There was a fourth sister. She wondered who that tree represented in her life. Her daughter Alex, maybe? She looked up at the four intertwined trees, eternally bonded no matter how far apart they were.

She stayed there for a long time, her eyes closed, before continuing along the path. It was wide and well-sealed, as if expecting a large number of tourists. Cora hoped it would remain silent. Far away from the crowded areas on the East Coast, she was enjoying her stay in Hokianga Harbour. Swimming each day, enjoying the beautiful sunsets and quiet days, she still missed Alex. It was the first time she had travelled without her. At sixteen, her daughter had presented her arguments in favour of staying in Wellington with her friends. Cora couldn't deny that times had changed. A profound wave of heaviness pressed on her chest again. It had started a few months ago. Her little girl was growing up, and in a couple of years she would be moving out and starting her own life. It seemed like only yesterday that she had been holding her baby in her arms, a gentle face with deep blue eyes looking back at her.

She took her jersey off, sweat running down her back. The day promised to be hot and humid like yesterday. A woman in her sixties approached her, a smile on her face.

'Lovely morning to walk along the giants, isn't it?'

She was wearing light brown tramping trousers and an old red pair of boots. She carried a walking pole and a small backpack, and looked as if she had used them for many years.

'Yes. It is. And I love the silence.'

'That's the best thing about this place. No matter how crowded it can be nearby, it's always peaceful down here.' She offered her hand. 'I'm Kath.'

Cora shook her hand. 'I'm Cora.'

'Nice to meet you, Cora. Where are you from?'

'Originally from Spain. But I've been living in Wellington for nineteen years.'

'That's a long time far away from your home country.'

'To be honest, I don't know where home is anymore.'

'Well. Home is where you make it. I'm from Hawke's Bay, but I lived in Auckland for many years. I moved here after my husband died thirty years ago, and I don't regret it. This is home now.'

'It's a wonderful place to call home.'

'Yes, it is. I live half an hour from here, in Hokianga Harbour.'

'I'm staying there for a few days. I'm enjoying it.'

'Why don't you come and visit me, then? We could have a tea and a piece of cake and watch the harbour.'

'That sounds lovely.'

'Well, I'd better go and get Sandy, my dog. She'll be getting impatient by now. She likes to go for a long walk along the harbour after my walk here, where she's not allowed.' She winked at Cora. 'You keep going. Many people miss it, but Te Matua Ngahere is my favourite kauri. Follow this path until the end, and enjoy.' She smiled. 'My house is the blue one at the end of the town, towards the east. It can't be missed.'

She turned around and left. Cora stayed still for a few moments. What a breath of fresh air that woman was. There was a sense of peace about her that Cora wished she could feel. Maybe age gave that to you. Or maybe it was the quality of your life. Cora didn't feel like she was on the path towards feeling that kind of peace herself. Too much self-doubt, too much disconnection from her dreams. It was all feeling very messy inside her soul lately.

She kept walking, past a wooden gate. The path meandered downhill for a while. With the sun shining through the branches, colouring the forest in dark gold, she felt like she was walking in a fairy forest.

And then the path ended in a cul-de-sac. She looked up. A thick trunk stood before her. Not as tall as the rest she had seen, this tree was surrounded by a magical aura, emanating a sense of majesty and eternity. Cora sat on the bench in front of it, tears falling down her cheeks. She trusted this ancient soul. Her heart was beating fast against her ribs. She had a deep feeling of having found home. And then she started to speak. About her frustrations, her loneliness, her love for her daughter, her nostalgia for her friends and her childhood. She talked until there were no more words inside her. Her body started spasming out of control, moved by a hidden force. She cried and screamed, bending herself over on the bench, gasping for breath. With her head between her legs, she took several deep breaths. Slowly she raised her head. The kauri was surrounded by golden light, a mist covering it in a layer of protection. She gave one last deep breath and closed her eyes. She felt clean, free. With a final sigh, she lay on the bench and fell asleep, feeling more peaceful than she had felt in a long time.

A few days later, Cora walked along the road south of the Hokianga Harbour, looking for Kath's house. It was a warm, sunny afternoon and her forehead was already covered in sweat. There were a few houses along the road, all facing north towards the sea and the sun. Except for a dog barking in the distance, it was quiet. The blue house appeared in front of her. A two-storey timber house from the twenties, surrounded by mature trees and a palm tree in the front garden, it smelt of happy childhoods and warm summers.

Kath was tending her roses with garden scissors in one hand and a bag of natural fertiliser in the other. She smiled at her. 'Over here, Cora.

It's so nice to see you.' She put her garden supplies on the ground and went to embrace her. 'You look radiant!'

'Thank you. I feel so energised after having spent a few days here.'

'That's what the harbour does to you,' Kath said with a smile. 'Come and let's have a cold drink on the deck.'

They walked inside the house. The lower part had a garage and a storage room. Upstairs were two small bedrooms, a kitchen facing the back garden and a cosy living room full of old furniture that reminded Cora of her grandmother.

'This is lovely,' Cora said.

'It's my refuge, where I'm the Queen of my own life,' Kath said.

'I like that feeling.'

'Maybe you should try it. It's good for the soul,' Kath said with a wink.

They sat in old wooden chairs on the deck facing the harbour.

'How peaceful.'

'Yes, it is. Well, unless you get a possum at night climbing that palm tree searching for eggs.'

'Really? Are they able to climb that?' She could see the knots and spikes along the trunk.

'Oh, yes. That and much more. But I've ordered a metal band to stop them, just like the other big trees have. That way they won't be able to climb to the leaves.'

Kath fetched lemonade and two pieces of cake, which she placed on a metallic table next to them.

'So. What's brought you here on your own?' she asked. 'Getting away from the noisy city?'

'Yes. I live in Lower Hutt with my daughter, who's sixteen years old and not that keen to travel with her mother anymore. I love the countryside, and I needed to get out of Wellington. After having lived there for nineteen years I need a change.'

'Oh yes, I know that feeling. I used to live in Auckland. But since

I moved here I haven't looked back. I want to spend my old age alone next to the sea.' She looked at Cora. 'No partner?'

'No. Alex's dad and I separated when she was four, and I've lived on my own since.'

'That's hard. A single mum for so long.'

'Yes. But it's also given me a strength I didn't know I had before.'

'Yes. I can relate to that.' Kath smiled at Cora. 'I was a solo mum for some time too, after my husband died when my son was twelve. It was hard, but I reconnected with myself in a way I hadn't before. That's when I started painting again. I took night lessons and I loved it. I had a very supportive old woman as a neighbour who would care for my son.'

'That is so nice. Yes, I've noticed how women on their own seem to reconnect with long-forgotten dreams. I wonder why that doesn't happen so often for women with partners.' She sipped her lemonade, closing her eyes with pleasure. 'This is delicious.'

'Thank you,' Kath said with a smile. 'Oh, women. Such silly creatures, thinking that men should always take priority. They always find excuses to put themselves last, after their partners, children, even the dog. Ah, and their elderly parents, when the time comes.'

'How very true.'

'So, what is your passion?'

'Writing. I've always loved writing, ever since I was a child. I've slowly rediscovered it over the years. I've written half a novel. Now I have no excuses, as Alex is grown up and I'm on my own. But I don't feel inspired.'

'Why is that?' Kath's eyes twinkled.

'A need for a big change,' Cora said. 'I need a change of scenery.'

'Yes. I can see that. Where to?'

'I don't know. Being from overseas, I have wasted many years wondering where home was. After my divorce, Alex and I went back to Germany for a year. It didn't go well. I felt out of place. We didn't make friends. And Alex was not doing well at school. So we came back. I got my job back. Europe is just not my place anymore.'

'Congratulations on doing all this on your own.'

'Thank you.'

'Maybe you need to move to a quieter place, like me.'

'I'd love to. But I have no finances to do that.'

'Well, in faraway places sometimes you need to be creative to survive financially. People tend to have several jobs. Or they become artists and sell their creations,' Kath said with a wink.

Cora smiled. She liked Kath. 'I think I'm too scared to make that move yet.'

'Well, don't wait too long. You have connected to your soul and listened to your needs. Don't keep longing.'

'I guess you're right.' Cora looked at the sea, deep in thought. Then she looked at Kath. 'What about you? What's your story?'

'Well, after those years painting, I found the love of my life, Charles. He was a good father to my Tom, and we spent fifteen wonderful years together. I did manage to keep painting, which gave me hope that I could maintain a healthy relationship without forgetting about myself.'

'That's nice to hear. And a breath of hope for many women.'

'Yes, it is. And then one day he was gone, lost to a short battle with cancer, and it broke my heart.' Kath's face crumbled, distorted with pain.

'Oh, Kath.'

'My son Tom was living in Dunedin, so I was alone again. It was so much harder than after my first husband. So I sold my house and moved here.'

'To run away from the world?'

'Yes,' she said with a smile. 'But I've also reconnected. With nature, with my soul. And I've made peace with life. From the other side, you get a great perspective on things.'

'In what sense?'

'Well, for instance, I could see how unhappy Tom was with his wife, a selfish woman who was sucking up my son's energy. I never said a word. But I was so happy when it was over. Now Tom is still there, to be close to his daughter and my granddaughter, Sylvia, whom I rarely see. But I can tell he's lonely, and in great need of a change.' Kath looked at Cora. 'Something tells me our paths will cross again in some way. I felt that since I saw you in the kauri forest. I wonder what life has planned.'

'Do you think life has a plan?'

Kath smiled. 'Oh, yes, it does. Life is a big planner. She moves us from here to there, making people meet, learn lessons and enrich their lives. And I have a feeling you'll find what you're looking for. Just don't leave it too long,' she said. 'Life is too precious. And you don't know what ideas it might have for you.' She sipped her lemonade and closed her eyes.

CHAPTER 18

The Healing of the Mountains

Alex

Mayrhofen, Tirol, Austria, September 2021

Alex looked up at the peaks ahead. She closed her eyes and took a deep breath, drawing into her lungs the clean air from the mountains. A smile appeared on her face. *God, this feels so good.* The sun was warming her heart, thawing it from the deep sadness that had overcome her in the weeks since her mum had died.

She opened her eyes, taking in the breathtaking beauty of the Alps in front of her. She couldn't believe she was here on her own. Her mum had talked to her about the Alps so often when she was little. 'One day I will take you to see them, ponytail,' she used to say. But it never happened. And now it was too late. Alex felt a hole in her chest, which had become a guest determined to stay; one she didn't know how to handle right now.

With a shake of her head she took her walking poles and kept going along the ridge. She knew she needed to keep going or she would drown. It was warm, but the sun was not burning her skin as much as in New Zealand. It was a relief to know she didn't need to be as careful in Europe with the sunscreen. A group of German middle-aged men and women passed, their soft and gentle language tickling her ears. She loved to sit down outside a restaurant, close her eyes and listen to others speaking German. She didn't know what they were talking about, as she couldn't understand the language. But she loved the cadence. It soothed her, listening to their voices.

A few people asked her where she was from and what she was doing there. They seemed intrigued to see a twenty-year old woman travelling on her own. A waitress almost cried when Alex managed to explain half in English and half in German. 'That is so sad,' she had said. 'It makes me want to call my mum and ask her to come along with me on the trip to Egypt we've always wanted to do.'

'You should do it,' Alex had replied. *Before it's too late* were the unspoken words left in the air.

Alex had also thought they had time. She had imagined finishing her veterinary assistant degree, helping at the vet clinic in Tākaka and living close to her mum. If she closed her eyes she could imagine herself in a few years with a partner and children, her mum singing her baby to sleep with her beautiful gentle voice. *God, I can't do this*, she thought now. *If I only think of the what ifs, I'll drown.* She sat on a bench looking at the mountain chain in front of her. The village of Mayrhofen was down the valley, the lovely geraniums on the balconies spots of red here and there.

Today she thought she would exhaust herself all day and see if it would help her sleep better. But she wasn't feeling like much anymore. She was ready to descend. Who said she needed to get to the peak, anyway? Bloody ambitious climbers, who didn't enjoy the journey and only wanted to add another peak to their set of life achievements. She was not like that. She would prove it and go down now. But half an hour later she was still sitting on the bench, unable to move, her face red with too much sun. Enough time under the European sun and she would get burnt just like anywhere else.

A woman in her sixties sat down next to her, her face red with exhaustion. She must have been part of the group that had passed ten minutes ago, speaking a mixture of languages. Italian. German. French.

'This is lovely, isn't it?' she said in a British accent.

'Yes. It's breathtaking,' Alex replied.

'But I can't keep up with the rest. They only want to conquer the peak. Not enjoy the journey.'

Alex looked at her. She had blonde hair full of white threads tied in a long braid. With blue leggings and a t-shirt, walking poles and a small backpack, she looked as if tramping (or hiking, as they called it in Europe) was a common activity for her. 'Is it different for you?' she asked.

'It was when Mark and I used to go hiking in Wales or Scotland. We would pore over the map in winter and write down all the peaks we would do over summer. And we achieved quite a bit, including most of the Munros in the Scottish Highlands,' she said with a smile full of memories.

'What happened?'

'Well. It stopped being a race when I got a hip replacement, and became an achievement to just walk.' She looked up at the mountains, then sighed and looked at Alex. 'And when Mark fell sick, I got angry with all the stupid hikers for being so determined to get up there instead of looking down and seeing how far they had come.'

'I feel the same. I thought reaching a peak would help me feel better today. But I don't want to bother.'

'No. Hiking with Mark was the reward. Spending time together in the outdoors. I wouldn't mind walking in circles around our town if only he could be with me for a bit longer…' she said with a trembling voice, trying to hide her eyes full of tears.

'I'm so sorry for your loss,' Alex said, a lump in her throat.

'Thank you, dear. I can see loss in your eyes too,' the woman said in a gentle tone.

'Yes. I lost my mum to cancer two months ago. It happened so quickly that I still wake up hearing her voice.'

'Oh no. That is so hard.' She took Alex's hand and smiled. 'I'm glad to have found you, dear.'

'I'm glad too. I feel so lonely.'

'Where are you from? I can't quite grasp your accent.'

'I was born in Wellington, New Zealand. My dad is Kiwi and my mum was from Spain. She spent many years in her childhood coming to the Alps. She always said she would take me one day.'

'Oh, darling.'

They spent a few minutes in silence, enjoying the company and the view. Zillertal Valley stood before them. Green, with steep slopes and little towns here and there, it looked like a postcard.

Alex sighed. 'Would you like to come down with me? It's time for me to try one of the famous bananensplit that my mum used to talk about.'

'I'd love to,' the woman said with a smile. 'By the way, I'm Nancy.'

'Hi, Nancy. I'm Alex.'

'Mmmm! This is delicious!' Alex scooped up another spoonful of chocolate ice-cream, banana and whipped cream. Seated on a balcony at one of the oldest and most elegant hotels in Mayrhofen, facing the back of the beautiful church, Alex felt like she was indulging herself for the first time in months.

'I haven't had anything so nice in a long time,' Nancy said, a smile on her face. Alex thought her face was so beautiful when she smiled, bright and full of light. She decided she wanted to grow old like her: fit, sweet and easy-going.

'Well, I can rest for the rest of the afternoon now,' Alex said.

'I thought about having a look at the church later. I'm not Catholic, but I'm intrigued by these pretty little churches and would like to know what they look like inside.'

'That's a good idea. But you'll be surprised. They are much more decorated and extravagant than you can probably imagine from looking at the outside.' Alex remembered the gleaming of the golden statues, how she had felt so annoyed with the church for spending so much money on gold rather than helping the poor. 'But I'd love to walk in the cemetery at the back of the church. It's so beautifully decorated. Most tombs have fresh flowers. It's a place that gives me so much peace. I like the feeling that nobody is forgotten there. So different from big cities.'

'Yes, I like that idea,' Nancy said. 'We used to live in London years ago, until one day, when we were in our forties, Mark and I decided we had had enough of noises and feeling unheard, and we moved to the north of England. We loved it there. The peace of the countryside. The lack of noise and cars. The ability to live your life the way you want without judgement and criticism. But most of all, without needing to fulfil any external expectations. I'm still living there.'

'I like that. In New Zealand there are lots of open spaces, so it's quite easy to feel at peace.'

'That's nice. I'd love to visit New Zealand one day.'

'You would love it. It's such a special place. Well, I was born there. But I remember hearing my mother say how much easier life was there compared to Europe. Without so much bureaucracy or judgement. You're free to make your own choices, Mum used to say.'

'That's great to know that there's still a place where you can be who you are.'

'Yes. But it's not all perfect, you know. And it's different enough that Mum never really felt part of the culture. I don't think it's easy when you've grown up somewhere else.'

'No. I guess not.'

'*Mochten sie etwas noch?*' the waiter asked. With Tyrolean brown lederhosen and a red and white shirt, he looked like he was from a Brothers Grimm folk tale. Would they like anything else?

'*Nein, danke,*' Alex said.

'OK, let's go to see that church,' Nancy said. They paid, took their belongings and crossed the road.

This is so magical, Alex thought while walking amongst the beautiful metallic crosses in the cemetery. All handcrafted, with an edelweiss or a native bird, she marvelled at how people would spend so much on decorating the tomb of their beloved ones. *Maybe I should have brought Mum's ashes here*, she thought. *This would have been a beautiful place for her to rest in, and for me to visit. And I know how much she loved this place.* Alex sighed. Her mother had chosen her resting place and she would honour it. She heard a soft noise behind. Nancy was approaching her cautiously, leaving her some space. She loved the way this woman was respecting her privacy. How much she must have gone through in her life. She wanted to embrace her like a second grandmother.

'This is so nice,' Nancy said.

'Yes. Maybe Mum would have preferred to be buried here instead,' Alex said.

'Was she cremated?'

'Yes,' Alex sighed. 'Her ashes are currently being taken to the Scottish Highlands, the place of her choice. Her sister and best friend are taking them.'

'I see. Why didn't you go with them?'

'I had the feeling that my mum wanted it this way. That she wanted the two people she loved most in the world (apart from me) to take them. The ones she needed to resolve a few things with.'

'You are very generous and perceptive, Alex,' Nancy said. 'And it'll be a very special trip for them.'

'Yes, it will. My Aunt Sofia is in shock. I was with her a few weeks ago. She's extremely angry with my mum. But I think mostly she is angry with herself for all the excuses she made to not come and visit us. Or even more so, not being brave enough to change her dull life.'

'Oh, wow. I can relate to that. But she is brave already if she's decided to go on that trip.'

'Yes. She's taken some time off work. I'm proud of her.'

'I'd love that to happen when I die: let my beloved ones change what they need to by asking them to do something for me.' She smiled at Alex. 'Your mum was a very clever woman.'

Alex smiled. 'Yes, she was.'

'What about you? Do you know your path ahead?'

'Good question.' Alex looked up at the mountains surrounding the town. 'I used to know it so clearly. I was planning to finish my degree and then help at the vet clinic in Tākaka, near where my mum lived.'

'That sounds like a good plan. I bet you love animals?'

'I do. They're honest and direct, unlike people. I love to be surrounded by them.'

'What about relationships? Would you like to do all this on your own?'

'Yes. At least, that's what I always wanted. To be strong and manage on my own like my mum.'

'And now?'

'Now I feel lonely without her. I'd like to take a break from my studies and travel for a while, see the world, live in the moment. There's plenty of time to work hard and get old.'

'Beautifully expressed,' Nancy said. 'I would do exactly the same if I were you.'

Alex looked at Nancy. She was still so young and full of energy.

'Why don't you do the same?'

'Me? Where would I go?'

'Wherever you've always wanted to go. Explore. Be adventurous.'

'Oh, I don't see myself doing that. This is the most adventurous thing I've ever done.'

'But it's the first step. It's easier after this.' Alex's face suddenly brightened. 'Why don't we start by travelling together for a few days?

There are some places I'd like to go, but I've felt lazy and lonely. Why don't we make a plan and choose a couple of places each? I would love to spend a few days with you, and we are both in no hurry to go back home, are we?'

'Well, I still have my garden to tend, and that neighbour who needed me to take care of her dog when I come back…' Nancy said. She stood still, a hand on her check, deep in thought. Then she smiled back at Alex. 'Why not? Let's do it!'

Nancy hooked arms with Alex, and they walked back to their hotel.

Discoveries

Sofia and Irene

Inverness, Scotland, October 2021

The pub was almost empty. Made of solid stone like most houses in Inverness, it gave Sofia a sense of permanence and strength. The fireplace made her imagine lovely warm nights listening to live music. The wall was decorated with old photos of Inverness, framed dried thistles and an old painting of Bonnie Prince Charlie, the hero of the 1745 uprising against the English King. She tucked up her jacket. The smell of autumn was in the air, with that whiteness in the sky announcing the cold weather.

Sofia and Irene were sitting next to the window, looking towards High Street. A few music stands, a trumpet case and a double bass lay against the wall. *Ceilidhs*, music and dance social events, were as alive in the Highlands now as they were in the eighteenth century. Sofia wished they could stay over the weekend and come back to the pub. She could imagine it full of Scottish farmers, laughing with beers in their hands, a few of them with that small glass of the 'water of life' that only they could drink in one go.

'So how did you find the day?' Irene was sitting opposite her, a wide smile on her face. She had changed in the last few weeks. She somehow looked more alive, enthusiastic about everywhere they went, explaining as much about rocks as Sofia was able to absorb. It was as if a flower had grown through the snow and was now showing all its beauty to the world. Sofia loved it, but for a few days now she had been quiet. Sofia wondered why.

Today they had visited Cawdor Castle. Sofia had fallen in love instantly with the small stronghold full of history (they even said *Macbeth* was inspired there, as they did of so many other Scottish castles). The fascinating rugs covering all the floors. The holly tree around which a tower was built. The peaceful gardens. The drawbridge made her feel like a medieval knight on horseback, heavy armour over her clothes.

'I liked the castle,' said Sofia. 'I must confess I wasn't expecting such beauty.'

'Cawdor is special. It was Cora's favourite castle.'

'Oh.' Sofia felt bile rise in her throat. Why had her sister never shared that with her?

Irene was looking at her, frowning. 'Cora didn't talk about Scotland with you, did she?'

'No, never.'

'Maybe she wanted to keep it to herself. She always said she would retire in the Scottish Highlands. She would buy a small place near a lake and end her life writing novels in the winter and hiking the Munros in the summer.'

'Yes, that sounds like her. Although I always thought she would do that in the north of Spain, maybe near the Picos de Europa,' Sofia sighed, and picked up her glass of Best beer. She had first tried it in Edinburgh and now always ordered it when she saw it.

'I think we both need to face the fact that Cora was not meant to return. New Zealand became her home,' Irene started slowly. She didn't want to say that Cora had secretly lived in Germany. It might be too much for Sofia to take on right now.

'Yes. Maybe I have been waiting in stand-by for her to come back. First when she got divorced, and then when our father died.' Sofia swallowed hard, trying to get rid of a lump in her throat. 'I think I was expecting my big sister to come and save me from my miserable life and take me on adventures around the world. I've wasted so much time.' Sofia was looking through the window, watching people passing by.

'Oh, sweetheart,' Irene's eyes were warm and dark, full of concern. 'It's never too late to live a fulfilling life. Actually, for some people that starts in their forties, after realising they need to throw away what they have.' Her eyes were sparkling. She hid them by taking a glass of her red wine.

'What's wrong, Irene? You've been quiet for a few days.'

'I've been thinking about my own life. About how, like you, I've let too much time pass by without listening to my needs. And children are always the perfect excuse not to take care of yourself.' She looked at Sofia now, her eyes clear as the sky. 'I'm not sure what to do now, but I will never let my needs be the last ones on the list. You never know how much time you have left, and it's time to take responsibility for my own happiness.'

'I feel like I should do the same, but I'm not sure where to start.' Sofia took some chips from the basket on the table, trying to hide the tears.

Irene finished her glass of wine.

'There's something I want to show you, Sofia. Come with me.'

⁓

They were in a second-hand bookshop along the main street in Inverness, not far from the pub. The first thing Sofia noticed were the high ceilings and the huge granite fireplace. Knowing the weather after a few weeks in Scotland, she predicted it would be used in a few weeks' time, maybe even that week. The armchairs on each side of the fireplace invited you to take a pile of books and spend the rest of the afternoon reading, immersed in books on any theme you could think of. There were books everywhere. Some shelves were fixed, others moveable to make more space, and there were even books on the floor in unorganised piles.

There weren't many people. It felt safe and peaceful. There was a café upstairs that was closed for the day. Sofia wondered how noisy it would be when the café was open.

They had been there for more than an hour, browsing through books. Sofia had started to read about Scottish history and had bought a few books in Edinburgh. A biography of Flora MacDonald and Bonnie Prince Charlie. A history of the 1745 revolution. She loved the passion of the Highlanders, at the same time welcoming and vengeful. She had become very emotional when Irene took her to see the statue of Flora MacDonald in front of the castle in Inverness. Up the hill, looking towards the river, Flora showed the conviction of a strong young woman who managed to save the Bonnie Prince from the British soldiers. Sofia envied her strength and determination.

'How are you doing?' Irene approached her, a pile of geology books in her arms.

'Good. I could stay here for hours.'

'I know. But I'm hungry. Let me show you one more thing and then maybe we can go and have dinner? We can come here again tomorrow if you like.'

'I would love to, yes.'

Irene took her to one of the shelves at the back, moved it towards the right and showed her a small ladder. 'You go first.'

'Are we allowed to go up there? Isn't that for the owners?'

'Yes, their office is up there. But I've asked the man at the counter, and he's given us permission. There's a group of old photos on the wall outside their office that I'd like to show you.'

Sofia went up the ladder, holding on to the rail. Made of sturdy oak, the steps creaked under her weight. Upstairs was a narrow corridor that led to two small offices, each one with a man typing on a computer as if his life depended on it. Irene pointed to the wall between the offices. It was covered with photographs from different periods, all taken inside the bookshop.

Sofia looked at them. Some seemed to be from the late nineteenth century, almost worn-out and colourless, full of men smiling with books in their hands.

And then she saw it. A photograph outside the bookshop with a few young men smiling, full of life. Something caught her attention. A familiar blue bonnet with a white ribbon. She now knew it belonged to the Jacobites. But this one had a familiar pin with a thistle that had fascinated her since her childhood. She looked at the face under the bonnet. He had the same hazel eyes as Cora's. They were full of life and expectation. There, ten years before she was born, stood her father. A shiver went through her. She turned around to look at Irene, her eyes welling up a little.

'Is he…?'

'Yes, he's your dad. Cora and I discovered this photo when we came here in our twenties,' Irene said with a smile. 'Cora had so many unanswered questions that day. I hope she got her answers from your dad.'

'He never mentioned having been to Scotland.'

'Maybe it was a dream buried in his heart. Maybe it was something he couldn't share with your mum.' Irene sighed. 'We all have secrets that are only for us, Sofia. And sometimes it's better to leave them where they are.'

It was getting cold. Sofia was walking along an island that led to the River Ness, draining water from Loch Ness down south. After dinner she had told Irene that she needed some time to herself. Irene had smiled, kissed her on the cheek and gone the other way towards the hotel. She needed no words. Sofia was starting to realise what a wonderful friend Irene must have been to her sister. She must be missing her terribly, like her, but Irene had a silent, peaceful way of grieving Cora.

A forest, mostly cypress and fir trees, lay beyond, with swing ropes here and there for children to enjoy, and even a small hut made of branches. Except for a couple with a dog, Sofia was on her own.

She had a lot to think about, but somehow the pieces of the puzzle were starting to make sense. Why Cora loved that place. Why her sister must have felt connected to their dad, whose story Sofia may never know. Why she wanted her ashes here, where she would have loved to spend her last days, an elderly woman fulfilling her deepest dreams.

But there was more than that. Sofia could sense a shift inside her. This country was making her feel more alive than ever. She wasn't so angry at Cora now. She was angry with life, leaving her thinking that she only deserved what she had. A life full of fears following a traumatic experience with a guy during her teens. And all her dreams of living elsewhere and becoming a writer had vanished.

She reached the tip of the island. A flat granite stone stood there, inviting. She skirted around the comfortable bench next to it and sat on the stone, looking at the dark water holding a secret. Like her dad. Like Cora. Like herself. A monster lay underneath. It could be a gentle creature, but the ones above had turned it into a monster that scared everyone to death. It had been years since it had last been spotted. Maybe it had gone down a channel and was now living a happy life in the sea, with a family of its own. Sofia smiled. She would love to believe that.

It was time to leave her past behind and stop making excuses to herself. She could now see a path ahead. And there was a bright light at the end of the tunnel. She stayed there, looking at the river, her heart beating slowly, the peace of the place invading her soul. After a long time she stood up and walked towards the hotel. It was time to open her sister's letter. She was ready.

At 4 am, Sofia still lay awake on her bed. She had opened the curtains and was enjoying the moonlight on her face, turning the tears running down her cheeks to silver.

She had read the letter three times. Irene had been right. Cora had not found a way back to Europe. She had built a life far away and had failed at finding a way to connect her past and present. Sofia suddenly realised that Cora had been as trapped as she herself was, not knowing the way out. And when she had listened to her soul it had been too late. Her sister's letter was honest, open. She was surprised to realise how much Cora understood her; her fears from a past she was terrified to talk about, about a future she didn't have faith in, about the loss of a loving father who had left a hole in both of their lives. And the expanding distance between them that none of them had managed to cross.

Dear Sofia, take your dreams and follow them, no matter the obstacles. Your fears are not real. They will vanish as you follow the voice inside you. Her sister had never been that straightforward with her. But now she had opened her heart. Sofia was shocked when she realised that Cora had not been the happy one. She, too, had been trapped.

What now? She wondered. She felt it was time to make the change she had needed for so long. But how? She couldn't just leave her job and pursue a chimera, becoming a writer just out of the blue without any training or experience. Since the start of the trip a month ago she had been asking herself: *Where to from here?* They would be at Neist Point in two days, Irene had told her. They would scatter Cora's ashes and then each would go their own way. But where? She still had some months before she needed to go back to her work. How could she spend that time in the best possible way to help her towards the next stage in her life?

Lately she hadn't been able to stop thinking about Peter. The lovely time they'd had. How connected they had been to each other. They had only spent three days together. The weekend in Picos de Europa had been lovely, but her head had been somewhere else after she'd learnt about Cora. Then he had left with his Kiwi friends to hike in the area. She would have loved to have joined them. They exchanged email addresses and phone numbers. Somehow it felt unfinished, like there could be so much more.

She was scared. But Cora's letter had touched something inside her. The desire to not let 'what ifs' hang around in her life, to be brave and move forward. But what if it was wrong? Peter had lived a fulfilling life with his wife. He had mourned her since her death and was now trying to move on and find a purpose in life. How could she compete with that? She had lived a life imprisoned by her own fears, painted in the colours of the grey apartment she lived in. How had she let this happen? Fear. Fear of life. Fear of being hurt like she had been at seventeen, when she was starting to live and a boy had forced her to do something she wasn't ready for. And since then she hadn't been able to move on; she hadn't been brave.

Cora had been all that Sofia hadn't. She had kept going for the sake of her daughter following her separation, despite being so far away from her family. And with a heavy weight on her chest, Sofia realised that she hadn't been there for her older sister when she had most needed her. She remembered a summer hiking together shortly after the divorce, how quiet she had been, how she didn't know what to say to her. Now the words would have come so easily.

'Oh, Cora.' Sofia said out loud, feeling warm tears run down her cheeks onto her pillow.

CHAPTER 20

Sunset

Sofia and Irene

Neist Point, Isle of Skye, Scotland, October 2021

The road towards Neist Point was windy and endless, through meadows full of the black-headed sheep that Sofia had learnt to admire in the last few weeks. She had seen them in whirling winds and awful thunderstorms, peacefully grazing.

Sofia felt calm, at peace, as if heading towards her destiny with grace, knowing she had no option to turn around and run and feeling no need for it. She was holding her sister's ash urn in her hands, almost embracing it. She had spent so little time with her in the last twenty years, she wanted to keep her for as long as she could.

On their trip to Skye from Inverness, surrounded by the wild beautiful scenery of the Scottish Highlands, Sofia had remembered long-forgotten childhood memories. The time their father had taken them to learn fishing one spring morning. How much she had enjoyed the freedom of being outdoors after a long cold winter. She had been so frustrated not to have caught a single fish. Cora had been very successful on her first day; she'd caught two big trout. 'You can have one, baby girl,' she had said to Sofia, and gave her the largest. The picture of the two of them and their dad, each girl with a trout and a big smile, was still standing on her mum's bedside table.

Looking at the steep slopes, Sofia remembered the time she had rolled down the slope of their garden in Santander. They had been there on holidays when she and Cora were young. They had loved it there. The beach, the sense of being free after having spent all winter in a crowded city. Sofia was slowly starting to understand why her older sister had cut ties with so many things and tried to find a better life in an unspoilt country like New Zealand. Peter's Kiwi friends at the lodge in Picos de Europa had talked with fondness of their country. It seemed to her like the last piece of paradise, unspoilt by the modern world. She had felt a strong connection with a long-lost need for more freedom in her life.

'We are almost there now,' Irene said, focused on the road.

―⁀―

A few minutes later they parked facing the sea. There were no trees, and a slight breeze was swaying the grass as if singing a gentle nursery song. The sun was bright in front of them. It was still about two hours till sunset, Sofia thought.

'We still have time to say goodbye.' Irene put a hand on Sofia's shoulder, reading her thoughts.

'Yes,' Sofia said with a sigh. 'Yes.'

'The lighthouse is at the end of the path.'

They descended the path in silence. A few seagulls were swirling, sailing in the sky, drawing circles and endless twirling shapes. *The symbol of life and death, without end,* Sofia thought. *What the Celts were trying to transmit to us.*

Irene had been silent all the way from Inverness, immersed in her own thoughts. No more stories about the geology of the region. Just silence.

Beyond a small hill, Sofia caught her breath. The lighthouse, bright white in the afternoon sun, lay in front of them as a symbol of eternity, its windows shining like mirrors.

They walked up a hill on their right and sat down on the soft grass.

'What are those islands?' Sofia asked, pointing west. They looked dark grey in the afternoon sun.

'Some of the Outer Hebrides. That's Lewis, the largest.' Irene was pointing to the one on the right. 'The one on the left is North Uist. And if you have good sight you'll see tiny Benbecula in between.'

Sofia squinted, but couldn't see the little one. Had she read something about it? The name was slightly familiar. Ah, yes. The Bonnie Prince had hidden there for a while.

'Cora and I sat at this same spot twenty-three years ago,' Irene said. 'Full of hopes and dreams for the future.' Her eyes were fixed far away on the sea. 'None of them came true.'

'Yeah. The same as with my dreams and projects. Stuck by life and a mountain of fears.'

'Well, I don't want to be fearful anymore.' Irene was looking at Sofia now, her eyes filled with an immense pain. 'It's over, Sofia. It's time for me to take a step towards my happiness and stop blaming it on others.'

'What do you mean?'

'I've called the head of the geology department at Stirling University. I saw an ad in the local newspaper about a fieldwork assistant needed. They've given me a job taking students to the field four times a year to remote areas in the Scottish Highlands.' Irene looked at Sofia, a smile shaping in her eyes. 'It's my dream job.'

'Wow. I'm so impressed and proud of you, Irene.'

'Yes, so am I. Impressed and scared at the same time. But excited about the challenge.'

'You'll need to spend quite some time here, then.'

'Yes, around a month every term preparing the trip, first going on my own, and then with the students. It's like going hiking with Cora.

I know she'll be by my side now.' Her eyes were fixed on the islands beyond the sea.

'That's perfect.'

'Let's see how it goes. I might contact the university in Karlsruhe too, and see if I can do something similar there. It's not teaching geology in class. It's doing the fun stuff that I always dreamt about.'

'I'd love to see you in action. I … I hope you'll keep in touch, Irene.' Now that their time together would be over soon, Sofia was scared to say goodbye. She had loved having Irene's calmness enveloping her. It had soothed her through her grief.

'We won't let long periods of time pass anymore.' Irene squeezed Sofia's free hand, the other one still tightly holding the urn.

'I'd love that.'

'What about you? Any plans until you need to go back to work in Madrid?' Irene's eyes shone bright in the sun.

'Well, yes. I'll stay for some time in Scotland. I'd like to walk the Great Glen Way. It sounds exciting and not as famous as the West Highland Way.'

'That's wonderful, Sofia. I know how much you and Cora loved to go hiking together. I'm so happy for you.' She looked at her, sparkles in her eyes. 'Alone?'

'No. Peter is coming from London in two days. We'll meet in Inverness and go down to Fort William to start the hike.' Sofia had told Irene about Peter. It had comforted her to speak to Irene about him. She'd had a feeling that Irene would understand, and she did. With few words or questions, their conversation had helped her realise how much she had missed him.

"Brave and courageous. As it should be,' Irene said with a smile.

They were in silence for a long time, watching the seagulls flying in circles above their heads.

'May I take the urn for a bit? I'd like to say my goodbye now,' Irene said.

'Of course.' Sofia gave it to her, tears in her eyes.

Irene took it, walked towards the edge of the cliff and sat. Sofia could see her hair whirling with the wind. She sat there for a long time.

⁓

Sofia walked towards the lighthouse, giving Irene some space. Her heart felt light as a feather now, somehow knowing Irene had taken the opportunity of a lifetime and grabbed it with both hands. Irene had no way of knowing if it would go as expected. It probably wouldn't. But that was not the point. She was taking a step towards her self-fulfilment. She was doing what felt right to her. And that's all that mattered.

But what about her? She was taking a first step with Peter. That was a start, no matter what the outcome was. But there was so much more. She simply couldn't go back to Madrid. She knew that now. That city was drowning her. And she had lost motivation at the university. But she felt lost, like when she was four and got lost in the forest. One minute she was following her parents and Cora, the next she was on her own. She had followed a hare and its baby to their hollow. She felt so proud of herself. But then she looked around. She was alone. She felt a lump in her throat and couldn't scream for help. What now? She sat next to a tree and waited. It took several hours for her family to find her. They said she had walked deep into the forest. It was almost dark and she had fallen half asleep.

Sofia had nightmares for years in which she was spending the night alone in the forest, surrounded by all sorts of noises that made her tremble in bed until the morning. She hadn't thought about them for a long time. This wasn't the forest. But the heavy lump in her throat was the same.

Then she saw them. A big whale's tail splashing down in the ocean, followed by a smaller one. Mother and daughter. Or big and little sister. They were crossing the channel towards the south, looking for warmer waters. She remembered Cora talking to her about how the whales passed through Cook Strait between the North and South Islands in New Zealand, heading from Antarctica to the warm waters in Tonga. They were taking their time. Whales didn't rush. They didn't need to, as if life would wait for them no matter how long it took. The larger one was in front, leading the way. For a moment Sofia couldn't see its immense tail. It was hidden by the sea. The sun disappeared behind a cloud. Sofia held her breath. An albatross shrieked above her, giving her a fright. Where were they? Her heart was beating fast. Before she knew it she was next to the cliff, looking down. In slow motion the sun came back, bathing her in its golden rays. In the distance she saw the two whales again. Something had changed. They had changed direction, heading towards Lewis Island. But the smaller one was leading now with confidence, the larger following.

A deep sense of peace embraced Sofia. And then she knew. She would finally go to New Zealand. Visit the places her sister had lived in and loved. She would spend some time at Cora's house in Golden Bay. Get to know Tom. Spend some time with Alex. And imagine how it would have been visiting Cora instead of always being afraid. She would even ask Peter if he would like to come with her. He might say yes. For a few moments she fantasised about the places she would visit on the way. Maybe Fiji, with its sandy beaches. Or Tonga, where she would swim with the whales, cousins of the ones she had just seen. It was time to set off and live her life. She would take a year off from the university and see. She didn't want to rush anymore. Not now. She would need to sell her apartment, leave a few boxes with her mum. *I don't need that dull furniture anymore*, she thought with a smile. It was time to give it all away.

The wind came from the sea, warm and inviting. She took out her hairclip. How many times had Cora told her to loosen her hair and let it breathe? And how often she hadn't listened to her. It wasn't about being comfortable or looking serious. It was about letting go, allowing herself to just be who she was. The wind and her hair started dancing, slowly then frantically, catching up with all the lost years. She opened her arms wide and looked towards the sky. She felt the sun warming her face, almost burning it with hunger. Sofia could imagine the sun saying, 'Yes! I'm finally allowed to play with this soul and show her the world!'

She opened her eyes. The whales could not be seen any more, but deep within her she knew they were there. Together, heading towards the sunset, in an eternal dance where each would take turns to lead and be led, help and be helped, no words needed. For the heart didn't need any words to express its feelings.

'Oh, Cora,' Sofia said, talking to the sea. 'There is so much I would like to say now. And somehow there's not much left to say.' She swallowed hard. 'I wish I had known about your passion for Scotland. I wish we were sharing it now. I've found out about dad. I would have loved to talk about it with you, and with him. What a discovery it would have been to share that passion between the three of us. Why didn't mum ever mention it? Maybe she didn't know about it. There's a mystery for me to solve now.' She breathed in slowly, releasing the tension in her chest. The sun was shining on her in tones of dark orange, warming her face, making her tears shine golden on her cheeks.

'I will get to know you better, Cora. Through all that you've loved and cared for in New Zealand. I wish I'd been brave enough to visit you there. I think I was scared of comparing your success with my failures. But now I know that your life wasn't easy either, and I wasn't there for you. That won't happen again. From now on I'll take care of the people you love, my dear sister. I will look after Alex.' She swallowed hard. 'And most of all, I promise you that I'll take care of myself. Of my needs and hopes. I will feed my dreams and never ever let them go.'

A gust came from the sea, swirling her hair around. She heard steps behind her.

'It's time,' Irene said.

'Yes.'

'Do you want to spend some time with the urn now?'

'No.' She was ready.

Irene took Sofia's hand and they headed towards the cliff facing the sun. She looked at Sofia, who nodded and opened the urn. Each took a handful of Cora's ashes. They were warm, full of Cora's sweetness.

They looked at each other, and scattered the ashes into the sea.

Taking their time, they repeated the process. In a silent agreement they left one handful each inside the urn. The sun kissed the horizon now. They both took the last remains of Cora. Shining in gold, the ashes flew in the air, taking their time. In a flash of orange, pink and red, the sun sank behind the horizon.

CHAPTER 21

A Castle by the Sea

Sofia and Peter

Scottish Highlands, Scotland, UK, October 2021

Sofia was tired. They had been driving all morning, heading up north along a narrow road that seemed to have no end. The sky was grey and full of clouds. She was getting accustomed to this type of weather, not knowing if it would rain or not.

'What do you call a grey and gloomy day in Scotland?' she asked.

'Depressing?' Peter asked.

'Summer,' Sofia said with a smile.

Peter laughed, relaxing his arms on the wheel. 'That's a great one.'

'I heard an old man tell another man at a pub in Inverness.'

'Well, the Scots have a good sense of humour.' Peter looked at her with a half-smile, his untamed hair swirling in the breeze. 'Anything interesting to stop and see? I'm getting tired of driving.'

'Let me see,' she said, looking at the map. 'Oh, there's a castle next to a cliff coming soon. The Old Keiss castle. What about that one? It looks like there's a half-hour walk to get there.'

'That's perfect. A stop to do some exercise and visit something new,' he said, winking at her.

They had been travelling for a week, getting to know each other. They had stayed in separate rooms, spending the days visiting new places and the evenings enjoying dinners together. Sofia had discovered that Peter had a great sense of humour. When he was joking a dimple would appear on his left cheek. She loved to see it, smiling inwardly.

Peter had travelled quite a bit in his youth. He had spent three months in India learning zen meditation, then six months hiking in the Himalayas in Nepal. 'Those were the most precious months in my life,' he had told her. 'When I discovered the profound meaning of everything that happens to you in life.' He had taken her hand then, his eyes intense. For her, these days had been a balm for the emotions. Somehow she felt like a different person; as if the grey woman she had been for years had been peeled back to reveal a rainbow-coloured person, full of dreams and hopes. She felt lighter, as if an elephant had been taken off her shoulders, letting her stretch.

—

Half an hour later Peter and Sofia were walking along a cliff. A strong wind was blowing from the sea, making Sofia's hair cover her eyes. She stopped to make a ponytail.

'How long do you think until we get there?' she asked.

Peter frowned, looking ahead. 'We should have arrived by now. Let's walk a bit more. If it wasn't for the wind I could keep walking for hours.'

Sofia was imagining life in the old days. The place was isolated. She had seen a couple of farms scattered here and there. No other remains of civilisation. Lords and servants would have lived isolated for months in this place, the wind constantly blowing from the north, the waves crashing on the cliffs.

'There it is!' Peter yelled. 'Look!'

A castle in ruins lay in the distance. As they approached it, Sofia realised how impressive it was. A pillar was holding up the entrance through an arch. The castle was on a promontory, about five metres from the mainland. It was tall, with one high wall and a chimney standing on one side, rubble on the other. With the waves crashing below she could imagine it in stormy days; how it could feel like the end of the world. She was speechless. She closed her eyes and imagined she was a young maid with a white cap, full of hope for love and children, spending months on end in this desolate place. She opened her eyes and crossed the bridge.

Peter was ahead of her, exploring. 'This is amazing!' he said. He walked round the castle, went in and out, then joined Sofia. The sea was dark grey with threads of silver. There was something glowing from inside, expressing its beauty in ways not many would understand. *If the sea could speak, what stories would it tell?* Sofia thought. *Of love and betrayal, hope and honour.*

She looked at Peter. His eyes were glowing.

'Thank you for bringing me to Scotland,' he said. 'This place … well, it speaks to my soul.'

'Yes,' she said. 'Even though I have no connection to this land I feel at home here, and I don't understand why.'

'I like it when there are things I don't understand,' he said. 'When life just throws something at you and helps you find a meaning deep inside that wakes you up.' He took her face between his hands. 'I feel alive, Sofia. Alive for the first time in years. This place is making me realise how much life and joy there is still inside me.' He swallowed, his Adam's apple bouncing up and down. 'I … I don't know where this is leading us, Sofia, but I'd like to give this a go, wherever it takes us. I would like to be with you, spend the next months together, explore the world, get to know each other. For the first time in too long I feel I can share everything with someone. My grief. My sorrow. But also the man I used to be, and the man I'd like to become. Would you like that?'

Sofia felt a lump in her throat. She was unable to breathe. This man had helped open something inside her, like a dam gate that had been closed for too long, blocked and rusty, now releasing all the contaminated water, finally free to flow down the hill towards its destination. This good man was giving her hope, making her believe that maybe men were not trying to harm her anymore. Making her trust again.

She embraced him and kissed him, watching his deep blue eyes as their mouths explored each other. He embraced her now, bringing her close to him, tightening her to him, their kisses becoming deeper and searching. And there, on a cliff over the North Sea, Sofia knew she was closing a chapter in her life and opening a new one.

A week later Sofia was staring at Loch Ness for the second time in a few weeks. Standing on a steep slope with a forest full of fir trees in front of her, she just couldn't believe the beauty of the place. The lake was silver, like the old mirror in her grandmother's attic when she was little. She used to stare at it for hours, feeling there was another world on the other side she wanted to explore. She felt an impulse to jump in the water and explore its mysteries. But there was more to it than that. She had been thinking of her dad lately. She felt him close to her these days. Why had he never talked to her about Scotland? What had connected him to this country? Had he ever regretted moving back to Spain? Had it just been a short stay? Or had he lived here for a long time? So many questions that might always remain unanswered. She wondered if she would feel brave enough to ask her mum one day. She was such a distant woman; more so after Cora's death.

It was their last day of the Great Glen Way, and the longest, all the way to Inverness. They had been mostly walking on their own, being late autumn. This morning they had passed an old man with a hunting dog covered in mud. 'Ay,' had been his salute. Sofia was loving the sparse but friendly conversations with the Highlanders.

It had been drizzling early in the morning but it wasn't too cold. Somehow she had managed to become accustomed to the weather. There was something that connected her to this land. Her soul felt at home here. Was that what her dad had felt? She wanted to explore this land of mystery, of fairy tales and drama combined in the most astonishing way.

She looked at Peter sitting below her, watching the lake. He had been quiet today, sensing her need for space. As if he had felt her looking, he turned around, a deep smile on his face. He stood up and went to sit beside her.

'This place is special,' he said.

'Yes,' Sofia smiled. 'I'm so grateful that you feel this too.'

He looked down to the lake and then up to the mountains on the eastern bank. 'Scotland always felt like a land of savages, where it was always cold and damp, where there was nothing interesting to see or do. I always imagined people drinking beer and whisky in pubs, walking home along wetlands and always feeling wet and cold.'

'That's an image that has been forced on us.'

'Exactly. But there is so much more to this land. Passion. Loss. Drama. And beyond all this, the people's fierce love for the land and a deep connection to nature and the fairy world. You can breathe in magic everywhere you go.'

'Yes.' Sofia held Peter's hand and smiled at him. He smiled back and looked down at the lake.

'When I first met you I felt like I was cheating on Mary, just by the mere act of speaking to you.' He swallowed hard. 'It made me hate myself and want to vomit. But I sense now that there is something pushing me towards you; a force that I cannot control.' He looked at her. 'I feel like there's a reason why I met you; that there is something for you to show me, and something for me to show you. And I've decided that life is too precious to miss a moment like this. I'd like to explore the world with you, Sofia, wherever it takes us.'

Sofia looked at him. He had wrinkles around his dark blue eyes. She felt she wanted to know everything about him and share and explore the world with him.

'Thank you.'

'For what?'

'For having found your way to me.'

He hugged her. His hair smelt of jasmine. She rested her head on his shoulder and they both stared at the lake.

'One day I will come back to this place. I'll buy a small house near a loch and spend my days walking up Munros and evenings next to my fire with a book in my hands and a dog at my feet.'

'That's a nice dream,' he said.

She liked that he hadn't asked to be part of that dream. It was her choice, and he was leaving that to her.

'I won't go back to Spain,' she said softly.

'No?' he asked.

'No. I've asked for a sabbatical from the university. I'm flying to New Zealand. I want to get to know the country where my sister lived for so long. I should have done that years ago, when Cora was alive. But I'm not waiting anymore for my life to take off. I want to meet Tom, Cora's partner. I want to spend time with Alex, my niece. And I want to see how big the world is.'

'That's a big step,' he said. 'And a brave one, too.'

'Yes.' Then she looked at him. 'And I'd love you to come with me.'

He looked at her, his face still, his eyes intent, penetrating her to her core.

'Would you?'

'Yes. If that's what you want.'

'Yes, it is. It's time for me to come out of my shell too. To find out what life has reserved for my mature years.'

Sofia smiled. 'I think life is full of surprises. But above all, life is what you make of it.'

He tickled her face slowly and then kissed her with the warmth of a new love and the wisdom of love lost and found.

—

Later that evening they walked alongside a small forest. Sofia put on her coat. She felt as if she was in the seventeenth century, walking for days to get to the largest town. Although she felt tired, her legs warm and heavy, she would have never exchanged this walk for a drive from Drumnadrochit. And there in front of them stood Inverness, ancient and full of wisdom, with no sign of the modern times. They could see the castle on the hill, Flora MacDonald's statue in front of it. And at the centre of it all, the Ness River heading north to its destination, the ocean at the Firth of Moray. Then she saw the island where she had walked that day after seeing her dad's photo at the bookstore. It had only been a month ago. Somehow she felt older; a different person with a weight off her shoulders and a whole new life full of hope ahead of her.

She looked at Peter next to her. She extended her arm towards him, inviting.

'Shall we?'

And with a smile on his face he held her hand and they ran down the hill towards the town.

—

The following day they hired a car and drove to Cawdor castle. Sofia wanted to show it to Peter. It had made a deep impression on her when she had visited with Irene a few weeks before. With a moat and a drawbridge, a holly tree that had grown inside one of the rooms and the most amazing gardens, it was the perfect ending to Sofia's time in Scotland. The following day they would take a train to Edinburgh and from there a flight to York. Peter had asked her to come and visit his family and his house in Yorkshire. She had accepted.

They were walking in the garden, admiring this small castle that somehow represented all the magnificence of its owners, of what a Scottish castle might have looked like in the past. She snuggled inside her feather jacket, her hand warm holding Peter's. It felt so natural to hold his hand. She smiled, looking at him sideways.

'What?'

'Oh, nothing. Just thinking,' she said.

'I hope it's good,' he replied.

'Couldn't be better.'

He kissed her. 'I'm glad to hear that.'

—

An hour later they were seated at the pub in Cawdor Town. With a fireplace and dim light sparkling in all the glasses, she felt at peace. She would miss Scotland, its wild nature, its strong people and the feeling of belonging it had left inside her.

'Well, to our future,' Peter said, raising his glass of red wine.

'To our future. And to Scotland, which without knowing me has given me so much.'

'To Scotland,' Peter said. They clinked glasses and drank. She loved the fact that he had taken the double toast well, without judgement.

'You've been thoughtful today,' he said.

'Yes. I … I'm thinking about my sister Cora, who loved this country so much. And about me; how I've fallen in love with it in such a short time.'

'You're wondering if there's a connection in your family to this land.'

'Yes,' she said, amazed at his perception. She had told him about her dad's photograph at the bookshop in Inverness. 'I just wonder why Dad had that photo there. Cora and I adored him. I thought I knew him well. But now I realise there is so much from his past I don't know. I'm intrigued by that photo. I wonder why he was here?'

'Maybe he was on holiday and spent a few days in Inverness.'

'Maybe. But something tells me it was more than that. I think he felt strongly connected to Scotland, and I'd love to find out more.'

'Why don't you ask your mum?' he asked.

'No, Mum won't be helpful. And something tells me she won't know much. It's as if Scotland was a very personal and treasured part of dad's life that he wanted to keep to himself.'

'Maybe you should respect that. You and Cora feeling this connection to Scotland is all that matters.'

Sofia smiled. 'Yes.'

He leant against the table, getting closer to her, his eyes bright in the candlelight. 'This trip has given you so much, Sofia,' he said. 'You are not the shy woman afraid of the world I met in that train to Santander a few months ago. You're now a strong woman who has laid her sister to rest and has gone on an amazing quest to find herself, and part of her has found the past along the way.'

She smiled at him. She was starting to get used to his deep insights into her thoughts and feelings. 'It's more than that. I've come to know what I truly value in life, and what I want.'

The waiter came with a tray and their meals. 'So here we are. A roasted chicken and a salmon.' He served the meals with a smile and left.

Sofia looked down at the salmon. It was beautifully presented with potatoes, carrots and parsley and a piece of rolled butter on top of the fish. She felt her stomach grumbling.

'*Buen provecho*,' she said with a smile.

CHAPTER 22

The Challenge

Sofia

Golden Bay, New Zealand, December 2021

Sofia was sitting on a wooden Adirondack chair in the garden, a glass of pinot gris in her hand. Looking towards the wild and impregnable Kahurangi ranges, she was waiting for another beautiful sunset. Since she had arrived at Cora's house in Golden Bay she hadn't missed a single one. It was her new way to connect with her sister, following her farewell in the Scottish Highlands.

It was warm, but comfortable without being too hot like in Spain. She was enjoying the temperature in New Zealand, but not the infamous sandflies. Not unlike the Scottish midges, they seemed to love her blood for some reason. She scratched her left ankle, which by now was red and swollen.

'There you are,' Tom said, coming to join her with some nibbles and another glass of wine. 'This is sauvignon blanc from Otago, if you'd like to try it after the pinot gris,' he said with a smile.

She was starting to find her way in New Zealand by now. Otago was further south. A region that could get Spanish-like hot in summer and Central Europe-like cold in winter.

'Maybe later,' she said.

'Would you like some company?' He had a gentle way about him that she really liked. Despite Sofia having invaded his space, he seemed to be enjoying her company. After three weeks they were getting to know each other and coming to understand the parts of Cora they hadn't known. It felt as if they were putting together the pieces of a puzzle.

'Yes, please. I'd like you to stay with me for a while, if you don't mind.'

Tom sat on the chair next to hers, picking up some olives on the way.

He looked at her, his face serious. 'How are you taking all this?'

'It's hard to absorb it all,' she said.

'Yes. Cora was all that you knew of her, and all that I knew of her, plus more.'

'Yes. But I've also realised how much alike we were.' She looked at the mountains in front of her, wishing they had had time to go tramping on their own for a few days. 'This place is so peaceful.' She was starting to understand why Cora had moved here. She was feeling closer to Cora now than in their childhood. Somehow her sister was speaking to her through this place, with its rare beauty and wilderness. The impossibly long white sandy beaches north of Collingwood, the orange paradise of the Abel Tasman National Park beaches and the inviting mountains ahead of her were speaking directly to her heart. They had awakened a part of her that had been asleep for a long time. A part that spoke of longing, of wasted years, of time that would not come back.

'Cora needed to find herself through nature. She needed space, peace and solitude.'

'Yes, she always did.' *And so did I*, Sofia thought. 'Was that what connected the two of you?'

Tom took his time to reply. 'Partly, yes. I also needed space and more connection with nature,' he said. 'But it was more than that. I think we both needed to find someone who would make time for us to get to know each other,' he said, sighing. 'No more rushed relationships. No more expecting to know the other person in five minutes.'

'I understand that.'

Tom looked at the mountains, searching for the right words. 'We also somehow needed to go back to basics. Get away from technology and the need for more, and return to writing with pen and paper, listening to the bird song instead of watching TV.'

'Oh.' That was something Sofia hadn't thought of. But then she realised there was no TV in Cora's place. Only a small music stereo and a laptop if needed. All the pictures were of nature. Both from New Zealand and overseas. She remembered when she had first seen the huge picture of Glencoe in Scotland hanging in Cora's living room. Both here and there, in Europe and New Zealand, Cora's heart had been split between the two worlds.

'I wonder where home is,' Sofia said.

'Mm.'

'I don't know if there is a place to call home anymore.'

'Well, I'm not an expert. For some people home is very straightforward. It's where they're from and where they have always lived.' Tom tossed his head backwards, a gesture she was starting to associate with him deep thinking. 'But for others it's more complicated. Home is where the heart is. And the heart can be divided between different places, different people.'

'Yes.'

'I think it was like that for Cora. She was searching for a place to call home.'

'Do you think she found it?'

'I think she did in the end. Despite all of it happening so fast, she did come to terms with it, yes.'

She looked at him. His eyes were surrounded by wrinkles, his face contorted. Sofia knew how much Tom had loved her sister. She wished Cora had met him earlier and that she had introduced him to her and they had shared a dinner right there, the three of them. A lump in her throat was not letting her breathe.

'Well, I need to refill this glass and look after dinner,' he said. 'And you need a bit of alone time.'

'Thank you.' She loved how he saw things without words.

Oh, Cora, she sighed. *Why did you not tell me about all this?*

'This is delicious,' Sofia said. Seated at the dining table, they were having a dinner of fresh salmon and baked feijoas. She looked out the window. The sunset had been spectacular, colouring the mountains with pink and purple.

Tom was a great cook. She liked his dishes and was being surprised each day.

'I'm glad that you're enjoying my meals.'

'More than that. I think I could stay here forever.'

'Maybe you should stay for more than three months and explore the country with Peter.'

'Maybe.' Peter was coming in a few days. She was looking forward to seeing him. She needed to feel loved and protected from all the emotions of the last few weeks.

'Would you like some more wine?'

'Maybe not now, thank you.'

He stood up and took the plates, a strange expression on his face. 'There's something I need to show you,' he said before leaving with the dishes.

A few minutes later he came back with a large folder in his hands. 'This is for you,' he said, and gave it to her.

She took it and opened it. Cora's neat handwriting welcomed her.

A Novel, said the first page.

'What is this?'

'Cora published a novel a few years ago,' he said. 'It was her most personal endeavour in her life. But she wanted to write something even

more personal. She started this one two years ago. She tried to finish it when she knew she was terminal. But the last months were difficult.'
His eyes were full of pain.

'Oh.'

'She asked me to hand this over to you.'

Sofia couldn't say anything. What would she do with it? This was a treasure of a lifetime.

'You will know what to do with it, Sofia. Believe in yourself. Just take your time.' And with that he left her, a treasure from her sister in her hands.

—

Two days later Sofia was sitting on the same chair in the garden, a postcard on her lap. Irene had written her from the Grampian Mountains in the Scottish Highlands. *This is beautiful, and so fulfilling,* she said. *I wish I had done this earlier. But it doesn't matter anymore. I have the rest of my life to live fully, no matter how long it is.*

How could it be the same Irene? Sofia smiled. Life could go round and round again, in an eternal loop, as the Celts always knew. She had been thinking about the Celts a lot lately. About eternity and forms with no end. She used to love squares and rectangles. They would keep her safe and imprisoned. Not anymore. She looked back at the outdoor table next to the house, where a stack of paper was being held down by a large basket full of seashells. She had started a collection. Yesterday she found her first pāua shell. It was not polished like the one José had given her years ago. It was white and rough on the outside. It probably wasn't worth much. But the blue and gold shone in the sun and caught her attention. A treasure hidden by the sand, waiting for the right soul to uncover it.

Cora had written from the heart, leaving a legacy for the future. But more importantly, she seemed to have written it for Sofia. The novel was based on Cora's life, on what could have been but never was. It was a succession of parallel lives. How things would have been if she had stayed in Europe. In one life she was living in Germany near Irene, raising their children together, and then one day they had an argument that tore them apart. In another life she was a hiking guide in the Scottish Highlands, living a simple life in nature. And one day she fell off a cliff and died. There was no daughter or partner. A life of self-fulfilment but she lived on her own.

The novel was written with her and Cora as elderly women telling each other stories by the fireplace, the wind howling outside. 'Now it's your turn,' the main character said. The novel ended there. A shiver went down Sofia's spine when she finished reading. Her sister hadn't left an unfinished novel for others to complete. Cora had explicitly left it to her, knowing that her younger sister would continue where she had left off. How would she manage with such a huge task? It was brilliantly written, another novel for her to analyse and admire. But that was not its intention. There was no way back. She knew it. She had found a note at the back of the last page.

You can do it, Sofia. And when you are done, you will know what to do with it, it said in Cora's neat handwriting.

She didn't have a clue. How to start. How to write as beautifully as her sister.

She heard a car arriving. Tom had offered to pick up Peter. He instinctively knew she needed the extra space before his arrival. Sofia stayed seated, her heart beating fast. How would she feel when she saw him, here, so far away from where they had met? What if it didn't work?

She heard Peter's footsteps on the grass and turned around. He was taller than she remembered. With a rain jacket in his hand and a tramping backpack hanging off one of his shoulders, he looked ten years younger and happier than the day they first met.

'Here I am,' he said, a huge smile on his face.

'Yes,' she replied, and went to embrace him. His arms held her

against his chest. How could she have doubted it? She closed her eyes
and sighed.

——

Two weeks later Sofia and Peter were walking along a path above the
hills. The wind was sweeping Sofia's hair, swirling it around her face.
Tom had recommended they visit Wharariki beach, at the northern
tip of the South Island. He said it was a good day and the wind wasn't
too bad. He said it was almost always windy there, as the beach was so
exposed to the northerly winds. They passed a family returning from the
beach, the girl and boy barefoot and wet. Sofia and Peter had crossed
a few farm gates, watching the sheep grazing on the nearby green hills
as they passed.

Sofia looked back at Peter, silently walking behind. She smiled. He
had become a calm presence in her life. She loved the fact that they
didn't feel the need to rush into anything. They were simply enjoying
their time together.

The path now became steep and sandy. She looked up. She could
see the sea in the distance, hear the waves crashing against the beach.
After reaching the top of the path, she stopped. The deep blue sea
was before her. Waves crushing and spreading foam everywhere. On
her left were two large promontories jutting out of the water, one of
them with a large arch. The beach was long and wide, full of dunes.
She heard kids screaming in delight and saw they were going down
the dunes with boards. She put her sunglasses on to avoid sand getting
in her eyes.

'Wow.' Peter said next to her. 'So much beauty!'

Sofia held his hand and they walked down the dunes towards the
sea. Without any words they left their belongings, took off their clothes
and walked to the water. It was cold, but she didn't mind. Hand in
hand, they went in and started jumping the waves. Sofia took some
water and washed her face. She closed her eyes and let the sun warm

her, the sound of the waves sooth her. She could feel Cora close to her. She knew her sister had been in that same spot not that long ago.

Sis, I wish I had been here with you, and let you show me all this beauty. How am I going to keep living without you? She choked, and then a big wave came over her, rocking her back and forth. Unable to breathe, she threw her arms up in fright. A hand pulled her up.

'Are you okay?' Peter asked.

She was gasping for air, coughing and spitting water.

'Yes,' she managed to say, before turning back to the beach.

⸺

Later, sitting on the beach having a sandwich, Sofia looked at Peter.

'Well, I must confess the sea has a bit of a character here. I'll be careful from now on.'

Peter looked at her, a frown on his face. 'I'm glad you see it that way. Tom has told me about what they call rogue waves. They're quite common here, especially along the West Coast. But he also said he's seen them down in Dunedin. The sea can be calm, and suddenly a huge wave comes and takes you out. Many people have drowned. It's not something to take lightly. We should be careful.'

Sofia looked his face, which was full of concern.

'I'm okay. I promise.' She smiled. It felt good to have someone taking care of her.

'Come here.' Peter got closer and hugged her. 'All this is too much for you. Coming to the country where your sister lived for so long. Getting to know her life after she's gone. And then having this huge task of finishing her novel.' He looked at her with his deep blue eyes. 'You don't need to take that burden on, Sofia. Your sister asked for too much. I've been wondering for some time why she asked that of you. It's a big thing. And you want to take your time before you decide on your next step.'

She looked at him, amazed at his deep understanding.

'Thank you. Yes. I'm not sure what to do with it, or how to start. Or in fact, what to do with my life.' She looked at him. 'But I'd like to stay here for the next six months. Explore New Zealand, maybe even go to the Cook Islands or Tonga. And not think about my past life for a while. I don't think I can go back to that.'

'I know. These last few months have changed the way you see things.'

'Yes. Cora's death. The trip to Scotland to scatter her ashes. Meeting you. It's all helped me realise that I need to start over again.' She looked at him. 'I've always wanted to be a writer, Peter. It's always been part of my dream. I'm still not sure what to write about. But somehow, with this task, my sister has given me an opportunity to get started on a project that's not mine. And I like the idea. But I'm terrified. Of not being able to do it. Of failing before having even started.' Tears were falling down her cheeks.

Peter gently took her sunglasses off and held her face with both hands. 'The only thing you ever need to be in this life is yourself. Truly and genuinely you. You do not need to fulfil anyone's expectations. You do not need to win a Nobel prize. You don't even need to climb Mount Everest or travel the world.' She smiled at that. Peter swallowed hard. 'For so long, I thought I needed to achieve something in life, to win the acceptance of others. My parents first. Then Mary. But not anymore. From now on I will close my eyes and follow my instincts.' He looked at her. 'I want to be with you. Explore this country. And take my time to decide about my next steps. We have all the time in the world now. Let's take it one step at a time.' With infinite gentleness he moved closer to her and kissed her deeply, slowly. She savoured the saltiness on his lips and embraced this man that had changed her life, the waves still crashing against the white sandy beach, the wind swirling around their faces in the afternoon sun.

CHAPTER 23

Hope

Tom

Tākaka, Golden Bay, New Zealand, March 2022

Tom was walking along the beach, his head low, the warm breeze caressing his curls. He stopped and looked back. A young red golden retriever was sniffing a large piece of driftwood.

'Lukas! Come here!' Tom said.

The dog looked at him and moved on.

He was a good dog, Tom thought. Well-behaved and easy-going, he had been a great company since Cora had died. Some neighbours gave him the dog when they moved overseas to take care of a grandchild in the UK after her parents had suddenly died in an accident. They said it was too expensive to take Lukas and too much to take care of him and the little girl. They were devastated at having lost their only daughter and were looking forward to hugging their granddaughter.

He had not been sure if it would work. He just didn't have the head to take care of any living being. But after a few weeks he realised that having Lukas was making him wake up every day and go for long walks.

Lukas came to him and licked his hand.

'Was there anything interesting over there? You're a good boy,' Tom said, patting the dog's head. 'And great company. Now let's play in the water for a while. Would you like that?'

'Woof!' Lukas was twirling in excitement.

'OK. One, two, three!' Tom threw the tennis ball towards the sea. Lukas ran like crazy, his tail going round in circles and almost unbalancing him. When he reached the water he jumped as high as he could then pushed himself into the sea until he got the ball and turned around.

Tom burst out laughing. His friends with dogs had always told him how wonderful they were. But sharing flats with friends for many years in Dunedin made it impossible for him to have a dog. He hadn't felt like he had a home he could share with a pet.

With Cora, he had talked about having a dog. She used to talk about her spaniel from when she was little, and how it had changed her life. But there had been no time for dogs.

Lukas kept trotting along the beach. It was almost deserted, a man and his rottweiler far away. The beaches north of Patons Rock were not usually very busy, and he loved to be there, just Lukas and him. Pakawau beach had become his favourite, especially in the early morning.

Tom felt as if he needed something, as if it was time for him to recover part of his childhood. He had this strong feeling that a part of him was pushing up from a hidden place deep inside him, rising to the surface. The psychologist had told him to give himself time and have no expectations. After all, he had planned his future with Cora, and now that plan was shattered to pieces.

He remembered the last time he had walked along this beach with a fragile Cora holding his arm. She was pale and cold. Despite that she insisted on going for long walks to look at the sun, the birds.

'I need to see life and enjoy every minute I have,' she said. That had been two weeks before she died. She had been silent that day, deep in her thoughts. Then at some stage she stopped and turned to him.

'Recover your inner child, Tom. Don't stop fighting until you recover part of who you are. It took me too long to do that myself, and now it's too late. But writing has been the most satisfying thing I've done in my last years, and I don't regret making all the sacrifices to get there. I just wish I had more time. So please, promise me you will find the dream of your childhood and pur*sue it, no matter what.*'

Looking at those deep brown eyes, full of warmth, Tom had promised. He still had no idea what that dream was. After interminable walks, he was still unsure.

Shrugging his shoulders, Tom turned around and called Lukas. It was time to head home.

That afternoon, someone knocked on his door. A young woman in her twenties with a long blonde ponytail and pale skin was smiling at him.

'Hello, Dad,' she said.

'Sylvia!' With a force he didn't remember having, he embraced his daughter. 'What … what are you doing here?'

Despite all his efforts to be close to her, Sylvia had kept to herself, especially after Tom had moved to Golden Bay and started his relationship with Cora. Tom had wondered if her mum had something to do with it.

'I just felt like paying you a surprise visit to see how you're doing.' Sylvia was smiling at him.

'That's wonderful, sweetie. Come in!'

Sylvia had been there once, when Cora died, and had stayed briefly for the funeral. He guided her to the guest room, a small room with a queen bed covered in a white duvet and a large window looking towards the mountains.

'This is lovely, so full of light!'

'Thank you. Yes, sometimes I forget how much light there is here. I guess I'm a local now.'

Sylvia sat on the bed and sighed.

Tom sat next to his daughter. 'There's more than just a surprise behind this visit, isn't there?'

'Yes.' Sylvia looked at him, tears falling down her cheeks. She laid her head on his shoulders. He held her by her waist. She felt so fragile, as if she could fall apart with a simple gust of wind.

For a while there was only silence. Two hearts beating at the same pace.

'It's still warm outside. What about we get a cup of tea and sit on the deck?' Tom asked.

'Sounds lovely.' Sylvia wiped her tears and stood up. 'I just need to go and wash my face.'

Half an hour later they were sitting in two Adirondack chairs, looking west towards the mountain ranges.

'You've found a good place, Dad,' Sylvia said.

Tom looked at the peaks, bright in the sun, and smiled.

'Yes. I have. But it's not easy enjoying it all by myself now.'

'You really loved Cora, didn't you?'

'I still love her.' Tom looked at her. 'You never stop loving, no matter what.'

Sylvia sipped her tea. 'I guess so. I don't really know. I've never found true love.'

Tom looked at her. He noticed dark hollows under her eyes and a twitch near her left eye that didn't use to be there. 'You're still young, sweetie. Anything can happen to you. I was in my late fifties when I found Cora.'

'Yes. Well, a bad relationship can suck the life out of you, can't it?

'Yes, it can.'

'Dad, I think I now understand why you left Mum; how it was draining you of all the good you had inside. When I was a small girl I hated you both for doing it to me. But now … well, now I understand better.'

Tom stayed silent.

'Even with children, you need to do it. An absent or unhappy mother is much worse than a single mother.' Her eyes were full of tears waiting to fall.

Tom looked at her again. He noticed her swollen face and legs. 'Are you…?'

'Yes. I'm pregnant, Dad. And I have nowhere to go.'

'Oh, sweetie.' Tom stood up, knelt next to his daughter and held her hand. And Sylvia burst into tears, holding her dad like a log in the open sea. A roar came from deep within her, like a protective lioness ready to attack any potential threat to her cubs. Then the sobs started, making her shudder in spasms.

Tom pulled her up and held her, without too much pressure, as if she were a porcelain girl needing to be held to stop her falling and smashing to pieces.

They stood like this for a while until the sobs turned almost inaudible, transformed into small sighs.

'Sit down.' Tom helped her back to the chair and gave her a glass of water. 'There.'

'Thank you.'

Tom smiled. 'That's what I am here for. I wonder why you didn't go to your mum?'

Sylvia frowned. 'Mum. She wouldn't have known how to handle this. She's too afraid of her new partner, who wouldn't have approved.'

'I see.' Tom wasn't surprised. 'By the way, you do have somewhere to be,' he said. 'You can stay here for as long as you want. You'll keep me company, and maybe I'll enjoy spoiling my little girl.'

'Oh, Dad.' Sylvia smiled.

A week later Tom was in bed, unable to sleep. He felt as if a lion was roaring in his ear.

He got up, made himself a cup of tea and went outside. It was a silent and warm night. A half moon was up in the sky. It felt like a perfect night for ghosts, Tom thought. 'Cora, are you there?' he asked. But there was no answer.

Sylvia had left a few magazines on the outdoor table. He looked at them. They were for mothers, full of baby clothes and photos. He smiled. He hadn't asked her about her plans, letting her find her own way. A grandfather. The word was too big to capture all his feelings. He sat on a chair under the moon, a magazine on his lap. A few minutes later his snoring echoed in the valley.

The sun on his back woke Tom up. He was surrounded by gold and copper colours everywhere. He went inside and opened a drawer in the living room. A folder with paintings in it was there, green and old. He didn't open it. He knew what it contained. A picture of ducks in a pond from his teenage times, a baby girl lying on her cot, a happy family having a picnic.

Tom turned around and ran to the shed.

That morning Sylvia woke up late. Tom heard her walking through the house then coming out towards the shed where he was. Tom had a straw hat on and a brush in his right hand. There was an easel in front of him.

'Oh, there you are!' Tom had turned around and was smiling at her.

'Sorry, Dad. I didn't want to spy on you.'

'It's all good, darling. I wanted you to see this.' He held her hand and pulled her towards the canvas. A woman with blonde hair and long eyelashes was sitting on a chair in the garden, smiling. On a picnic blanket an older man was holding a baby girl, a flower in his hand, a smile on his face. She looked at her dad.

'Oh, Dad.' The words were struggling to get out.

He smiled at her and held her tight, tears falling down his cheeks.

—

Three months later

Tom was sitting in the shed, holding the planer with both hands, bits of sliced wood flying everywhere. Despite the fan next to him, he was sweating. This was the sixth wooden toy he was making for his grandchild-to-be. Despite it being too early to know, he was sure it would be a little girl. He had started making toys for both boys and girls. A duck. A cat. But as time passed by, for some reason he had started focusing more on creating toys for girls. The coffee table in the living room had a flower and a sun. This was his most ambitious piece. He had been working on it for a week, mostly in the evenings, until he would go to bed exhausted.

He stopped to look at his creation. Yes, it was looking as it should. He then moved to a rocking chair with a knife and started carving.

Things had been good with Sylvia. They had shared memories from when she was a child and hopes and dreams for the new baby. Each day Sylvia looked better, with more self-esteem, growing in strength as well as weight. He was proud of her. Raising a child on her own wouldn't be easy. But he was sure she would be OK. Somehow, he knew it would give her faith in her own capability.

She had been silent for the last few days. Tom knew she had made a decision. But he didn't ask. She would tell him when she was ready. In the meantime, he was happy to have his daughter around him. Lukas had been great company since Cora had died, but he had missed being able to share things with another human being. When things had ended with Samantha he had dreamt of living on his own and having space to himself. But now that he was reaching sixty, loneliness was becoming like a huge basket full of laundry on his head, like (as Cora had described to him) older people in Spain's northwest walking to the river with their laundry. His neck felt numb, holding a weight he couldn't stand.

He had never considered finding another partner. Cora had been the person he wanted to grow old with. It had taken him so long to find a soulmate. And then she was gone… No, a partner was out of the question. But having his daughter with him and helping her raise a baby had brought him hope again. He would wake up smiling. He had taken to whistling in the house. Life was good.

His eyes started to close. With a start, he looked at the wooden toy. It was almost finished. He could continue in the morning and have it ready by breakfast. He left it on the table covered with a cloth. He turned off the light and the heater and closed the door of the shed, heading towards the house and his bed.

In the morning Sylvia was sitting at the breakfast table, a plate of toast and jam in front of her.

'I've finished my last piece,' Tom said as he came in and laid a wrapped parcel on the table in front of her.

'Oh, Dad.'

'Come on, open it,' he said.

With trembling hands, she opened the package. A wooden crafted doll about fifteen centimetres tall lay in her hands. She had a dress with puffy sleeves and a pair of high boots. Her hair was long and curly, with a bonnet with a bow. She had big eyes and a huge smile. It was a toy made with love.

'Oh, Dad.' Sylvia stood up and hugged Tom. 'You're the best father I could have.'

Tom embraced his daughter. 'You deserve it, sweetie. And I love you so much.'

She looked at him. 'Dad, I, er…'

'You have something important to tell me, but you don't know how,' he said.

'Yes, I…' She was looking towards the wall, trying to avoid his gaze.

'You don't need to worry, sweetie. You've decided to live on your own, raise the baby on your own terms, be a single mum. Is that right?'

'Yes! How did you guess?'

Tom smiled. 'Well, age can do some strange things to you, you know? And developing intuition is one of them.' He looked at his girl. 'I'm proud of you, sweetie. And whatever you do, I'll support and help you the best I can.'

Sylvia was quiet, looking out the window, her lower lip trembling.

Tom moved close to her and lifted her chin. 'You're going to be a great mum.'

'How do you know? I have no idea how to raise a baby.'

'Because you've chosen to have her. Because you're a caring woman. Because you are strong and will do whatever you can to protect her and make her happy.'

'Yes,' she smiled. 'I want to protect this little creature inside me. And I have so many projects in my head.'

'Where are you planning to move to?'

'Back to Dunedin. It's my home, Dad. I've been offered a job as a curator at Otago Museum. I'll be in charge of the fossils collection. And I've asked to organise programmes for kids. I have so many ideas!'

'That's wonderful, sweetie.'

'Yes. And they know about my pregnancy. As long as I work for them for three months, they'll keep me on after my maternity leave.'

'They're good people.'

'They are. My friend Monica has a small house that used to belong to her granny, who died a few years ago. She's renting it to me cheap. It's the perfect place for me and the baby. Sunny, near the botanical gardens, a little garden.'

'Oh, sweetie. I hope the sofa bed will be comfy enough for my visits.' Tom grinned at her.

'It will be.' Her face became serious. 'And one more thing: I have a name for her now.'

'Oh. Would you like to tell me?'

'Cora,' she said with a smile.

Tom's face contorted, tears rolling down his face.

Sylvia approached him and he embraced her, sobbing on her shoulder. 'Cora would have loved that,' he said in a whisper.

CHAPTER 24

Home is Where the Heart is

Sofia and Peter

Fox Glacier, New Zealand, March 2022

Sofia looked into the distance, beneath the peaks covered in ice. 'There it is!' she exclaimed, her cheeks red with excitement.

'Where?' Peter asked, searching.

Sofia held his arm and pointed. 'There, to your left.'

'Yes!' Fox Glacier appeared in front of his eyes, steep, majestic, more full of ice than he would have expected for a receding glacier. 'Wow!'

Sofia wished she could reach it. She remembered when Cora had told her she had gone to the foot of both Fox and Franz Joseph Glaciers many years ago. Both had receded so much now that it wasn't possible to get there anymore. *I was too late*, her old voice said. She pushed away that voice. She wasn't going to let it ruin her life. She closed her eyes, said a little prayer for that voice that was trying to keep her safe, and told it she didn't need it anymore, as she had learnt in the mindfulness classes she had been attending in Tākaka. It had been hard to pull it back, but somehow that voice was not coming out that frequently anymore, and that was good.

She clung to Peter's arm, leant her head against his shoulder and sighed. She felt happy. Their months travelling in New Zealand had opened their hearts to life again. Sofia had been careful not to substitute for Mary, Peter's first wife. She had tried to be herself, acknowledging her doubts and fears about being loved. And it had worked. She had opened her heart to this honest man. And he had held it with care and accepted all of her, including her tendency to shed tears in the most unexpected places.

She smiled remembering when she had lost herself in his arms when they had seen Mount Cook for the first time. It had reminded her of her tramping trips in the Alps with Cora. The vision of her and Cora on their way to that mountain had been so vivid. She and Peter had been surrounded by a few people, mostly tourists and a couple of Kiwi families, all looking at her, surprised that the mountain had caused so much emotion in a woman from overseas. The mountain that Sir Edmund Hillary had trained on before going to the Himalayas and climbing Mount Everest.

'I'm hungry,' Peter said. 'What about we go to that café near Lake Matheson and for a walk around the lake afterwards? I wonder if we can take one of those famous photos with Mount Cook and Mount Tasman reflected in the water.'

Sofia was amazed at how much younger he looked now compared to when they had first met on the train to Santander. She just couldn't believe they were still together, building a life in this strange country on the other side of the world.

Well, for now you're on an eternal holiday, the voice again reminded her. *Soon the dream will be over and you'll need to make up your mind about what you're going to do*. This time it was more difficult to ignore.

'What's wrong?' Peter asked, a frown on his face. He knew her too well by now.

'Well…' She was unable to lie to him. 'I think I'm worried about the future.'

'Yes, I know. But if there's anything I've learnt in all those years of grieving, it's that the best decisions take time to arrive, and they don't need any thinking behind them; just a second when you realise what it is you really need.' He smiled. 'And somehow I think we both know the answer – to the short-term future, anyway.'

'Do we?'

'Yes, Sofia. You're finishing your book and finding yourself in the process. We don't want to cut that short, do we?'

'No. I wouldn't want that, but…'

'But you feel uncomfortable about living on someone else's salary, right?'

'Yes, I do.' Peter had been kindly paying for their trips and food, and Tom had lent them his house in Golden Bay for free once his old tenants had left, as he was living in Cora's house. He didn't need any extra money, he said. And they were family after all. It had been kind and natural. She liked Tom, and wished she had seen her sister Cora and him growing old together.

'You shouldn't, Sofia.' He held her chin to make her face him. 'I mean it. And we've gone through this many times. You just need to let it go.'

Let go. Yes. Such short words containing so much wisdom. And it was so bloody hard for her to do.

—

Half an hour later they sat at the table of a café facing the white peaks, two glasses of pinot gris, a dish of mussels and seafood chowder in front of them. It was a lovely sunny day, barely any clouds in the sky.

'This is to us,' Peter said, his eyes sparkling, and he clinked his glass against hers.

'To us and the future,' Sofia said. *To love each other*, her head continued, too shy to say it out loud.

—

Sofia's legs were heavy like stones as she dragged herself upstairs to the Airbnb she and Peter had rented on the West Coast.

It had been a nice day. They had gone for a walk in the native forest and had seen Mount Cook reflected in the famous Lake Matheson. They had been almost on their own in the forest, watching the birds. A tūī almost crashed into them, so focused was it on beating its wings as fast as it could. A robin came by to say hello and jumped on Peter's boots. Then there had been a wonderful dinner, with the best fish and chips she had ever tasted. She remembered staring at Peter as he was talking about their day, just feeling so happy.

'You're staring at me again, Sofia,' he had said with a smile. She was fascinated to see once again how he would never get angry or upset when she wasn't paying him attention.

'No, er … I'm sorry,' she replied.

'You shouldn't be.' And he held her hand between his own, the fish and chips left on one side of the table. 'I…' He swallowed. 'I am so grateful for having taken the step of going on that trip to Spain. It opened me up to so many things.' His eyes shone in the candlelight. 'It brought me back to life, back to wanting to live it in all its fullness.' He was playing with her hand, caressing it, holding it with one hand and then with the other. 'It brought me to feel such a deep love, such a warmth in my heart that I didn't think possible.'

She looked up then. He had stopped caressing her hand. His eyes were fixed on her. 'It brought me to you. I love you, Sofia, and I'm here to stay.'

Without her noticing, a few tears ran down her cheeks, dropping on her plate.

⁓

At the Airbnb she opened the bedroom door, and there he was. His clothes on the floor. The pyjamas neatly folded on a chair.

She walked towards him, taking her time. Her eyes were fixed on his, anchored to the safety of his harbour. She had no doubts about her life, its meaning or her future.

He embraced her, caressing her back, then taking off her t-shirt with a pōhutukawa flower, bought as a souvenir. With expertise he took her bra off, holding her breasts with gentleness. She held him tight, holding his head, kissing his forehead, tangling her hands in his hair until she couldn't wait any longer and kissed him, a soft kiss at first, a hungry one next. He took her in his arms, heading towards the large bed. He gently laid her down and unbuttoned her shorts, his hands searching. Then he put his hands underneath her underwear, and she couldn't wait any longer. She took everything off, gently pushed him on the bed and helped him move inside her, slowly but deeply at the same time, their mouths hungry for each other.

The next morning they were sitting at the deck outside their room, having breakfast in the sun. Peter was having a croissant.

'This is the life!' he said with a smile. 'I think I could stay here forever.'

'Me too.'

'Yes. But I truly mean it, Sofia.'

'What?'

'We don't need to go back to Europe,' Peter said. 'What's waiting for us there? A sad and lonely life full of rain in the UK for me, a dull life in Madrid for you. We deserve better. And I don't want us to live in either of those places.'

'Us?'

'Yes. Us.' Peter looked at Sofia, the wrinkles around his eyes more pronounced from squinting in the sun. 'There is an "us" now.'

'Oh.'

'And you need some time to explore your options, to fulfil your sister's wishes with that book. It's the project of a lifetime, Sofia, and it will change your life.'

'Yes. I need to work on it, even if I don't know how to start.' She had been avoiding getting close to the book, the challenge too daunting. She had told herself that she would start after the Christmas break, then after their visit to the North Island, then to the South Island … always making excuses. It was time she got serious about it. But she didn't even know where to start. Revisit the beginning of the book? Correct her sister's style in a "literature professor" kind of way? Analyse each sentence, as she had done for so many years with Shakespeare or Goethe? That was probably not what Cora had intended.

'I've been thinking.' Peter had taken her hand in his usual gentle way, caressing the back of it, moving it from one hand to the other. 'I'd like to stay in New Zealand for a while, give you time to write the book. And give me time to think about what I'd like to do with my life now.'

'But how?'

'I've talked to a real estate agent in the UK. I've put my house up for sale.'

'Are you sure?'

'Yes, Sofia. My life in the North is over now. I like it here. We could rent a house for a while and go from there. There is no hurry. Not anymore for me.'

'I … I've also been thinking that I want to stay, but not quite figuring out how. I'll talk to the Dean. My sabbatical will be over in a few months, but I don't think I'll go back. I can't return to that kind of life. And nothing is waiting for me in Madrid, either.'

She looked out at the mountains. Mount Cook, majestic, despite looking smaller than the impressive Mount Tasman. How she loved to see the mountains again, with nothing between her and them, the promise of the adventure before her. They had learnt about so many hikes (or "tramps", as they called them here) they could do. Great Walks, as the most famous ones were called. She was keen to try a few of those. And she felt at ease in this country full of gentle people who never seemed to be in a rush and were always interested in your well-being.

Sofia took a deep breath and smiled at Peter. 'Yes. Let's do it!'

'Yes?'

'Yes.'

—

Two nights later they were in Mount Cook Village, facing Mount Cook again. But this time he was the King of the show. That morning she had seen the most beautiful sunrise ever, painting the mountains in orange and pink. She had cried like a baby, held in Peter's arms.

Peter was asleep in the bedroom. She couldn't sleep; something was burning inside her. Her sister's book was lying open on the coffee table, challenging and terrifying at the same time. She went outside. It was a calm night. *No wind, but still a bit cold,* she thought, embracing herself. She felt calm, at ease, as if she was where she should be, as if the stars were aligned. She looked at them, majestic, strange, making her feel like she was from another planet, not recognising any of them. And then she heard it: the sound of the morepork, the ruru, as it was called in Māori. And then she saw it: Orion with its belt, and Sirius in the Canis Major. That was familiar. That was home. She looked at the sky for a long time. Then with a smile she came inside, sat at the computer and started typing.

CHAPTER 25

The Hidden Valley

Irene

Glencoe, Scotland, September 2022

Irene climbed the hills covered in heather. She reached a stone bridge above a small creek and stopped. Below her lay the valley of Glencoe, bright in the morning sun. The Three Sisters of Glencoe were behind her, impossibly steep, the road below her feet. The valley was silent, almost stopped in time. Later that day a few remaining tourists might come up, but only the ones who liked hiking. It was the end of the high season, with children already back at school.

She smiled, a hand on her heart. What wonderful set of circumstances had brought her to explore her favourite place in the world? She just couldn't believe her luck. After so many years dreaming of a job like this, here she was, exploring the area, preparing for a fieldtrip with the geology students from Stirling University. They would be looking at basalt formations, and there were plenty of them here, the area being the remains of an ancient caldera. She remembered when she had suggested The Lost Valley to Professor McKerrick. At first he had been doubtful, until she managed to win him over with her enthusiasm.

This last year had been a huge learning curve. Hesitant at first, she was regaining her self-confidence, finding the pure joy of being outdoors and showing the Highlands to the students. A few of them knew the area and had been hiking here and there, most of them in the Cairgorms near Aviemore, a famous climbing area in the Highlands. But few had ventured further, or 'gone bush', as Cora would have said. This year Irene had her favourite students, two young women from Italy, who expressed their enthusiasm about everything they saw. Passionate about rocks, they both wanted to do a PhD and work at the university in their home city, Milan. They reminded her of herself at their age, with a life ahead full of possibilities. They would love this place.

Irene took her water bottle from her backpack and drank, then continued climbing the last part of her journey. She had been here with Cora and could almost walk with her eyes closed. When the Campbells had massacred the MacDonalds of Glencoe in 1692, a few managed to flee to this valley. Considering it had been in the middle of winter, with probably frozen paths, it was incredible to think that a few had managed to get there and save their lives. When she'd come here with Cora she'd had so many questions. How long had they stayed here in the cold until they thought it was safe enough to return? What did they find when they went back? Dead bodies. Burnt homes. No food. No cattle. How did they survive their trip to the next town? Or did they die on the way? She shivered.

A movement above caught her eye. She looked up. A deer was standing up the slope, looking at her with curiosity. It looked young, no sign of antlers, with strong legs and a bright reddish skin. Irene was sure it was a female. Maybe she was looking for food for her fawn. Or just exploring. Slowly, Irene moved towards her. The deer just stared at her, standing still. She was probably one of the ones who used to go to the Kingshouse Hotel down the valley, to get food from humans. *They must have been doing this for centuries*, she thought. An iconic granite house in the valley, it was one of the most famous hotels on the West

Highland way. Irene loved to have dinner there, spend time in its lovely warm rooms, reading, having a beer or eating. She had booked several rooms for her students. She wanted them to experience what it was like to stay at a very old place full of history, so different from the houses in Stirling where they lived.

Irene continued walking. A few minutes later she entered The Lost Valley, a vast, flat valley surrounded by mountains, a treasure well kept by the Three Sisters. Vast, completely surrounded by mountains except for the small entrance where the creek ran down to the main valley, it was the perfect hiding place. She could see the path climbing up at the end of the valley, towards the peaks at the far end. The valley was deserted. Not a single noise. Not even the almost constant wind that usually blew fiercely here. Just silence. She looked up. The female deer was climbing up the path. Irene moved towards her left and sat on the slope. They would camp here for a night, experiencing the wild Highlands, feeling the ghosts of the lucky ones who survived that terrible winter. But the valley was full of peace. She didn't feel anxious, as she used to in a place where terrible incidents had happened. She had the ability to feel past events. Cora used to say she was like a feather, profoundly sensitive to any movement, real or not.

Then she heard a cry. The deer had reached the top and was making a call. To whom? Maybe her family. Or the morning sun. Or maybe the souls of the survivors. The deer's call, deep and guttural, echoed throughout the valley, vibrating inside Irene's heart. She felt as if she had closed a circle. Longing for something she couldn't put a name to in her twenties had led her to this moment of self-fulfilment and joy. How she wished Cora was here too. She closed her eyes. She felt her friend was there with her, somewhere between the deer's call and the valley echoing.

—

That evening Irene was having dinner at the Kingshouse Hotel. Sipping pumpkin soup, her hands were trembling from exhaustion. She was happy listening to the animated conversation of the locals. She closed her eyes and smiled. She loved the sound of their Scottish accents with their soft cadence.

After dinner she went to one of the living rooms. With brown old-fashioned sofas worn by time and a sense of history, the room was welcoming. She sat in front of an open fire with a book, but she was too tired to read.

Her mobile rang. It was Martha. With a smile, Irene took the call. 'Hello, darling.'

'Mum! How are you doing up north? Are you enjoying it?'

'Immensely, sweetie. I just can't describe in words how happy I am.'

'You don't need to, Mum. It seeps out of your pores,' Martha said. 'I've just received your postcard. It looks like such a special place.'

'It is.'

'You're fulfilling a dream, eh, Mum?'

'Yes. I am.'

'Was it … was it difficult for you when we were little?'

Irene smiled. Her older daughter's sensitivity would always surprise her.

'I loved having you and Beth, sweetie. But I left behind my career aspirations. A mother's choices are never easy.'

'I can see that. Life is so difficult!'

'Why do you say that, sweetie?'

'Well, here I am about to finish uni. And I have no idea what to do next.'

'I see. I thought you wanted to become a paediatrician and help sick children?'

'I thought so too. But now I'm not sure. I mean, I want to be independent, of course. But somehow I feel the need to explore the world.'

'Well, if you have that need, do it. Don't doubt it. It's your heart talking to you.'

'Thank you, Mum.' Irene could hear tears in her voice.

'Are you OK, darling?'

'Yes,' Martha sniffed. 'Well, I'm not sure what's going on with me, Mum.'

'Well, if you're having a crisis, follow what it's trying to tell you. So many young people just ignore those signs and keep going. They take all the steps society seems to impose on all of us: career, house, marriage, children … only to discover at fifty that they didn't want any of that. I'd rather you stop and search now than regret not doing it for the rest of your life.'

'Oh, Mum. Thank you. That means so much to me.'

'Have you thought about visiting Alex in New Zealand? I know you haven't had much contact with her in the last few years. But I think that since her mother died she's lost track of what she wants. It might do you two good to spend some time together and explore the country. Cora used to say it was the last piece of paradise.'

'I'd love to! That's a wonderful idea!'

'I'm pleased to hear that.'

'Why did you never visit Cora there?'

Irene was silent. 'I should have, darling. I could have made the effort. But I was scared. I used you and Beth as excuses not to go. I would have needed to bring you with me, and I thought the trip would have been too much for you and your sister. But you would have loved it, and it would have been a change of scenery for us. We had the money and the opportunity to do it. And I wasted it because of fear.'

'Oh, Mum. It's so sad to hear that! And now Cora's not there anymore.'

'No, she's not,' Irene said.

'She was your best friend, wasn't she?'

'She was the best of friends. Despite the distance and all those years without talking to each other. Cora was my soulmate, love. The one who would understand me without judgement. The one who would see through me without words. And that is so special. How many people never find someone like that?'

'Oh, Mum…' Martha was silent for a few minutes. 'You know what? I'm getting excited about going to New Zealand. I'll call Alex. But I'll only go under one condition.'

'What's that?'

'That you join me sometime soon. It's time for you to come and see where Cora lived for so many years. Even if you've released Cora's ashes in Neist Point, part of her soul is in New Zealand.'

Irene wiped her tears. 'Oh, darling. You're so right. And you know what? Sofia and I left some of Cora's ashes, thinking there was some other place for her.'

'Well, that's a sign. Let's find that place together. Sofia is in New Zealand with Peter anyway, so we could all gather there and say goodbye to Cora.'

'That's a great idea, love.'

'I need to go now, Mum. I'm glad I talked to you. I think we both have a plan now! I love you.'

'I love you, darling. Thank you for your call, and for being so understanding.'

'Of course, Mum. Take care.'

'You too, love.'

Irene lay down on one of the long sofas. She was astonished at her daughter's perception. Martha was so different from Beth. Calm, taking her time in life. Unlike Beth, who was there to conquer the world as soon as she possibly could.

Yes, she needed to spend some time in New Zealand. Get closer to Cora's heart, to the dreams she managed to fulfil, to the landscape she came to love. And take time to decide how she wanted her life to look from now on. She just couldn't ignore anymore that things with Mark were not going well. He hadn't taken well to her changes. She had stopped calling him every day. She only heard him complain that she was away, but he didn't seem to miss being with her – it was just that things were easier for him with her around. Lately she had been wondering if he had ever really understood her. Or if he had ever even tried. She felt as if she was dragging him around, heavy chains tied to her ankles making her move slowly and painfully. She was forty-seven. Enough of having chains. It was time for her to finally free herself and open to life and all its possibilities.

CHAPTER 26

The Search

Alex

Coromandel Peninsula, New Zealand, December 2022

The sun was warm and welcoming on Alex's face. She stopped walking and faced the sun, closing her eyes. It would be a hot day. She took off her backpack and grabbed her water bottle, drinking with pleasure. It had been a good idea to take some days for herself and explore this part of the country, so far away from where she had spent four years studying in Dunedin.

A shriek cut through the silence. She looked up. A hawk was hunting the skies, majestic above the landscape. The peaks she was heading to lay ahead, welcoming, golden bright from the morning sun. The Pinnacles Track was one of the most famous tramping tracks in the Coromandel. She vaguely remembered coming here with her mother when she was about nine. She had complained that it was too long, her mum gently encouraging her to keep going. 'You will love the view from up there, *mi niña*,' Mum had said.

Alex put on her backpack and kept ascending. Apart from a hunter, she had seen no one so far. Good. She needed time to think. Mum used to say that big decisions were not made by thinking, but by feeling. She had strongly believed in her intuition, which had taken her far in her last few years.

Everything had changed since Mum had died. Her plans to finish her studies and help Sarah at the local vet clinic in Tākaka, eventually taking over, didn't make sense anymore. She had been to Golden Bay a few times, spending the days walking along the beach and having deep conversations with Tom. She liked him. She wished Mum had had more time with this gentle man who had loved her the way she deserved. Now that she was moving into adulthood, she realised how hard it must have been for her mum to raise her on her own. Dad had found a woman with whom he seemed happy. But Mum had remained alone, holding all the weight of being a single working mum in a strange country, with no family around and few people she could rely on for help. She had been a strong woman, and had taught Alex to be strong too. That was a big responsibility: it meant she would be able to overcome anything life brought her and come out the other side – but sometimes at a cost. Loneliness. Suffering. Pain. She wondered what lay ahead for her now.

She stumbled against a rock in front of her, her red tramping boots shining in the sun. *OK, time to pay more attention. This is getting challenging*, she thought, looking above at the peaks.

———

Half an hour later she was sitting facing the cliff, The Pinnacles behind her. She could see in the distance the plains below her, green, welcoming. She ate a sandwich and some nuts, breathing in the peace of the place. She took some time to meditate facing the rising run. It would soon get too hot. *This is beautiful, Mum. You were right about it being worth it*, she thought.

She had felt closer to her mum when she had broken up with Finn. It had somehow not felt right to her anymore. Few things did lately. She even wondered if veterinary nursing was the right thing to study, even though she had kept going and recently graduated from Otago Polytechnic. It had been a warm November day, uncommon and special in Dunedin. All her classmates had come with their parents, their faces beaming with pride. At least Dad had been there with his partner, disappearing soon after the lunch celebration. Mum's absence had filled every moment.

Alex loved animals, that was clear. But in the last few months she had realised that healing animals had been like a balm for her when her parents separated. As if she could be with them and express to them how she felt without the need for words. Finding abandoned animals had helped her move on. A hedgehog with a broken leg. A fantail fallen from its nest. She had used all her energy to heal them and set them free, as if that process was part of her own emotional healing process.

Things were different now. She somehow didn't feel that need anymore. She needed something else. Lately she was feeling more useful helping her friends, like Patty, whose dad had cancer; she couldn't accept the fact that he might not make it. It had opened a dam of emotions for Alex, and somehow talking to Patty had helped her with her own grieving. Or Molly, obsessed with a guy who didn't love her, trying to accept it and move on. Alex had imagined walking in her shoes, feeling the pain of a broken heart. It had been a revelation to see things from a different angle, and she had loved feeling useful to other people.

But now her friends were going in different directions. Patty had returned to Greymouth with her family, wanting to spend more time with her dad. She said she knew the owner of the vet clinic there and might try to get a vet nurse position. Molly was heading back to Napier and would try to start a new business there. She felt full of energy about the task ahead. Alex felt so proud of her friend.

And what about her? She couldn't go back to Golden Bay. Tom was really nice. They had shared their love for Dunedin and for her mum. But it wasn't her home. It had always been her mum's choice, and now Alex felt like she didn't have a home to go back to. And that made her feel scared about the future. Shouldn't she be feeling exactly the opposite now, being young and free? She was free to go anywhere she wanted, knowing she had nobody to answer to, no one to tell her she was wrong (not that her mum ever said that), nobody to hurt her or drag her back. And yet … she also had nobody to encourage her, nobody to share her experiences with. Somehow that was making her wake up every night covered in sweat. While for many people she had met at college that was the dream, for her it wasn't the same anymore. After losing someone who truly loved you, you didn't want to "just be free" anymore. Freedom did not hold the fun and sense of adventure it would have held in other times. Not that she had planned many adventures. They seemed even less appealing now. And yet … maybe it was the only way for her to keep going. To start from scratch in a new place.

A panting noise brought her out of her thoughts. An energetic golden retriever was running up to the peak, its tongue hanging to one side. The dog circled the landmark indicating the top and then came to her, smelling her with caution.

'Hey, lovely. You've made it!'

The dog got closer to her and licked her face. She caressed its soft face. It looked like a happy dog, full of warmth.

'Beth! Where are you, kitty girl?' A voice sounded from behind. A girl in her twenties with short jeans and a pink top appeared next to the dog.

'You naughty girl! Have you been licking this woman sitting here in peace?'

'It's OK. I like her. She was brave to come all the way up here.'

'She loves tramping,' the girl said with a strong accent. Blonde curly hair partly covered her big green eyes. 'I'm Monique,' she said, extending her hand.

'Hi, Monique. I'm Alex.'

'Are you from here?'

'Well, I live in Dunedin, in the South Island.'

'I love Dunedin!' Monique said. 'I've spent three months there working for the Otago Museum.'

'That's a lovely place to work. I used to go there on weekends in winter and visit only a couple of rooms.' It used to cheer her up to read about something completely different from her degree. Physics, New Zealand history.

'It is. I miss it. But then it was my time to travel, as I only have four more months left of my working holiday visa.'

'It's nice to have that time. Where are you planning to go?'

Monique opened her arms wide and sighed. 'No idea! I just wake up each day and decide where to go.'

'I love that.'

'Why don't you do it too?'

'I don't know. I'm at a crossroads now.'

Monique smiled. 'So was I a year ago. That's why I made this trip,' she said, sitting down next to Alex and hugging her dog.

'Has it helped?'

'Partly,' she said, stopping to think. 'I still have no idea what to do with the rest of my life. But at least I've learnt how to live more fully. And I'm determined never to lose that.'

Alex liked this woman, so full of positive energy.

'Do you have plans for the next few days?' Alex asked.

'None at all.'

'What about spending a few days at Port Jackson, at the tip of the Coromandel Peninsula? I've always wanted to go there, but never felt brave enough.'

'Sounds great! Let's do it!'

Beth got up and started to walk down the hill.

'She knows we're done here and she's ready for the next adventure!' Monique said with a smile.

A week later Alex got out of her sleeping bag, trying to make no noise. Monique tossed around. Alex opened the tent's zip, grabbed her swimming suit and towel and clambered out. It was early morning and the beach was quiet. The waves had the usual calming effect on her: not rushed, simply being. She headed to the toilet and changed. The campground was now silent after the noisy parties at night. People would get up in two or three hours' time, lazily moving through the day till the evening. Except for the area with young families. In the distance she could see a little girl already playing with a bucket and spade.

There was a light breeze playing with Alex's long hair. She climbed the rocks near the cliff and sat down at her favourite spot, facing the sea. The waves were not too high today, unlike three days ago when a wave splashed over her and almost took her back to sea with it. Her heart started to beat fast recalling the experience. The sea was such an unexpected beast. And despite that, she adored the spot. It reminded her of Dunedin, of the wild beaches only good surfers would venture to, the wild beauty of the south.

She was missing it. This was beautiful, but still there was something about the North Island that made her want to rush, as if she were always late to something. Like when she was in Wellington, first at primary school, then at intermediate and high school. Always searching for good scores. Sometimes her mum needed to remind her to enjoy herself.

'Have some fun too, sweetheart,' she would say. 'Time flies, and if you don't include fun in your life it will never be present.'

'You were so right, Mum,' Alex thought, tears running down her cheeks.

Well, she could go anywhere. She could spend some time in Europe if she wanted to. She had enjoyed spending some weeks there last year. But deep inside her, she knew it wasn't her place. She didn't feel ready for the busyness of Europe, of not being special because there were too many people, of needing to *ganarse el pan* (earn her own bread) every day of her life. Since being back in New Zealand she had started to really understand how special this country was. Far away from the world, but still a Western country in all senses, it had a warm community feeling, probably inherited from the colony times. People would help one another, care for one another. Her mum used to say that the first thing that surprised her when she arrived in New Zealand was when the cashier at the supermarket would ask her how her day had been, looking in her eyes and actually waiting for an answer. She said in Spain they would just say it and look down, not waiting for you to respond. Here there was time to be polite, time to help people, time to just *be* without any rush.

Sometimes she had wondered why her mother had stayed. She remembered being sad and lonely when her parents split up, nostalgic for the life of her youth. They had moved to Germany for a year when she was ten. It hadn't worked out well. Mum was even more lonely there, and had complained of the amount of paperwork she had to fill in simply to take Alex to swimming lessons. School had been hard, and she had made a few friends (including Vanessa, with whom she still kept in touch), but overall she had been glad when her mum said they were going back.

'Why, Mummy?' she had asked.

'Because I have realised New Zealand is home,' Mum had said. And that had settled it. Irene had not understood when she found out years later about the year in Germany. She took it so badly that she had stopped calling. That broke Mum's heart. They saw each other a couple of times after that (for grandad's funeral, for a short visit a few years ago), but the tension was palpable, and they never opened up to each other in the same way again.

Mum had made her choices, Alex realised, tracking the beautiful flight of a young seagull along the beach. It was time to make her own.

'Life is so hard,' she heard a teenager say from the other side of the rocks. 'Now that I'm getting used to living in Auckland, Mum decides to go and live with the penguins!'

'Come on, Paula. Don't be so picky. Dunedin isn't Antarctica, for God's sake! It has nice beaches and…' another teenage girl replied.

'Bullshit! And it's never summer there! What about my swimming lessons?'

Without realising what she was doing, Alex was suddenly standing next to them, two girls around sixteen, one with long blonde hair in a ponytail, the other with short red hair and a face full of pimples.

'There are wonderful swimming lessons down there.'

Both girls looked at her, their mouths open.

'Sorry, girls,' Alex said. 'I was just sitting on the other side of the rocks and I heard you. I've lived in Dunedin for four years, where I was studying. And it's a beautiful town to live in, full of hidden treasures.'

'What did you study?' the blonde girl asked.

'Vet nursing.'

'My mum is a vet. She's bought a vet clinic and is starting a business down there.'

'Really?' Alex asked. 'I'd love to talk to her.'

'See that woman with long blonde hair swimming in the sea?' the girl asked, pointing. 'That's my mum.'

And with a shiver going down her spine, Alex left the two girls and headed towards the woman in the water.

CHAPTER 27

The Wharf

Alex and Sofia

Napier, New Zealand, January 2023

Sofia woke up and opened the curtains. A bright sun greeted her, sending sparkles around the bedroom. She could see the ocean extending as far as the eye could see. Calm, welcoming, glittering.

There was a knock on the door. 'Are you ready for a walk?' Alex asked from the other side.

'Er, no. I think I fell asleep.'

'That's OK,' Alex said. 'Can you be ready in ten minutes? I just want to show you something before it's too crowded.'

'Sure.'

Half an hour later Sofia and Alex were walking along Napier's waterfront. Beautifully built, with large gardens, flower beds and fountains, it filled Sofia with a deep sense of peace.

'This is a special place.' She looked at her niece. 'I understand why you chose to come here.' Sofia had been surprised when Alex called her from Coromandel, asking if they could spend a few days together in Napier. She hadn't seen her since their encounter in Madrid, shortly after Cora died. Despite a few phone calls, she wasn't sure how her niece was doing. She was aware that she was travelling around New Zealand. She looked older, more mature, her face more determined.

Alex smiled at Sofia. 'I feel at ease here. It's warm. It's relaxing. A favourite place for retired couples from Wellington or other major cities.' She shrugged. 'Dad is from here, so I used to come with him to visit my grandad before he died. I also came often with Mum. We liked it here.'

'I didn't know that.'

Alex looked at Sofia and her face crumpled. 'There are many things you don't know, Auntie.'

'Like what?'

'Like how hard it was for Mum to live here on her own. Or how divided she was between the life she left in Spain and the life she created here.'

'I can only imagine. And after having lived here for a few months, I can see how hard it must have been to be so far away from all she knew.'

'Yes.'

Decorated with flowers and fountains, Marine Parade had a track to walk and cycle along the beach. Sofia imagined it would be bustling with people in a few hours' time.

'Let's turn here.' Alex guided Sofia to the left, towards an open space around a big stone fountain. In front of her was a bronze statue of a woman sitting on a rock, a pin in her hair. She had an air of mystery in her smile, and Sofia wouldn't have been surprised if she had moved.

'Oh.'

'This is Pania of the Reef, our lady of the sea. She is on the shore here, but she is said to be under the sea crying for the fate that didn't allow her return to her beloved, Karitoki. She is one of our most precious souls, and a guardian of the fishermen who risk their lives every day out at sea.'

Sofia stood still looking at her. A warm feeling crept up her chest. Of love. Of gratitude. And a deep feeling of having arrived home. She shivered. For a few minutes, time stopped. A suite of memories filed past. Cora and her as little girls in a forest, being chased by their father. Both of them tramping in the mountains twenty years ago.

Sofia had never believed in fate, but now, in front of the most beautiful mermaid she had ever seen, she felt as if she was finally able to sit down and relax.

'Look at me?' Alex asked.

Sofia turned and her niece took a photo of her. She then looked back, and the spell was gone. With trembling legs, she followed Alex on the path along the beach.

A few hours later Sofia and Alex were seated at a café in town. They had spent the morning walking along the beach and wandering around the town. Sofia found Napier to be a treasure. Completely built in Art Deco style in the 1930s following a devastating earthquake and subsequent fire, the town seemed to be frozen in time. It wouldn't have surprised her to see carriages approaching the theatre, women in long dresses with colourful umbrellas holding the arms of men in tailcoats with high hats and walking canes.

'What is the likelihood of another earthquake like the one in the thirties?' Sofia asked, then sipped her spider, a drink consisting of vanilla ice cream and fizzy soda. 'This tastes nice,' she added.

'Good that you like my recommendation, even if it's more for children,' Alex said with a wink. She leant on the table and looked at Sofia. 'Look, Auntie, you need to understand something. This is a beautiful country; some people even say it's the last paradise on Earth. But it comes at a cost.' Alex lifted one finger. 'First, its distance from the rest of the world. Second, its natural hazards. We regularly have landslides and earthquakes, and at times tsunamis or volcanic eruptions.

Sometimes they are small. Sometimes devastating.' Alex looked at Sofia. 'Some time ago, the last time I came here with Mum, I asked a friend who works at the East Coast Lab (a research institute in Hawke's Bay), what would be the likelihood of another earthquake like the one in 1931. He said it would happen again, as the subduction plate boundary is just off the coast. They're just not sure when.'

'Oh! So you're in constant danger here.'

'You could say so, yes, coming from stable Europe.' Alex smiled. 'It's the same in Wellington. In my teens I was scared. I had nightmares about earthquakes ripping our house apart. But one day I just got over it. You learn to live with the danger. And you know what? It helps you appreciate life. You learn to enjoy every moment you have on Earth.'

Sofia was silent for a while. 'That's an interesting way of seeing it. I guess it also gives you perspective. As if the little things we're constantly worried about aren't that important after all. As if you should focus on the "big rocks".'

'Exactly,' Alex said. 'And then you realise it doesn't happen that often, and you can relax and enjoy.'

They were silent for a while, gazing at the deep blue sea in front of them.

A young woman approached them with two plates. 'Here's your food. Enjoy!' she said with a smile.

'Thank you,' Sofia replied, looking at her corn fritters with salad. 'This looks good.'

'It tastes even better,' Alex said, digging into her burger. 'Let's enjoy the food and then go to that café at the beach for a drink.'

'That sounds great. I'm already loving it here,' Sofia said, lifting her first forkful.

'Would you consider moving to Europe?' Sofia asked later, a chocolate ice-cream cone in her hand.

They were seated on two wooden chairs at the beach, a small shed acting as a café at their back, the infinite sea in front.

'This is the life!' Sofia added.

'I told you.' Alex was smiling at her, a cup of hot chocolate in her hands. She frowned. 'I go back and forth,' Alex said. 'Sometimes I want to leave all this and run away to Europe, where Granny is, where Irene lives.' Alex looked at the sea, deep in thought. 'But other times, when I travel around New Zealand, I feel I belong here. My trip to Europe when Mum died made me realise I wouldn't be understood there; I would always be a stranger. Here I feel I can be just me.' She looked at Sofia with a crumpled face. 'And I don't want to have Mum's contradictory feelings about where home is.'

'Yes. It's hard.' Sofia held Alex's hand. It was warm and young, full of possibilities. She thought about what a constant dilemma it seemed to be to live here. All that you always dreamed of at your doorstep. The nature, the beauty, the landscape. But also the freedom to create at your own pace, to live and let live, to choose where and when, without external pressures. But for some people like her sister, all this was at the cost of loneliness and feeling trapped, with her roots taken away from her.

Sofia reached for her handbag and took out a pile of paper.

'I've been longing to show you this for a while.'

'What is it?' Alex asked.

'It's a half-written novel left by your mum.'

Sofia looked at Alex. Her niece had frozen. 'Did you know she was writing a second novel?'

'No, I didn't.' Alex's hand was in the air, as if touching her mum's book would break her into pieces.

Sofia left the book on Alex's lap. 'This is the reason I've stayed in New Zealand. To finish it, as was Cora's wish.'

'Oh.' Alex was facing towards the sea, her lip trembling.

'It's about the options we have, and how they can all happen at the same time. How we are all alive and dead, in Europe and in New

Zealand, married with children and a big house or single and travelling the world.'

Alex touched the manuscript with trembling hands. 'That's what she talked about the last time I saw her. She was writing it down.'

'Yes.'

'Have you finished it?'

'No. It's not easy to do it justice. Your mum was a great writer.'

'Yes, she was. And she never believed it.'

'No.'

'I'm stuck at the moment,' said Sofia. 'And I wanted you to read it and give me some feedback on my new chapters.'

Alex looked at her auntie. 'Thank you for trusting me to do that.'

Sofia smiled back. 'I couldn't think of a better person. And I suspect you'll give me your sincere opinion, no matter how blunt it is.'

They both stayed silent for a while, the soft waves crashing against the beach. Sofia looked at the sea, her hair swaying in the gentle breeze. She closed her eyes. This felt right. After days of doubts, wondering if showing it to Alex would be a good idea, she felt she could relax. It would help her niece know her mum a little better. And in the process, she was envisioning the two of them having long conversations about the parallel lives Cora had created.

About all the 'what ifs' of lives not lived, of different choices.

After a long time, Sofia looked at Alex. Her niece had fallen asleep on the long chair, an arm hanging out, a slight smile on her face.

A few days later Sofia and Alex stood in front of the long wharf. Made of wood and half eaten by the sea, it had stood through time and storms, marking the first landing of Captain James Cook. Tolaga Bay wharf was an iconic place in New Zealand.

There was nobody else there. It was cloudy and with increasing winds, and Sofia would not have attempted to go on her own. But by now she knew that if she stayed at home just because of the weather, she would never go anywhere. *I have learnt a wonderful skill from the Kiwis: keep your plans despite the weather.* Sofia wondered how much happier European people would be if they adopted this habit from their Antipodean cousins.

They walked along the wooden wharf. Sofia felt like she was going back in time. Not back into New Zealand's history, still quite unknown to her, but in her life. Back to the times when she was little and free of fear. When Cora and her dad were alive, when they were a united family always on adventures. Her granny came into her thoughts too. What a strong woman she had been. She had taught Sofia about the pleasure of adventures. 'Don't be afraid to sail away, my dear girl. Travelling is the joy of the heart,' she used to say.

Sofia wondered why she was thinking of her now. Somehow, for several decades, she had lost the sense of freedom of her youth. It had taken her a huge effort to get to this point, through darkness and self-doubt. Now life looked wonderful. She had found a purpose, a place where she belonged, the love of her life. She looked up. The sky was a deep blue, with spongy clouds towards the north. All this had started when Cora died, when she was angry at her older sister for dying and not being there for her. In only eighteen months she had turned into a different woman.

Before knowing it they had reached the end of the wharf. A vast grey sea stood before them.

'Wow,' Sofia said.

'Chile is on the other side, about nine thousand kilometres away. Nothing else stands between America and us.'

Sofia wondered how she could have spent years in her oppressive apartment in Madrid feeling sorry for herself, missing so much in life.

'I've read the book,' Alex said.

Sofia turned towards her niece. Her gaze was fixed far away on the deep blue sea, slightly flinching. Then she looked at Sofia, her deep blue eyes covered by a shadow.

'Mum needed to see herself in different situations, ask herself what would have happened if she had never left Spain, if she had never met dad, if I had never been born. That's why she created a novel with the main character, Ellie, having different lives, each one leading to a different outcome,' Alex said.

'Maybe she needed it to make sense of her own life.'

'And there was always something in common in all of Ellie's lives.'

'What is that?'

'Passion. Whatever she was doing, she always managed to follow her passions. Whether she was a geologist exploring the Andes, a schoolteacher in Spain or a woman searching for gold in Otago, she had this engine that would keep her going, no matter how hard her life was.'

'Oh. I hadn't seen it that way. I like that. It's the way she was.'

'Yes. Even if things weren't easy for her, deep inside she always believed she would find a way to achieve her dreams.' Alex looked at Sofia. 'Thank you for letting me read it,' she said.

'Of course.' Sofia kissed Alex on the cheek and held her close. They stood like that for a long time, looking at the seagulls swaying in the wind.

'Your chapters add humour to the book. I like them,' Alex said.

'Do they?'

'Yes,' Alex looked at her aunt. 'You have a beautiful sense of humour and freshness I didn't know about. Like when Ellie found that crazy man in the desert and went for a ride on the motorbike with him and then ended up living in a town in the Andes for months on end. You've added colour to the novel; a sense of hope that wasn't there in mum's chapters.' Alex looked at Sofia. 'Passion from mum. Hope from you. It's such a rich novel. I'm sure many women will identify with Ellie and her choices, and laugh and cry with her.'

'Oh! Thank you,' Sofia said, her throat tight. Alex held her hand and they both looked towards the sea.

'There's something else in common in all of Ellie's different lives,' Sofia said after a while.

'What's that?'

'The girl. Whether she had a girl of her own or not, there was always a girl or a young woman helping her or giving her the advice she needed. Always there to give her the emotional connection and the grounding she needed.'

'Oh!'

'Look at the twelve-year-old girl she found in the middle of the Atacama Desert in Chile when she was lost. She showed her the way back to civilisation. Or the sixteen-year-old student the schoolteacher felt so connected to, and all the deep conversations they shared.' Sofia looked at Alex. 'That was you, always in her heart, the one leading her home.'

Alex looked towards the start of the wharf, the connection to Mother Earth. 'I wish she had lived to see me finding myself,' she said, her lips trembling.

Sofia took Alex's face and turned it towards her. 'She is still here with you, always, like in the book.'

'Yes,' Alex said, sniffing. They stood there hugging each other, two women at the end of the wharf, the wind swirling their hair.

Going for a Ride

Martha and Alex

Central Otago, New Zealand, March 2023

Martha was surrounded by a morning fog that had sunk inside her bones. She shivered. With only a thin jacket, she was not prepared for this cold. Suddenly the sun rose on the horizon behind a green meadow full of running rabbits. She stopped her bike to admire the scene unfolding in front of her. She couldn't believe the beauty and peace of the place. She was by herself, Alex probably ten minutes ahead of her. But she realised she didn't mind at all. After only a few weeks in New Zealand, she had already started to appreciate the vast spaces and the joy of rarely passing another person.

She had enjoyed Clyde, where they had stayed overnight. A small town she could easily imagine in the nineteenth century during the gold rush, it had kept its essence, with old stone houses, a pub, a mill and a few old houses adapted as Airbnbs. Alex had been the one to suggest they bike the Otago Rail Trail, a three-to-five-day bike trail in Central Otago. It was a favourite for both Kiwis and tourists. Martha had been reluctant at first. Had she travelled all the way to New Zealand to just go on a bike ride for a few days? Was that what she was looking for when she decided to spend a few months visiting Alex? She definitely needed a break; all the changes in the last few months had made her lose her way. Cora's death had destabilised her mum, who had gone on a journey to Scotland to scatter Cora's ashes with Sofia, Cora's sister. Then, out of the blue, her mum had decided she would go back to teaching geology and organising fieldtrips in Scotland. She said that would allow her to spend more time hiking in the Highlands, and that she was recovering a long-lost dream. Martha was happy about her mum's decision and was the first one to support her, unlike her little sister Beth, who at twenty-one had had a tantrum as huge as when she was two years old, only with worse consequences. Their dad had taken a week off work to visit some friends in Hungary they had never heard of, to get away from the stress. But Martha knew there was more to it than what her mum had said. Things had not been going well between her parents. There had been way too many nights with her dad in his office and her mum reading in the living room. And those were the few nights she had been visiting from uni, when they had had nice family dinners. She suspected the dinner conversation wasn't as light-hearted when she wasn't around.

'Martha! Where are you?' Martha could hear Alex calling her before she saw her friend cycling back towards her.

'Sorry, Alex. I just got carried away by the beautiful scenery.'

Alex smiled. 'Yes. You've got that look.'

'What look?'

Alex stopped next to her and sighed. 'The look of someone falling in love with this country. I've seen it many times. I can recognise it by now.'

'Maybe you're right.' Martha smiled. 'I don't know what I was expecting, but this is so much more.'

Alex looked at the rising sun dispersing the fog, a frown on her face. 'Yes. But my mum never felt at home here. Well, not until the last couple of years, when she settled into a life she had been searching for for a long time. And then … well, then it was too late.' She swallowed, a lump forming in her throat.

'It wasn't your fault that she waited so long to move where she felt home was, searching for a better life.'

'I know,' Alex said. 'And yet…' She looked at Martha. 'Don't you feel the same with your mum? So many years yearning to go back to geology, looking after you and Beth, and not making the move until you two had gone to uni?'

Martha looked at Alex. She was so mature now. She remembered seeing her as a teenager, talking about boys, make-up and actors; how she had felt so much younger back then, the one-year difference a canyon between them. But her mum's death had changed Alex. Where she had once been all energy, she was now all depth and a deep sadness. They had never really been friends, living so far apart. And yet Martha had always felt connected to this girl one year younger than her, the daughter of her mum's best friend. It didn't matter that they hadn't been in touch for a few years. Martha knew her mum's friend, the one she would fully open to, had always been Cora.

'Yes. I feel sad and responsible. As if I should have noticed and pushed her to make this move years ago. But I was young, dealing with hormones and finding out what I wanted in life…' (*Only to lose it again*, a voice in her head said.) 'I had plenty on my plate. I think we need to face the fact that this is part of life: a mother just leaves aside her dreams until the right time comes.'

'Yes,' Alex sighed, flicking a fly away. 'I just wished she had had more time doing what she wanted,' she said, a single tear falling down her face.

Martha touched Alex's shoulder. 'I know.'

Alex forced a smile. 'OK, let's keep going. We have almost forty kilometres to go until we get to Omakau, and the sun is out now.'

'Yes, let's go!'

The following day Alex and Martha had an early start. It was a warm sunny morning, promising midday heat. Martha loved the sense of freedom and achievement, moving in her own power from town to town. Even though it was meant to be high season, there were not many people cycling the track. A large group of men and women in their forties that looked like old school friends, a family with young children cycling one section and three couples they would meet here and there. The towns only had a few accommodation options and usually one old hotel where they had dinner. Martha enjoyed being amongst so few people. Coming from Germany, with so many crowded cities, she just couldn't believe the amount of space there was in New Zealand. Space to breathe and enjoy nature. Space to be just herself.

With small backpacks on their backs and double paniers at the back of their bikes, they had all they needed for the day. The day before they had stopped for lunch to find simple cafés with rustic tables under trees, where they could rest and replenish themselves. She had noticed that nobody was locking their bikes, leaving them at the entrance of the cafés without any worries that they would be stolen. Martha was open-mouthed the first time she saw it. But after a few more stops she was getting accustomed to the relaxed and trusting Kiwi style.

They had established the routine of having Alex lead with a slow but steady pace, leaving Martha to follow and enjoy the scenery. Even though they hadn't seen each other for some time, they were soon connecting and sharing their recent life experiences, and Martha was slowly feeling as if she had a new friend in this beautiful country.

The path was almost flat, gently going uphill. They had been crossing beautiful old bridges above fresh water rivers. Martha felt as if nature was speaking through its features, each scenery more stunning than the previous one.

'Look!' Alex was pointing towards a group of white rocks on the slope to their right. Tall and slim, they looked like sentinels from another world.

'Wow!'

—

Two hours later they were sitting at a café with wooden tables and umbrellas. Three kids were playing on the slides and swings, a couple patting a llama in a paddock. They had ordered wraps for lunch. Martha's had a wonderful green sauce similar to pesto.

'Mum and I should have done this track together,' Alex said. She had been quiet all morning, deep in her thoughts, steadily pedalling.

'Why didn't you?' Martha asked.

Alex shrugged. 'Life, I guess. Too far away from Wellington. Too many logistics to get here, hire bikes…'

'And expensive too for your mum, I guess.'

'Yes. Bloody money. You're so selfish when you're young. But now, looking back, I realise how lucky I was. How, despite all the difficulties, we had a lovely life together.' Alex sighed, looking into the distance. 'And being just the two of us made it even more special. At times I wished she had a partner, especially when I was about to go to uni and realised how lonely she would be. And when I was a teenager and we had a quarrel and I wished she wasn't always on top of me.' Alex stopped to look at Martha with darkened eyes. 'I feel so guilty about those times now.'

'I can imagine,' Martha said. 'And despite that, your mum loved you more than anything in her life, Alex.'

'I know. She was the best mum ever.'

After a few minutes, Alex crossed her legs and looked at Martha. 'What about you?'

'What?'

'Why are you here? Why have you taken some months off to come and see me?'

'Well, I… A year ago I was sure I knew what I wanted: to become a paediatrician. Look after children and heal them from their diseases. Fill the world with happy kids.'

'That's a nice dream.'

'It is. But it doesn't feel right anymore. I don't trust myself that I can do it. Who am I to do anything differently to all the other great paediatricians in the world?'

'Well. I don't have a reply to that. All I can say is that you need to find out what's special about you. What you can offer that others can't. And I don't mean from a competitive point of view. I'm talking about self-esteem. If there's something I've learnt in the last few months, it's that no matter your career or the amount of money you have in the bank, if you don't have faith in yourself and know your special place in life, you have nothing.'

'Wow. That's profound, Alex.'

'I had a lot of time to think after mum died. And I know that I don't want to achieve anything grand in life. I don't want a Nobel prize or to win the lottery. Or (goodness me!) to be flattered by others. I only want to leave this life knowing that I've made a difference to someone. That being in this world has made someone feel loved, cared for and happy. That is all that matters to me.' Alex touched Martha's arm, and with tears running down her face she headed towards the toilet, leaving Martha alone with her thoughts.

That afternoon Martha and Alex reached the first tunnel, a dark hole in front of them. They left their bikes and went up a steep path to the side to look at the scenery. The Poolburn Gorge stood before them, majestic, with a drop full of green bushes, immense rocks and trees hanging from impossible angles. Martha was speechless. She felt a sense of achievement she hadn't felt for a long time. She had missed that. Focused on her studies, she hadn't paid much attention to doing regular exercise. She thought it required too much effort. But doing the Otago Rail Trail had been a great decision. A gentle path, although at times slowly grading uphill, she was able to focus on the scenery and work on resistance, while being able to stop at any time without feeling guilty. A gentle smile appeared on her face and a light feeling spread through her chest.

'This is so beautiful,' Alex said next to her, her face beaming. She took a few photos and they took a selfie with the gorge in the background. Alex put away her mobile phone and hugged Martha. 'Thank you,' Alex said. 'Thank you.' Tears were running down her face.

Martha held Alex, a warm feeling in her heart.

'Thank you,' she replied.

They pulled back and looked into each other's eyes.

'I feel whole again, as if I have recovered a part of me that was hiding for a long time,' Martha said.

'That's good. You need time, Martha. Time to redirect yourself. I took that time when Mum died, and it's been like rediscovering who I really am and who I'd like to be. I thought I knew before, but I didn't.'

'You were always so confident. I was surprised you needed to stop. But then something similar happened to me. And stopping society's push to move ahead without thinking was the best thing I could do. I'm glad I did it and came here, far away from the crazy world, to reconnect with nature, to find out who I want to be. You can't do that in Europe, where you have so much pressure to keep going, to not stop. Being rejected at a job interview if you've had a gap of two months. I hate that. I don't want to live that way anymore.'

'I see what you mean. Here it's different. We live at a different pace, especially in the South Island. The world is somewhere out there and we're aware of it, but we live in a parallel universe. That's what Mum used to say.'

'Yes. That's how I feel.'

'Have you thought about staying in New Zealand for some time?

Mum's house in Tākaka is open for you to stay for as long as you want, and I'd love to have you nearby.'

'Mm. It's tempting.'

'Well, take the next few days to think about it.' Alex turned towards the tunnel. 'And now we should tackle the darkness and find the light at the end.' She smiled at Martha and walked back to her bike.

Martha looked at the scenery, wondering how she could feel so alive after just a few weeks in this remote and beautiful country. She shrugged. Maybe she didn't need to understand everything after all. She got on her bike and followed her friend.

CHAPTER 29

The Dolphins

Irene and Sofia

Golden Bay, New Zealand, April 2023

Irene followed the long queue at Auckland airport. It was six in the morning and she was exhausted. Surrounded by people with sleepy eyes, Irene couldn't believe she had made it all the way to New Zealand. Now she understood how far away Cora had lived all these years and why travelling to Europe to see her family had been so sporadic. Irene didn't think she could do this very often. Her legs felt as heavy as Greek columns, her eyes puffy under her glasses. She didn't feel capable of putting in her contact lenses.

A little girl was fast asleep in her mother's arms. The mother looked worn out, with dark circles under her eyes. Irene smiled at her.

She moved forward in the queue and looked at the policeman at the counter. With dark hair and blue eyes, he was smiling at her. She gave him her passport.

'Good morning. Did you have a good flight?' he asked while examining her passport.

'Yes, thank you.'

'What's the purpose of your trip?'

'I'm visiting some friends and will take time to explore the country.'

'It's a beautiful country, ma'am. Enjoy it. Welcome to New Zealand.' He gave Irene her passport back and she moved on. Wow. What a friendly policeman. She had never experienced such a warm welcome at an airport in Europe.

After collecting her luggage and going through customs, she went through the arrivals doors.

'Mum!'

Martha was waving at her. Wearing blue jeans and a pink t-shirt, she looked relaxed.

'Hello, darling!' Irene embraced her daughter.

'You look tired, Mum,' Martha said. 'Just take it easy in the next week or so. It'll get better.' She smiled. 'I've taken the liberty of hiring a car. I thought we could spend a couple of days exploring Auckland before going to Tākaka. What do you think?'

'That sounds lovely.'

'OK, let's go pick up the car and we can head off. I'd like to see the beaches on the West Coast. I've been told they're spectacular. And you should stay awake until this evening to avoid your jetlag getting worse.'

She picked up her mum's luggage and they went out into the sunshine.

A few days later Irene and Martha were in a taxi heading to Cora's house in Golden Bay. They had spent a nice few days in Auckland. Being the largest city in New Zealand, it had a lot to offer. Irene had particularly liked the zoo. Designed with care, it provided plenty of space for the animals. Set in a large green area that included a park and a playground, it didn't feel as if it was in the middle of a city.

Karekare beach had been spectacular. It was vast, with black sand and wild waves, and Irene just couldn't believe such beauty could still exist. When she had watched *The Piano* she had felt depressed when the main character arrived at that same beach. It looked like the last place on Earth, the piano standing on the beach as if screaming to get out of there. It must have felt that way in the nineteenth century. Now, coming from crowded Europe, a place with such open spaces and wild nature had warmed her heart.

The flight to Tākaka from Nelson had been quite an experience. In a small plane with just three seats, Irene had felt sick when taking off and almost threw up. But then she looked down. Green forests and dark blue waters shining in the sun. She felt as if she were part of a documentary about the last paradise. With islands here and there, what left her open-mouthed were the bays with golden beaches and turquoise waters. The pilot, a young man with a deep smile and long hair in a ponytail, had told her that the name Golden Bay was not because of the colour of the beaches, but due to the gold that was found there in the nineteenth century.

'Mum, are you all right? Are you over the dizziness from the plane?'

Irene looked at her daughter, a smile on her face. 'Oh, yes, I'm better now, thank you.'

'I haven't been to Cora's place yet either. I wonder what it'll be like to be there,' Martha said.

Irene had been thinking about Cora since she had arrived in New Zealand. Wondering if Cora had been to each place she visited. She hated not to have been here when her friend was still alive. She looked at her cabin bag. Cora's ashes were in a small urn. Just a couple of handfuls; a small sample to bring to the place that had been her home for more than twenty years.

Cora's home was a wooden house with red shutters and a blue roof, bright in the midday sun. A nicely tended front garden full of colour, with geraniums against the windowsills that reminded her of Tirolean houses, and two large trees with beautiful red flowers she had never seen before.

They got out of the taxi, paid and collected their luggage.

The front door opened and Sofia came out in a long white summer dress and a straw hat, a big smile on her face. 'Irene!'

The two women embraced.

'You look so young, Sofia, and so happy!'

Sofia smiled back. 'I am, Irene. And you look different too; more open to life.'

While Sofia hugged Martha, Irene walked towards the front door of her dear friend's house, tears falling down her cheeks.

———

A few days later Irene was sitting at the beach. Wild and welcoming, the waves soothed her spirit. The sand was a bright orange she had never seen before. A large, curved bay, the beach extended forever between two high cliffs to the north and south. She had been told that Tōtaranui was full of people in the summer, as it had the largest campground in New Zealand. She wondered how crowded the beach would look then. She could see a young couple walking in the distance.

Sofia had lent her an old Subaru, and she had taken the day to explore. She had headed south, leaving Golden Bay to enter the Abel Tasman National Park, a very popular place due to its turquoise waters. It was like being in the Caribbean, but without the sharks. It had been a long drive down a gravel road, but she felt exhilarated. She wondered if Cora had ever been there, if she had come for a swim or a walk. There was even the option of taking the ferry to other beaches and returning on foot.

The last few days had been full of emotion. She had met Tom, Cora's partner, a calm man looking for peace. His daughter Sylvia was visiting. She had a small baby girl. Tom's face gleamed every time he looked at her.

Alex had arrived a few days ago. She looked different. Her outward energy had been replaced by an inner glow of self-confidence. She spoke calmly, taking her time to express her thoughts and feelings. She had returned to Dunedin and had started a job as an assistant at a vet clinic. She looked happy, relaxed, at ease.

Irene and Peter had shared a few conversations. She had seen him look at Sofia with a light radiating from his face. They had decided to stay in New Zealand for a while. Sofia had started writing, and it made her happy. It was as if through her writing she was expressing all her hidden feelings from the past twenty years. She was very private about what she was writing. She said it had to do with Cora. Irene had not asked any more questions.

Martha had changed. She didn't look like the serious and responsible girl she used to be. She had turned into a woman looking for things that made her happy; things that gave her pleasure and a sense of self-esteem. She and Alex had become friends. They were going horse-riding on the beach each morning and were planning to do the Heaphy Track in the spring.

Irene had asked her daughter what her plans were. Martha wanted to stay for a while. In a few weeks she was moving to Dunedin to stay with Alex. Being a paediatrician was not what she wanted anymore, she said. Irene was happy for her. The search for happiness had become her priority. She wished she had learnt that lesson a long time ago.

A couple of children flying a kite had stopped and moved closer to the water, screaming in delight. Their mother was with them, pointing at something. Irene stood up, looking. And then she saw them: a pod of small dolphins swimming next to the beach, diving in and out of the water. There was a little one following her mother, and then one jumped above the others, making an arch of light.

One of the children waded into the water. She reached a dolphin and touched it. The dolphin swam around her, playful. Irene approached the family. The mother was beaming.

'Hector's dolphins,' she said. 'It's so rare to see them get so close. My brother and I used to swim with them in Bay of Plenty when we were little. I never thought my kids would ever experience something like this.'

The girl was screaming, her face beaming as she splashed around and turned in circles, following her friend. Until the dolphins turned around and headed towards deeper waters.

After the family left Irene stayed, looking at the place where the dolphins had disappeared. Now she was sure Cora had been there. And then she knew where they would scatter her remaining ashes. In these deep blue waters, to swim with the dolphins.

—

Two weeks later

Sofia looked at the sea in front of her. It was silver-grey, reflecting the colour of the sky. She had a lump in her throat. She didn't like to throw her sister's ashes in a dark sea. The waves were gentle, producing a soft sound in her ears. The beach was deserted. It had been raining over the previous few days, and the road from Tākaka had been flooded in places.

She had enjoyed having Irene around. She and Peter had rented a house on the West Coast, and would be moving there in a few days. It had been nice spending so much time with Tom, but they wanted to give him some privacy. His daughter and granddaughter were staying for a while, and she and Peter needed some privacy too. Besides, she was stuck with the novel. She hadn't been feeling close to Cora's soul lately. She needed to have her sister beside her to finish it, and she was starting to despair. The wind was picking up now.

She looked down to the urn in her arms. The last remains of Cora. She was holding it tight, her knuckles white, her lips pressed.

Alex approached her.

'Hi, Auntie.' She looked bright and happy. After having made the decision to move to Dunedin had fallen into a serene mode that fascinated Sofia.

'Hi, darling.'

'Hey.' She held her hand on top of the urn. 'We don't need to do this if you're not ready,' she said, her eyes full of concern.

Sofia smiled. 'That's a very kind gesture, Alex,' she said. 'You're her daughter. You also have a say.'

'Yes, but we all need to be ready.'

Sofia looked around. Irene and Peter were walking along the beach. Irene was collecting something, possibly some shells. They had been getting to know each other in the last few weeks. Peter said how much he liked her, how she deserved to follow her dreams and live a happy life. Irene had told her that she was moving to the Scottish Highlands. It was easier for her to organise the fieldtrips from there. She had also told Mark that their marriage was over. She said how much she realised what a toll it had taken to be with a man who was never around to help her with the girls, never interested in her dreams and hopes, never supportive of her. Sofia was proud of her. Irene had so much courage and passion within her.

Martha and Tom were near the water, pointing at something in the sea.

'Look, Sofia!' Tom said.

'Where?'

'There!' Sofia squinted her eyes. And then she saw them. Three small dolphins were swimming towards the beach, jumping with an elegance that reminded her of her childhood, when she was flexible enough to do cartwheels in the sand.

'Irene! Peter!' Alex was calling them. They came running and formed a circle.

'What are they doing?' Peter asked. The dolphins were coming close to the sand.

'I don't know,' Sofia said. 'Maybe…' she swallowed. 'Maybe they're coming for her,' she said.

Peter squeezed her arm. 'Are you OK?'

'Yes, and it's time.'

She looked at Alex, who smiled at her. Then she looked at Irene. Her face was peaceful through her tears. Irene nodded.

Then Tom held Sofia's hand on top of the urn. 'Let's do it all together,' he said. Sofia looked at him. After so many months together, she had grown to appreciate and love this gentle man who only wanted to live a quiet life in the countryside. He was smiling at her.

Sofia looked down at the golden urn. She swallowed. And then the urn brightened up. She looked at the sky. The sun had appeared from behind the clouds, shining on her face. She closed her eyes.

Cora, wherever you are, I love you, dear sister. I wish we had spent more time together over the last few years. I am proud of who you became, following your instincts no matter what. She could feel Alex next to her, squeezing her shoulder. *You have raised a wonderful daughter by yourself. She is kind and gentle, and she will be OK. We are all here for you, and we love you. Goodbye, dear sister.*

Sofia opened the urn and walked to the water. It was cold but welcoming. They were all holding hands behind her. Tom, Irene, Martha, Peter, Alex. They walked behind Sofia. She lifted the urn and released the ashes, a cloud of grey above the sea which had turned dark blue, like the Aegean Sea in Greece where she and Cora had spent a summer in their childhood.

The Hector's dolphins swam towards them, their fins like silver, shining in the sun. They swam in circles around the ashes as if holding Cora's remains.

Peter held Sofia's hand. She looked at him through watering eyes, smiling.

The dolphins swam around one last time then headed back out to sea. The group stood watching them until they reached the horizon. And then the three dolphins jumped against the bright sky in a beautiful farewell dance.

'Goodbye, Cora,' Sofia whispered.

CHAPTER 30

The Attic

Sofia

Madrid, September 2023

Sofia was reading a book on a bench in her mum's garden. It was a warm day, typical of the Indian autumn that never failed in Spain. A couple of late summer days before the cold returned. She could hear the bees buzzing from flower to flower. The roses were magnificent, tended by her mother with the utmost care. Sofia had never been interested in gardening. Her mum hadn't shared her passion for gardening with her daughters. It seemed to have been her hobby to escape the daily routine, the hard work of raising two girls and tending a house. The roses matched her mum's character quite well, Sofia thought. Beautiful to admire but prickly if you got too close, ready for an attack at any time.

She had returned to Spain for a few weeks to visit her mum and arrange a few things. After selling her apartment some months ago, she had left a few boxes at her mum's house until she had time to decide which things to ship to New Zealand, which ones to get rid of, which to keep. Well, that wasn't an option anymore: her mum had stated very clearly that she didn't want to store any of her boxes. She already had too many from Cora that were occupying space in the attic, and she didn't want more from Sofia. As if all that was left of Cora was a pile of annoying boxes to get rid of; a soul lost without voice or memories.

Sofia looked up. The old brick house from the 1920s stood before her, steady through years of her dad's care, only to be left to her mum's abandonment in the last few years. Above her was the dormer window of the bedroom she had shared with Cora. She remembered Cora spending hours seated on the windowsill, looking outside, unable to leave and find out for herself what life was like. Sofia was the outgoing one who would spend every weekends in and out, going to discos with her friends, skating, riding her bike; anything that would keep her in the outdoors. Except for tramping, which was shared with Cora and sometimes their dad. And then, when Cora left for uni, Sofia's life changed. She had shut down to the world and taken her sister's place at the windowsill. Her friends stopped passing by to invite her out. They moved on with their lives. A few days before she had seen one of them at the supermarket. She looked old, with two small kids and complaining about her husband and how difficult it was to keep her too-big-to-clean house. It made Sofia wonder what kind of life would have awaited her had she continued hanging out with those girls.

She could hear a hose being turned on. Her mum must have woken up and was watering the garden. After a few moments she appeared round the corner. In her usual faded blue dress and pink apron, her grey hair tight in a bun, she looked tired.

'Oh, there you are,' she said, raising the hose to water the bushes at the back.

'Shall I help you, Mum?'

'No, thank you. I like to do it myself and make sure all the roses get water. Besides, who is here to help me usually anyway?'

Sofia was silent. Over the years she had learnt not to reply to her mum when she started complaining.

'What? Are you mute? Is that what you learn overseas?'

'No, Mum. We learn to be kind. And I can't reply to this with kindness.'

'How do you dare say this to me?'

With a sigh, Sofia stood up and took her book. 'I'd better have a look at the boxes in the attic.' She turned towards the house.

A beam of light from a skylight in the roof illuminated the attic. Sofia could see old pieces of furniture covered in white sheets that had been there ever since she could remember. She wondered who they had belonged to and why they had never been used or disposed of in her lifetime. Her boxes had been neatly stacked by the movers in two piles to her left, just under the light. She opened the first one.

After a couple of hours she stood up and smiled. She had made some decisions. Three big boxes stood on one side. She would ship them to New Zealand. They had books she wanted to keep; those that made her feel at home wherever she was. She had missed them. *Wuthering Heights*, *Rob Roy*, *The Persian Boy*. Her most precious dolls were there too. An old teddy bear with a broken ear that had lost most of its stuffing. A soft doll without an arm. She couldn't leave them behind. They had been her bed companions in her early childhood, and then in her late teens. But they needed attention. Tom had told her about a doll hospital in Palmerston North where you could send your broken dolls and get them back fixed. She might try that.

She went downstairs to grab some water. The house was silent. Her mum was nowhere to be seen.

Back upstairs, she looked over at a pile of four boxes that looked damp and abandoned. Cora's boxes, left there twenty-five years ago, when Cora didn't know if she would come back.

'I'd like to take enough with me to feel at home, but not everything in case I decide to come back and I can't afford to ship it all back,' she had said. They had never been opened since.

With a sigh, Sofia opened the first box.

—

Half an hour later Sofia was sitting on the floor. The foulard on her head was full of dust, her forehead wet with sweat. She was getting some fresh air using an old Spanish fan of Cora's she had found in one of the boxes. They were full of memories from her childhood. The whole collection of *The Happy Hollisters* by Jerry West, which she and Cora had loved as children. A necklace made of small seashells her sister had won one summer. Sofia had a vivid memory of her older sister walking along the beach with the necklace shining in the sun.

She didn't know what to do with all this. She should donate the books, maybe take them to the Cuesta de Mollano, the steep street near Atocha train station with the small second-hand book shops. It was a good opportunity to go there again, spend some time searching for interesting books. She had loved doing that as a child, going on Sundays with her dad and her sister, holding her dad's hand and being enthusiastic about everything she saw. She missed her dad. He had been a warm light in her heart. He had taught her enthusiasm, trust and faith in a life full of hopes and dreams.

'Go out to the world and explore it, *mi niña*,' he used to say. 'The world is there to show you that it's full of light and colours.' The last time he had said that to her was a few weeks before he'd died. She remembered him lying on the deck in this house, facing the spring garden in bloom. Even then, he still had hope. Sofia's eyes filled with warm tears. So many wasted years. She had felt trapped for so long. Now that she was back in Madrid, she felt pity for the woman who hadn't found a way out of that grief. Now she, Sofia, was out of all that thanks to Cora, whose gift after death had been to push her out of her comfort zone. Her dad would have liked that. She imagined him smiling at her from wherever he was.

The sun shone on something bright in the half-opened box before her, waiting to be inspected. It was a silver metallic box with an old-style painting of a girl with a bonnet holding an orange cat. With trembling hands, she opened the box. It was full of letters. She opened the first one. It was a letter from her dad to Cora, dated 2006. He was writing about how worried he was for her after her divorce from Nick, being alone in New Zealand with little Alex. It was full of warmth and care. She felt nosy, invading her sister's privacy. She would take those letters and read them later.

When packing them up, one of them fell on the floor. It was an older letter from 1994, before Cora had moved to New Zealand. Her dad was writing about her, Sofia.

Someone has deeply hurt your sister, Cora. I don't know the details, and I probably never will. They're too painful for your sister to share. But you and I need to do the best we can to get her out of her cocoon. Otherwise she'll stay there for the rest of her life and never live a fulfilling life. Promise me you'll help me with this, darling.

With tears rolling down her cheeks, Sofia leant against a box, holding the letter to her chest. Oh, Dad. He had known all these years and had never asked her any questions. And then she knew Cora had kept her promise. Every time she had visited she had planned a tramp for the two of them. The Picos de Europa, the Pyrenees, even the Alps. Despite her efforts, nothing had worked. Cora had gone back to New Zealand and Sofia in her cocoon, amongst her books at the university, inside her apartment in the city. It had only been after her death that Cora had helped her open up to life again. Sofia had finally explored the country that had been Cora's for so many years. She had found love. She had discovered a passion in life, a purpose. But it was too late to share that with her dad and sister. Her body shook, and with tears falling on her clothes she lay down and embraced her body, rocking herself from side to side, alone in the attic of her parents' home, surrounded by objects full of memories of her happy childhood. A few minutes later, she fell asleep.

'Sofia! Where are you?' Sofia could hear her mum's steps up the stairs.

Sofia opened her eyes. Her mum's face was next to her, frowning with worry.

'Too many memories here, *pichi*, ey? Come on,' she helped Sofia stand up. 'Let's go down and have something to drink.'

Sofia hadn't heard her mum use her nickname since she was a little girl.

Two days later Sofia entered her bedroom. The afternoon sun was coming through the window, bathing it in golden light. She looked around. The room was an ode to her childhood. A porcelain doll with a blue dress and a broken arm was sitting on a chair. The poster of Elijah Wood in *The Adventures of Huck Finn* was on the wall behind the door. A photo of Cora and her as girls stood next to her lamp. They were outside the summer house they had hired in Pontevedra, on the northwest coast of Spain. She must have been eight and Cora thirteen. They were holding hands in front of an *horreo*, a traditional grain storage house made of granite. Sofia was holding a Colajet, a rocket-shaped Cola ice block, a smile on her face. That day, Cora had won an extra one and had given it to Sofia. With trembling hands she picked up the photo and packed it in her bag.

Then she saw it. A letter yellowed from time and with a couple of dark stains, lying on her pillow. It had a stamp from Scotland from 1964 and was addressed to her father. A shiver went down her back, making her feel cold and sweaty. She opened the letter. It seemed to be from a friend of her dad's who lived in Scotland and missed him after 'the wonderful years we have spent together exploring the Scottish Highlands.' Sofia sat on the rocking chair, moving the porcelain doll aside, and read it twice. After a long time staring out the window, she stood up and went downstairs.

Her mum was sitting on a bench in the garden, enjoying the afternoon sun, her face turned up to the sky.

'Mum?' Sofia asked.

'Yes, darling?'

'You look happy.'

'I am relieved. I feel free,' she said, looking at her. She had the brightest smile Sofia had seen for a long time.

'What is this?'

'A letter from your father's best friend, Robert.'

'I can see that. But… How did we never know of his existence?'

'He lived far away, and your dad kept that part of his life apart.'

'But why?'

'I think he didn't want to have regrets. I knew you would want to know more, so I thought it was good that you have the letter. It's all I have of Dad's past. He kept it in his bedside table till he died.' Her mum's hands were shaking.

'Oh, Mum.' Sofia hugged her mum. She looked thin and fragile underneath her clothes.

'Mum, I … I saw a photo of him in a bookstore in Inverness.'

'Oh, yes. That was his favourite bookstore, where he spent many days reading with his friends. He even worked there for a few months.'

'If he liked Scotland so much, why did he come back?'

'His dad was very sick, and his mum, your granny, asked him to come and help her with the farm and the rest of the family, as he had small brothers and sisters. During that time our friendship turned into something else,' she said with a sad smile. 'When his dad died, we got married. He wanted to go back to Scotland and build a family there.' She looked at Sofia. 'But I was a selfish girl, too scared to move to a different country. And so we bought this house and never left. Your dad never went back to Scotland. He sacrificed himself for me,' she said, her bottom lip trembling.

Sofia swallowed hard. 'Did he ever regret it?'

'Well, he never showed it. But his heart belonged there. We could have lived there. He had a good job at the historical archive in Inverness. You and Cora could have been born in Scotland. And it would have been a good life.'

'Why did he never tell us?'

'He didn't want you or your sister to think he had regrets. Besides, everyone should always keep deep secrets;, secrets that make them whole and special, that are never shared with anyone else.'

Sofia had always had dark secrets inside her. They had swallowed the light in her heart. Those were not the ones to keep.

'Are you thirsty? Shall I bring some lemonade?' Sofia asked.

'That would be lovely, darling.'

Sofia stood up, leaving her mother gazing at her garden.

~

Ten minutes later they were seated at the outdoor table in the garden, two glasses of lemonade and a plate of olives between them.

'It's been a while since I last had a visitor, and I miss it,' Sofia's mum said.

'It seems to me that you've closed yourself off since Dad died.'

'It's true. I was lost,' she said. 'I had spent all of my life attending to his needs and those of you and your sister, and I had forgotten to look after myself. I didn't even know what I wanted.'

'Oh, Mum.' Sofia looked at her mum. She saw wrinkles around her eyes and mouth that hadn't been there the last time she had bothered to look closely at her. 'Do you feel lonely?'

'Every day,' she said with a smile. 'Dad and Cora are gone, and now you've settled far away.'

'I'm still here if you need me.'

'Yes,' she said with a smile. 'But it's time for me to move on.'

'What are your plans?'

'Well, I've joined a reading group. They're all widows like me, who love to read and need company. It was weird at the start. But I discovered that they make me laugh, and have shown me what friendship is.' Her face was beaming.

'That sounds wonderful, Mum. I'm very happy for you.'

'Thank you, darling. I'm happy too.' She stood up. 'There's something else I'd like to show you.'

A few minutes later Sofia's mum returned with a book in her hands.

'What is this?' Sofia asked.

Her mum was seating next to her, smiling. 'This is the job of a lifetime,' she said.

Sofia opened it. *Memorias de una mujer*, it said. A Woman's Memoir. The book included old photos of their family and of the farm she grew up in Cantabria, in the north of Spain, and even scanned letters.

'Is this Dad's handwriting?' Sofia asked.

'Yes. It's one of the letters he sent me from Scotland when he was living there.'

There was a photo of her mum in her twenties in front of a granite house. She had a big smile on her face and a bunch of flowers in her arms.

'That is the day I got my first job as a secretary.' It was a smile of triumph, the only one Sofia had ever seen.

Sofia took her mum's hand and squeezed it. 'I'm so proud of you, Mum.'

Her mum had tears running down her cheeks. Sofia couldn't remember the last time she had seen her cry.

'Thank you, darling.' She pointed to the book. 'Read the first page.'

Sofia turned to the first page.

To Arturo, the love of my life. To Mum and Dad, who gave me a happy childhood. And to Niebla and Pichi (Cora and Sofia), my lovely two girls whom I lost due to my fears. I love you so much, and I am so proud of you, my brave and strong girls.

Sofia's hands were trembling, the book shaking on her lap. She closed her eyes. An image came to her. Cora was running around in the garden, pretending to be barking. She was spreading out her arms and flying, making *tweet tweet* sounds. Niebla and Pichi, Heidi's dog and bird from Johanna Spyri's nineteenth-century book, the first heroes in their lives and the nicknames their mum had given them.

Sofia thought how little she knew of her own mum, how her mum had always been angry with her or too focused on her dad, a gentle man full of warmth and light. But her mum had been there all along. In the shadows, providing a security she hadn't been aware of, the security she had before that terrible incident in her teens she had tried to forget for most of her life. And while focusing on that, she had forgotten about what she still had. Wonderful friends who loved her. Health and a future ahead. Cora and Dad were not there anymore. But her mum was.

Sofia stood up and embraced her mum, feeling her fragile body against hers, her warmth that had always been there.

'Thank you.'

'For what, darling?'

'For being there for me all the time, despite it all.'

'Oh, yes. I was always there and will always be.'

'And now I'm far away, and you don't have anyone else.'

'You're wrong there: I know I have you when I need you. But most of all, I finally have myself. And that is all I need,' she said with a smile.

Sofia looked at her mother, the mother who had always seemed distant and cold to her, who had been overshadowed by her dad's huge personality. A woman who had lost her husband and older daughter within a few years. There she was, standing before her as a new woman, strong, with a whole future ahead of her and with so much to say.

'My friends are coming over tomorrow for our weekly meeting. Would you like to meet them?' Her mum was beaming, her lip trembling.

'I'd love to,' Sofia said. She took the lemonade and drank it, memories of her happy youth mixing with her present. She looked at the garden. The roses her mum had tended for so many years were blooming in reds, yellows, even purples. Her mum had created a haven of light and colour, and Sofia was seeing it for the first time. And with tears falling down her cheeks, Sofia smiled.

A Light Through the Roof

Sofia

Madrid, Spain, September 2023

Sofia was sitting at a table outside a café in the centre of Madrid. It was warm in the sun, but under the big umbrella she could feel the cool breeze swinging her hair.

She looked around. A couple of women walked past, several bags in their hands. She smiled. She remembered how many times she had come to the city centre and looked around clothes shops. But most of all she used to love spending hours on end at the bookshops, reading the blurbs of dozens of books, a notebook in her hand. She missed that. Just being on her own exploring her inner world. She had spent so much time longing to leave the big city, explore the world, have new adventures. She drank her Coke and picked up some potatoes with aioli. Oh, wow, she had had plenty of adventures in the last two years. She now lived in a country so far away that it felt like something in a dream. She looked around. Nobody would believe that this woman, with her long dark hair and brown eyes, had a life at the other side of the world.

She loved her life in New Zealand with Peter. She had rediscovered her passion for writing. She lived in a beautiful place that many people in this big city would envy. She was in love with a good man who respected her just as she was. But she now realised she had denied part of who she was: her origins, her culture, her background. These last few weeks with her mum had brought back where she came from. She was Spanish. It was in her blood. She belonged to this city she had hated for so many years. But now she could see how many things made her feel like she belonged. Sitting outside a café having a drink and sharing tapas with a friend. Going to the wonderful *Teatro Español* to watch a classic play. Laughing out loud without anyone feeling uncomfortable around her.

She crossed her legs, feeling the cool breeze coming up under her long white dress. Oh, she had missed being able to wear summer dresses for weeks on end.

The phone rang.

'Hello?'

'Sofia!' a familiar voice said.

'Maria? Is that you?'

'Yes! I can't believe you're in Madrid!'

Sofia smiled. It was so good to hear her friend's voice. 'Yes. Just for a few more days. I'd love to see you. Are you around? Shall we meet in the centre?'

'I don't live in Madrid anymore, Sofia.'

'What! How? Where do you live now?'

'In Cercedilla, in my old granny's house.'

'How did that happen?' Sofia asked, a knot in her stomach. She hadn't been checking on her friend as much as she should have in the last few months.

'Oh, Sofia. That's a long story… Why don't you come and stay for a few days, and we can catch up? Do you have time?'

Sofia looked into the distance. Staying with her mum had been good for her soul. She had finally found a connection with her that she hadn't realised she'd been missing. But she needed some space for herself too.

'I'd love to,' Sofia said. 'I can come on Thursday, if that works for you.'

Maria squealed. 'Yes! Please come! There's a train that brings you here directly. I'll send you the details by text. Just let me know your arrival time and I'll pick you up.'

'That sounds lovely. See you on Thursday!'

Hearing her friend's voice was making her nostalgic, bringing back so many memories. It had been a good idea to come to Spain to visit friends.

Sofia raised her hand towards the waiter, paid and stood up. She had a few days to do some shopping and browse the bookshops the way she used to.

—

A few days later Sofia was sitting on a train heading towards Cercedilla, at the foot of the Sierra de Guadarrama mountain range northwest of Madrid. She looked through the window. The meadows were all yellow after the hot summer. But there, in front of her, stood her beloved mountains. Almost silver, they shone in the morning sun. How many good memories she had from her childhood and youth, scrambling from rock to rock in La Pedriza, a well-known rock-climbing place She gave a deep sigh. She had missed this. There was a family nearby with small children with tiny backpacks, jumping around in excitement. It felt like only yesterday that she and Cora were doing the same on their weekend tramping trips with their dad.

Cercedilla train station was just as she remembered it. Small, made of the same granite as the mountains above, the cool air creating goosebumps on her arms. She remembered there was a tiny bakery nearby where they would get their sandwiches. She wondered if it was still there.

'Sofia!' a woman with long dark hair was waving from the driver's seat of a red SUV opposite the train station.

'Maria!' Sofia crossed the street. Maria got out of the car and embraced her, a huge smile on her face. 'Look at you! You look so much younger!'

'You look fabulous!' Sofia said, looking at her friend who wore a blue dress down to her ankles, a silver bracelet on her right ankle.

Maria smiled. 'Well, I take better care of myself now,' she said. 'But get in the car and we can talk at home.'

⁓

'Wow!' Sofia said. Maria's house was just as she remembered. It had belonged to her grandparents back then. They used to spend so many weekends together when they were thirteen, doing their nails, watching films, giggling all day. It was a small granite house with blue wooden shutters and a red door, surrounded by mature trees. There were red and white geraniums on the windowsills and flowers everywhere in the front garden. A yellow rose climbed the front wall, near a pond surrounded by red and white tulips.

'You've taken good care of it,' Sofia said.

'Yes. It's home now.'

Sofia looked at Maria. The wrinkles around her mouth were gone.

They went inside. The cool kitchen surprised her. She had forgotten how stone houses could be so cool even when it was hot outside. A big fireplace on one side would keep it warm during winter. There was a small pot with a yellow flower on the big wooden dining table.

'What would you like?' Maria had opened the fridge and was getting out some cheeses, then cutting some bread. 'I have lemonade, orange juice or cold water.'

'A lemonade would be great, thank you.'

A few minutes later they were seated at the outdoor wooden table, facing the garden. With a pergola with hanging vines and buzzing with bees, it was fresh and cool.

'Wow!'

'I know. I can hardly believe it myself,' Maria said. 'Sometimes I need to pinch myself to believe I'm really here.'

'How did this happen? Last time we talked you were still trying to save your marriage.'

Maria sipped her lemonade and sighed. 'Oh, yes. That feels like eons ago.'

'So?'

'So one day, when I was determined to talk to Carlos about going to a couples' counsellor, I found a note in Carlos's coat pocket that changed it all.' Maria looked at Sofia with a blank face. 'Yes. There was a woman after all. Not sure when it started. I didn't bother to ask for all the details. It actually made things so much easier. At that very moment I realised that it was the perfect excuse to break up with him. I hadn't noticed how tense I had been until I released my breath that afternoon.'

'Was it easy?'

'It was. Easier than I thought it would be. He didn't fight for anything. We sold the house and split up the rest: the cars, the furniture, everything.'

'And then?'

'Well, then I realised I could come here. I had had a lovely childhood coming to this place, and I needed to get away from the big city, get all of us some fresh air.'

'How did they take it?' Sofia looked around, a frown on her face. She had forgotten about the kids.

Maria smiled. 'Don't worry. They're spending the day with my mum. We have a couple more hours.' She took some cheese and bread. 'They actually took it better than I expected. They soon made friends at the small school in Cercedilla. They now run wild with bare feet in the garden. You wouldn't recognise them!'

'Wow! That's hard to believe. And what do you do for a living?'

'Come with me.' Maria stood up and offered her hand. 'There's something I'd like you to see,' she said with a smile.

They went up the ladder in the middle of the living room and climbed to the attic. Sofia remembered it as cold and damp and dark. Now there was a big window on one side and it was bright and golden. In the middle of the attic, in the part where the ceiling was higher, there was a big easel with an unfinished painting of the mountains at dusk. The walls were covered with finished paintings. Maria's kids running in the garden, a white cat on top of a fence, an old man with a walking stick playing chess with a boy.

Sofia looked at Maria, her mouth opened, tears rolling down her cheeks. 'You've made it.'

'Yes,' Maria said. 'I'm taking painting lessons in Villalba, and I'm practising a lot. Actually, last month I sold my first painting.'

Sofia took Maria in her arms. Her friend had gone through hell and come out the other side into the bright sun. She saw something new in Maria's beautiful grey eyes: pride and self-fulfilment.

Half an hour later they were walking around Cercedilla. There was a cool breeze, and Sofia was glad she had remembered to bring a jacket with her. She hugged herself.

'What?' Maria asked.

'Uhm?'

'That smile on your face.'

'Uhm.' Sofia said again. 'You seem to notice everything.'

'Yes, I do. You know me,' Maria said with a smile.

Sofia looked at Maria. 'You know something weird? I've spent decades dreaming of moving somewhere else. Hating Madrid because it was noisy and suffocating and there was nobody who loved me.'

'Which is absolutely not true.' Maria had turned and was facing Sofia, a frown on her forehead.

'Yes,' Sofia said to those eyes she knew so well. 'Now I know. These days I've started to appreciate Madrid. All the things I was missing, from Serrano ham to the professional waiters always attending to your needs to the buzzing of a city that never sleeps. And oh, I missed the city centre. Having Zara, Desigual and FNAC within metres!'

'Good. It seems you needed to live thousands of kilometres away to appreciate that.'

Sofia noted a tone of sarcasm that she hadn't heard before from her friend.

'Yes. I needed to get away to see that Madrid and Spain were not the problem. It was me. I was stuck in a life that I hated. I couldn't find the way out. And until I managed to find it I couldn't see the light of the life I had left behind.'

'I hope that includes me,' Maria said with a smile.

'Of course it does.' Sofia took her arm and they kept walking.

'So… Are you planning to come back anytime soon?' Maria asked.

Sofia stopped and looked at her.

'What? Maria,' Sofia said softly. 'Please. You need to understand that I need to explore this part of my life. But I don't want that to ever destroy our friendship.'

'It won't,' Maria said solemnly.

'Well. It could. That's what happened to Cora and Irene.' Sofia looked at her friend. 'I'm not sure what will happen in the future, where I'll be living in three years' time, even six months' time. But I do know that your friendship keeps me grounded. Having you and my mother here helps me explore the world without forgetting where I come from. I need you to be my anchor here.'

Maria kept walking in silence. 'You're asking me to be a different type of friend than I have been until now.'

'Yes, in a way I am.'

Maria looked up at the mountains, lit up in gold. Then she looked at Sofia.

'If there's something that I've learnt in the last few years, it's that life changes, and we need to embrace those changes the best we can.

They define who we are even more than the fixed parts of ourselves. Yes, I will. I will be the friend you need of me.'

Sofia smiled. 'Thank you.'

'But I want you to promise me that we'll have quality time regularly. Every year or two. Whatever it takes. But we'll go away for a few days and just be us. Sofia and Maria.'

Sofia looked at Maria with her long hair in a bun. 'Yes. I promise. I'll need it.'

'No,' Maria said. 'You are the one who is having great adventures. It'll be me who needs it most.' She kissed Sofia on the cheek. 'And now it's time to go back. The kids will return anytime.'

They walked back in silence, the gold and red of the setting sun behind their backs. Maria's hands were cold against Sofia's arm. Sofia could see a tear falling down her face. She looked away before noticing she had tears on her cheeks too. Once she had read a poem about friendships. About how there were friendships for a season, for a reason or for a lifetime. Through the years she had met many seasonal friends, those who came and went after a few months. Since she had moved to New Zealand, she had wondered if the friendship with Maria would last. How could she have doubted it? Now she knew they would keep in contact. It was as if a curtain had opened and let the light in again.

'Mami!' A boy of around seven was running towards them.

'Roberto! He is so big now,' Sofia said, looking at Maria. But Maria was running towards her son. And with a smile on her face, Sofia ran after her friend to greet the children.

CHAPTER 32

New Beginnings

Martha and Alex

Dunedin, New Zealand, October 2023

Martha looked at the narrow path ahead covered in mud, roots and leaves. Surrounded by silver beech and ferns, it meandered uphill. It was cold inside the forest. She was alone, the fantails her only companions. She closed the zip of her feather vest. Apart from a man and his dog, she had passed no one else. Alex had recommended that she climb Mount Cargill this way, from Bethune's Gully. She had been busy at the vet lately, a couple of urgent surgeries taking all her attention.

Even with her tramping boots, Martha's feet were slipping in the mud. She was thankful for her walking sticks. Dunedin was a quiet town. Despite its more than a hundred and thirty thousand inhabitants, it didn't feel crowded. Surrounded by dormant volcanoes and stunning beaches, farmland just at the edges of the city, there was so much green everywhere. It was a town alive with cultural events. Otago University was full of international students and there were interesting events happening every weekend. She would never forget the winter festival in the city centre near First Church, an impressive stone church dominating the town, illuminated with thousands of lanterns especially designed for the occasion. Surrounded by girls with long scarfs and boys with candy floss in gloved hands, she felt like a little girl again, next to fairies lit in blue lights and even a carriage pulled by two unicorns, with the Ice Queen to sit with and take a photo.

The trees cleared out and Martha approached a wooden fence. The hill was covered with native trees. She could hear a stream running down the hill. In front of her stood her destination, a large peak with a huge antenna. Suddenly the clouds moved aside and the bright sun shone on her face, warming up her red nose and cheeks. She closed her eyes, enjoying the change from winter to spring. Alex had told her how Dunedin showed the changes in season like no other place in New Zealand, from the cold winter to the hot summers. Martha liked that, each season bringing something new.

It had been a winter of letting go, of letting herself explore without worries or pressure. Sharing Alex's apartment, she was managing to sort out her finances enough to stay longer than expected. She had applied for a working holiday visa, which would entitle her to stay for a whole year, with a maximum of six months working. She still hadn't decided what work she wanted to do, but she needed to make up her mind soon. Money wouldn't last forever.

She continued walking, the cold and damp path making her shiver. But seeing the sun creeping through the branches made her smile. Spring was making her feel alive again, as if something dormant was now waking up inside her, trying to emerge from its shell and find some sun.

Her mum had changed, she thought. She was now permanently based in the Scottish Highlands, spending all day in boots and a rain jacket looking for good spots to carry out geology fieldtrips with her students. Alex hadn't seen her that happy in a long time. Her dad had somehow faded in her mind, living a dull life, as if the light in his life had been her mum and now that she was gone his life had turned grey. She was planning to spend some time with him when she returned to

Germany, to see if she could get to know him a bit better. When she talked to him over Skype he seemed to be truly interested in her life for the first time, his attention focused, his questions showing care and warmth.

Medicine was not what it used to be for her. It had been her life for five years. She hadn't been thinking of anything else. She had wanted to save lives, to cure small children and feel good about herself. But in the last two years she had changed. There seemed to be much more to life than just her profession. It was as if a transparent curtain that she didn't know had been in front of her had lifted to show her the light and colours of life. She liked what she saw, and when looking back she could only see grey days. What this meant, she didn't know. But she felt calm, and happy to explore her feelings. It was a new experience that she was enjoying while it lasted.

But today she would just focus on climbing up hill and breathing in and out.

—

Half an hour later the path had become steeper, muddy and full of rocks. She was going round a rocky outcrop and stopped to look down. The steep hill went all the way to the sea. She could see Blueskin Bay, close to where she and Alex had gone for a walk along the stunning Long Beach. On her right the Otago Peninsula extended towards the east, green and bright. She was surrounded by deep greens and dark bright blues, her face golden with the midday sun. A few minutes later, in front of her, she saw the column marking the peak, a large stone indicating all the key locations. She stepped onto a rock and looked down. The city of Dunedin lay below her, camouflaged in the beautiful scenery as if it had always belonged there.

Martha wiped the sweat off her forehead and took off her vest. The light wind welcomed her. And there, looking down to one of the southernmost towns on Earth, she stood fascinated at how far life had taken her. To a place where time seemed to have stopped, where catching your breath was not a sin, where she felt more connected to her soul than she ever had. Martha looked up and closed her eyes. *This feels so good,* she thought, a smile appearing on her face.

—

A few weeks later Martha and Alex were driving south. It was a warm morning, with a light wind moving the branches of the trees. Martha looked sideways at Alex, who was focused on the road, silent. Martha liked living with her. She was like the calm sister she could share things with; the kind of sister she wished Beth had been. Alex had been silent for a few days.

'Are you okay?' Martha asked.

'Yes.' Alex jumped slightly in her seat. 'Why are you asking?'

'Well, you're clenching the wheel as if you were fighting against an imaginary dragon.'

Alex smiled. 'Yes, you could say so.'

'Do you want to share with me?'

'Er…no. That will happen in its own time.'

'OK,' Martha said. 'You know what? I like it here. The South Island has an air of peace, of relinquishing the need to rush, to compete, to fight.'

'That's a nice way to express it,' Alex said. 'Yes. I didn't know I was rushing around in Wellington until I moved to Dunedin. There's something in the southern air that makes you stop, recover and start over again with what you always wanted to do in your life.'

'Exactly. That's how I feel now.'

'And has that brought you to any conclusion?'

'Maybe. I'm working on it. But you'll be the first to know.'

'That's nice,' Alex said. 'But whatever happens, I've enjoyed spending this time with you, Martha. Even though we haven't seen each other much, over the years you've always been part of my life, and the fact that our mothers were so close has made me feel as if you're family.'

Martha squeezed Alex's shoulder. 'Thank you. That means a lot to me. And I feel the same too. I feel like you're more like my sister than my own.'

'How is Beth?'

'Active. Crazy. Impossible to have a proper conversation with. She seems to be rushing to get to a destination only she can see. I can't keep up with her changes. But I love her anyway,' Martha said with a smile.

An hour later Martha and Alex were walking along the strip of land towards the lighthouse at Nugget Point. Apart from a young Chinese couple they were on their own. The wind was gusting, Alex's long hair moving in all directions.

'I thought you said it would be calm here,' Martha said.

'Well, as calm as it can be. It's never calm at Nugget Point. It's usually the windiest point in New Zealand. But it's worth the view.'

The flaxes around them were banging against the wooden fence, the seagulls making impossible turns in the air above them.

The white lighthouse stood in front of them, majestic in the midday sun, pointing towards the infinite sea.

'Wow,' Martha said. She wondered what lay beyond.

'Antarctica is about five thousand kilometres that way.' Alex pointed in front of them.

They stood in silence for a while, Martha holding the rail with cold hands. Alex hugged herself inside her feather jacket.

'Would you be OK if I stayed with you for a little longer?' Martha asked, her face still focused on the ocean.

'Of course! What are your plans?'

Martha looked at Alex. Her lips were trembling. 'Well, the point is, I can't be a doctor anymore. I thought taking care of sick children was my destiny. But I can't stand their suffering. I had always imagined myself talking to them after having done surgery, giving them lollies.'

'That's nice.'

'Yes,' Martha said. 'But it was the wrong career.' She looked at Alex now. 'I don't want to be a doctor, Alex. I want to be a coach for children.'

'Oh.'

'There's a great life coaching academy in Christchurch, and I'd like to take a few courses there. And if everything goes well, I'd like to work as a life coach for children here in Dunedin. In a smaller city, where maybe there are no other life coaches who can help them.' She looked at the sea. 'I need to do this. I want to be present for all the small children who are suffering. From their parents divorcing. From moving to a different city and struggling to make friends. From bullying. I want them to have a space where they can talk and be listened to, accepted, valued.'

Alex stood still. She squeezed Martha's arm. 'I would have loved to have someone to talk to when Mum and Dad split. Even though I was only four, my world crumbled and I had no way to express how I felt.' She looked at Martha. 'You're such a sweet person, Martha. Thank you for choosing to give love to the ones who need it.'

Martha threw herself in her friend's arms, all the fear and frustration from the last few weeks crumbling with her sobs.

After a few minutes she looked up at Alex. 'Thank you.'

Alex smiled. 'Thank you, Martha,' she said. 'You've helped me make a big decision in my life too.'

'What's that?'

'Well…' Alex looked at the sea. 'I've been thinking of my dad lately. He looks fragile. Mum's death has affected him on a deeper level, despite the fact that they'd been separated for so long. I'd like to go on a trip with him. Just the two of us. Get to know each other better.'

Martha smiled. 'That's a great idea, Alex. You're giving him a chance, and with that you're getting rid of anger and making peace with the past, helping the girl within you who is still in pain.'

'You're already a great life coach. Do you know that?' Alex said with a smile.

Martha smiled back. 'Where would you go?'

'To the Cook Islands,' Alex said. 'I always wanted to see them. And I need a change of scenery. My boss said the other day that it was time for me to take a long break. So I might do just that and take a couple of weeks next month. Well, if Dad agrees, of course.'

'He will,' Martha said. 'Something tells me he would love to go with you.' Martha hooked her arm through Alex's and they turned to walk back.

'What about getting a hot chocolate?' Alex asked.

'I'd love to,' Martha said.

CHAPTER 33

A Letter from the Past

Alex

Dunedin, New Zealand, February 2024

Alex was sitting on her sofa reading. She looked outside. It had been overcast all morning, but now she could see the blue sky, and the sun was shining. Maybe she should go for a walk. She got up, walked towards the kitchen and made a mug of tea. She was thinking that maybe a dog would help her get out more often. *It definitely helped Tom after Mum died,* she thought. She had been thinking of him lately. Maybe she should go and pay him a visit.

Martha was away. She had met some people through her studies, and they had gone tramping in Fiordland for the long weekend. She looked around the house. Martha had left some clothes neatly folded on a chair in the living room. There was a psychology book on the coffee table. Alex missed her quiet presence.

The trip to the Cook Islands with her dad had been a great idea. Even though she would never feel as connected to him as to her mum, Alex felt they had taken the first step towards a closer relationship.

She sat on the sofa sipping her tea, looking at the clouds pass by.

There was a knock on the door. With a sigh, Alex stood up and went to answer it.

A smiling Tom was outside, a large bag at his feet.

'Hello, darling,' he said, opening his arms.

'Tom!' Alex embraced him. He smelt of flowers and the strong scent of his perfume. It reminded Alex of nice walks along the beach in warm Golden Bay.

'How nice to see you!'

'Are you not surprised?'

'Maybe not,' Alex said. 'I've been thinking about you lately.'

'That's nice. It makes me feel like we're still connected.'

'Yes, we are.' Alex smiled. Would you like to come in?'

'Yes. Er…' He hesitated at the door step. 'Are you OK if I stay for a couple of nights? Sylvia has a new partner, and I don't want to impose.'

'That's so considerate, Tom. Yes, of course you can stay for as long as you'd like. Martha is away for a few days, so you can use her room. I am sure she won't mind.'

'Thank you,' he said as he stepped inside.

Half an hour later they were comfortably seated, mugs in their hands and some biscuits on the table. Tom was quiet, looking out the window.

'There's another reason you've come to see me,' Alex said.

Tom looked at her. 'You've become very perceptive in the last few years, you know.'

'Yes, maybe I have.'

'There's something I've been thinking for a while, and I wanted to check it with you.'

'Why me?'

'Because it's concerning your mum's house in Golden Bay.'

'Oh. It's your house now, Tom.'

'Well, only unofficially. It'll be your house one day.'

'I'm not sure I'll ever live there. I don't really know what life will bring.'

'Does Dunedin feel temporary?'

Alex raised her shoulders. 'I don't know.'

'Well … for a long time I've been thinking about your mum's dilemma, being from overseas and having lived here for so long. How she used to say that she would make friends only to lose them again when they went back overseas, and how she wished she could keep her friends from here and there.' He looked up at Alex. 'I'd like to turn her home into a place where people from overseas can come and connect with each other.'

'Like a retreat?'

'Not quite. More like a club, where people can connect, talk about their own culture, cook food from their country, sing songs… Maybe I could arrange a weekly meeting for anyone that would like to join. But it's more than that.' His eyes were shining. 'I'd like them to access life coaching services, to have books to read in their own language. I've been talking to a few artists in the area, and two of them are going to create sculptures of each country represented. I'm also in contact with several associations across the country to get donated books in German, Spanish, Italian, French.'

'Oh.'

'It won't be for tourists. This is for the people who feel nostalgic, disconnected. To give them a safe space to talk about how they feel, how they miss their families and friends, a place to share their feelings.'

Alex was quiet, tears rolling down her face. Tom moved closer to her on the sofa and put an arm around her shoulders.

'Sorry, darling. I got carried away. This is probably too much for you to take in.'

Alex looked at him. 'No, it's not. I think it's brilliant. Mum would have loved it. I'll help you. I could take some time off work and rearrange the house to make it work.'

'Really?'

'Yes.'

'That's wonderful, Alex!' Tom embraced her. Alex closed her eyes. It felt good to share such a lovely plan.

'Well, what about we go for a walk?' Tom said after a while. 'It's such a sunny afternoon.'

'Yes, let's go.'

They took their mugs to the sink, put on their shoes and left the house.

—

The beach was bright, endlessly stretching towards the far-away sea, the crushing waves the only noise they could hear.

'I love this beach,' Tom said. 'So far away from any other, so wild.'

'Yes,' Alex said. She had only been here once. Allan's Beach was tucked at the end of the Otago Peninsula, and getting there took quite an effort. Few people ventured this far.

There was a man running towards them, a black labrador following.

The soft wind swirled Alex's long hair. Her arms felt warm under the sun. She looked up at the sky, smiling.

Tom was looking at her. 'You look like your mum,' he said softly.

Alex opened her eyes. 'I miss her.'

'I know. I miss her too.' Tom looked towards the sea, deep in thought. After a few minutes he turned towards Alex. He took something from his pocket – a white envelope folded in two. 'This is the second reason I wanted to see you alone. I was tidying up your mum's desk the other day, and I found this letter at the bottom of a drawer. It's for you.' He gave it to Alex.

The envelope was sealed. Her mum's neat handwriting had been faded by time. *To Alex, 27th October 2020.*

'Oh,' Alex said, her hands trembling.

'I'm not sure why she didn't give it to you then.'

'Did she…?'

'Yes,' Tom looked at her, a serious face on his face. 'She knew about her illness then.'

'Oh.' Alex touched her chest. It felt as if she had swollen a stone.

'Do you want me to leave you alone?'

'No,' Alex said. 'I'd like you to be here while I open it.'

'Ok,' Tom said, a half-smile on his face.

They sat far away from the water. With trembling hands, Alex opened her mum's letter, written a lifetime ago.

My dear Alex,

You are my little girl, no matter how old you are.

You have started university, and are so enthusiastic about your future! I love seeing you like that.

Yesterday I got my fifth reply letter from a publisher about my novel. They loved it, and are planning to publish it next year. Can you believe it? It's taken me five tries and so many sleepless nights. Sometimes I wondered what I was doing, in my mid-forties trying to make a dream come true. It's been so bloody hard! But at the same time it's so worth it: having a dream of your own, something only you see clearly, something to follow no matter what others say.

I know what you think, darling. You've told me several times, in different ways: you think you've been an obstacle in my life. You think I could have achieved all this earlier if I hadn't had you. And maybe I would have. But it wouldn't have been the special life I've lived with you. If I could start all over again, I would do exactly the same. I would have moved to New Zealand, I would have met your father, I would have had you, then got divorced and lived with you as a single mum. And you know why? Because life is not so much about the successes. It's the small details that make life worth living: when you looked at me and said 'Mum' for the first time, your fist gripping my finger. When you learnt how to ride your bike without the training wheels, your face full of determination, fear and pride all at the same time. When you cried in my arms when your best friend moved to Australia in Class 9. The great majority of my best memories from the last nineteen years are about you, my dearest girl.

I am dying, my love. A brutal cancer will take me soon. I'm still not prepared to tell you, but I know I need to soon. I am at peace. I have had time to prepare, and to go through my life and see that, despite all its ups and downs and all my mistakes, I've done a few things well. I've learnt to follow my intuition, to say 'no' when I mean it. I've found a lovely man who loves me the way I am, impatient, lost, confused, funny (I've learnt lately that I can be funny!), loving, caring. And I have become the person I was meant to be. One who expresses her soul on a piece of paper. One who helps others find their true selves.

And I haven't achieved all this because you're now grown up and I have time. I've only been able to achieve this because of the life I have lived and the lessons I have learnt.

Motherhood is a beautiful gift, my darling. Sometimes it's bloody hard. Sometimes you wish you were somewhere else. But it's the moments the sun shines through my soul that matter, and to be able to value those and forget about the others. I have become a writer because I had you, not despite of it. Because I have learnt to be a bit more patient (only a bit!), I have learnt to love unconditionally, and to know what I like in life. And I have learnt all of this thanks to sharing my life with you, thanks to learning from you each day how to be kind, how to do silly things when you feel like them, how to sit down quietly on a sofa, reading a book with you, watching a film with a bowl of popcorn on our laps.

Motherhood makes women resilient. It teaches you to prioritise what is really important in life. And in the end, it shows you how to love and respect yourself like nothing else in life.

With trembling hands, Alex folded the letter. She covered her face. Her shoulders began to shake uncontrollably. Before she knew it, she heard screams coming from far away, pinching her ears to her core. Tom embraced her, holding her so tight her ribs hurt. She pulled his shirt.

"Why? Why?"

The breeze picked up, pulling at her hair. Why hadn't her mum given this letter to her before she died?

Half an hour later she was lying on Tom's lap. Her throat ached, as if she had eaten a thousand needles. The waves in front of her were calm, inviting.

Alex stood up and took off her leggings and t-shirt, revealing a red and white swimsuit. She walked towards the sea, letting herself sway by the waves. She swam fast into the ocean, fighting against the waves, her face full of foam and tears. Slowly, a sense of peace overcame her, relaxing her muscles one at a time. And then she raised her arms. Swirling around, her arms shining in the bright sun, she laughed until her throat ached. Before she noticed, Tom was next to her, splashing her, laughing with her, under the bright sun of Dunedin's summer.

Afterword

Sofia

Kahurangi Ranges, Golden Bay, New Zealand, December 2024

Sofia stood on a flat rock above the cliff. It was windy. A dark cloud in front of her warned of a storm, and she knew how fast they could move in. She needed to be quick.

She took the paper packet from her backpack and undid the cord around it. A five hundred-page novel, co-written with her sister Cora.

It hadn't been easy. She had been stuck for months. Peter would just look at her and know when she needed a break. They had been doing a lot of tramping. In Fiordland in the south, down the Whanganui River in the North Island on a canoe like traditional Māori people, and lots of walks in the bush in unnamed places that had melted her heart. She had somehow managed to go through it all and find the words inside her heart.

Peter had read it. *This will take you far*, he had said. *You can start a career as a writer.* Yes, she wanted to, and she would. But she needed to share it with Cora the best way she knew how. The novel was at the printer's now. They said it would be published in around three months.

She took a letter from the backpack with her sister's name on it. She knew its contents by heart.

Cora, I've made it. I've fulfilled your request. It hasn't been easy. At times I've hated you for it. But I kept going. I had support. From Peter, whom I wish you had met. He loves me for who I am, and I am happy. From Tom, that wonderful man who loved you to pieces. From Alex, who misses you terribly. And in the process, I have rediscovered my passion for writing. Thank you, dear sister. I love you.

But this hard copy was too personal to share. It was an extended version, into which she had poured her soul, as well as a few poems of her own; a version in which she added letters to her sister, camouflaged in the story. It was not for the world to read. This was for Cora, and for the scared woman she had been in her twenties and thirties. This was for the little Sofia who had been lost in the forest. It was a book of hope. Of all the 'could have been' moments that never were. All the ones that looked better than her current life, but somehow lacked something. Cora had chosen her own life, with all its flaws and failures, and had forged her own path and found fulfilment, no matter how brief. Sofia had found the courage to do the same through the book; to find lives that looked better than her own but somehow weren't. Where she had been more courageous, living a life of adventure just to realise in the end how meaningless it had been. She had needed to walk this path to get to where she really wanted to be, and no one else needed to know this but her.

She and Peter had decided to move permanently to New Zealand. They loved the little cottage they had rented near Hokitika on the West Coast. They had made an offer to the owner to buy it and she had accepted. They were thrilled. Small but warm and comfortable, with a garden where Sofia had started to grow her own vegetables, it was all they needed. On cold or stormy days they would sit on the sofa and watch the magnificent ocean with its wild waves crushing against the white sandy beach. They had very friendly neighbours. A young couple with two little girls, and an artist in her late fifties who painted the most stunning sunsets.

During the last months of writing the novel, Sofia had found a peace within herself that she never thought she could find. It was as if the storm inside her had disappeared to leave a bright and warm sun with soothing waves. But she had been feeling restless in the last few weeks. Now that she had finished the book, the need to return to the Scottish Highlands was pulling her. She felt the need to breathe the heather in autumn, see the mountains in purple and green. Watch the waterfalls with golden water that you could only see there. But it was more than that. She had been thinking about her dad and his mysterious time in Scotland, and she needed to find out more. A book had formed in her head. And the research for it would give her the clues she had been wondering about since her first visit to that beautiful country. She somehow needed to understand why her dad had been in Scotland; find out if she could track some of his friends from the time he was there. She wanted to know what had drawn him to that country, and if there was any family connection to it. She smiled, thinking that those were the kind of books she would love to write: the ones that filled her with a glow of hope and light, the ones where she discovered something personal and put it on paper. She had the feeling that the quest into her dad's past would help her find what she needed to move on with the new life she had chosen. She knew it would be inspiring for others at a crossroads in their lives, to help them find their way; their courage to look inside and follow their dreams. Yes. That is what she really wanted: to help others find their own truth. To work through their dramas and fears and find the courage to be themselves. No more. But no less.

She had shared her feelings with Peter. As usual, he had managed to surprise her by fully understanding her need; in fact, he had almost anticipated it. They had decided to go to Scotland for six months the following April and spend the summer there. Irene had managed to find a lovely cottage for them to rent, next to a lake west of Inverness. It was as if life had suddenly opened the path for her, decorating it with flowers; a shiny path of hope and dreams ahead of her.

With a sigh, she looked down at the manuscript in her lap. She wondered what Cora would have thought of it. There were certainly flaws. Lack of detail in the characters' descriptions. The faulty grammar of a non-native English speaker. Peter had helped her with that, and the editor did the rest. But Sofia hoped that beneath all this, Cora would have appreciated the love and care she had put into it, with all the 'what ifs' she had imagined for both their lives. She wished her sister was there with her. She would have loved to see how much she had changed in the last years. She closed her eyes. *Thank you, big sis, for knowing me so well and giving me the best last gift. I love you.*

With trembling hands, she opened the paper wrapping. The stack of papers perched on the edge of the cliff, bright in the sun. A gust of wind came by, taking the first sheets away. They swirled in an upwards spiral, dancing. Sofia, calm and at peace, watched her parallel lives take wing and fly. No more regrets in her life. Those were flying too, never to return.

'Goodbye, dear lives. I have enjoyed dreaming about you,' she said. 'But now I set you free. I don't need you anymore. I have the life that I want.' And without waiting for the whole stack to disappear in the wind, Sofia walked down the path, heading towards her future.

THE END

Acknowledgments

I love reading, ever since I was a little girl. And it always fascinated me to read how many people are included in the books' acknowledgments, as if the production of a book was like a movie, with the director, the producers, dressmakers, photographers, and so many more to thank, in addition to the actors and actresses. Had I known this book would have taken so much effort to come to light, I am not sure I would have had the courage to keep going, from the first years of passion, then determination, to the moment when the manuscript went out to the world seeking to be ready to publish. And here I am, like many authors before me, thanking a whole team of wonderful people without whom this book would have never come to light.

First, to my wonderful editor and amazing author, Patricia Bell, for her attention to detail, her believe in my project and her wonderful advice. I couldn't have had a better ally.

To Rosetta Allan, my manuscript assessor, whose enthusiasm about my book and advice significantly improved my manuscript. Thank you for believing in my vision.

To Holly Dunn, for designing such a beautiful cover design for me. It has been wonderful working with you.

To Suzanne North, Janice Charles and the team at CopyPress, for believing in my project from the start, and for the kind way they have led the publication of my book, delivered in such high-quality standards.

To my wonderful publicist Karen McKenzie from LightHousePR, for her enthusiasm and faith in me as a first-time author, and for leading the best marketing process I could have dreamed of.

To Georgia Gibbons from SideKit, for the newsletter template for my author's page, and to Stephen Martin from Virtual Innovation, for the fantastic author's website design. For their enthusiasm and belief in my vision.

To my amazing writing teachers, Helen Brain and Alex Smith, from the New Zealand Writers College. For their encouragement and support, and for believing in me before I did.

To my three beta readers. My dearest friend Natalia Deligne, whom I miss having closer, for believing in me and for her support and encouragement from the very start. For being the first one to read it and provide the best feedback I could have ever had, full of enthusiasm and attention to detail. To my dear friend Kath McCulloch, who is like a second mother to me, for being so enthusiastic about this book and for believing in me. For the wonderful chats, for being my tramping mate and showing me the secret jewels of New Zealand Nature. And to Marianne Jenner, for her enthusiasm and encouraging feedback.

I hope I have shown in this book my love for bookshops around the World. I'd like to thank the two that specifically appear here: Schrödinger's Books, in Petone (New Zealand), where Cora works, a bookshop where each book has been chosen with thought and care and where I love to spend time searching for jewels; and Leakey's bookshop in Inverness (Scotland), where Sofia and Irene find the photo of Cora and Sofia's dad, a true refuge for book lovers. I loved this place from the first time I came in. It captures the essence of a space to spend hours on end and let your imagination fly.

This book is a lot about opening up and showing your vulnerability. I'd like to thank the people who most recently have been there to support me when I needed it. For their warmth, immense wisdom and faith in me: Josh Roche, Billee White and Alba Reina. And a special thanks to Malcolm Wilson, for his warmth, care, wisdom and immense compassion towards me and my family when we most needed it.

This book is so much about friendships, in Cora's mother country and in her new home, New Zealand. Like Cora, I wouldn't be able to keep going without the wonderful support of my amazing group of friends. To my tribe in Spain: Almudena Gomis Moreno ("mi Almu"), the best friend I could have ever dreamed of, who, despite the distance, I feel closer to than ever; José Fernández Petrement, "my soulmate", for knowing without words and supporting me throughout my life; to Adrián Ávila Sánchez and Rudi Esteban Ferreiro, "my brothers"; to Miguel Parra Arrabal, and to my University friends, who help me recover myself when I feel lost. You mean so much to me: Almudena Gomis Moreno, Juan Luis Valera Rubio, Mari Carmen Rico García, Cristina Díaz López, Joaquin López Herraiz, Juan Matos Lafuente, Jesús Damián Lozano Ruiz, Jesús Enrique López, Manuel Lueiro Valencia, Carmen del Fresno Rodríguez-Portugal, Daniel García and Beatriz Gaite, and their families, and Paco Sánchez in Scotland, who followed his dream and I am so proud of. I love you all and I miss you. To my New Zealand tribe: Natalia Deligne, Melanie Hutton (my "big sister") and Daniel Harrison, Miko and Petra Fohrmann, Todd Ventura and Ariane Savi, Kath McCulloch and Zaytoon Noorbhai. Even though some live overseas now, they are lifelong friends. You have all made me feel so welcome in this beautiful country and given me so much.

To my family: my mother, Isabel Millán Martínez, who showed me the passion for books. I love you, mum! For my sisters Lara and Sandra Goded Millán, whom I love to pieces, for their support despite the distance, and for the lovely bonding and closeness we still have. To my beautiful nieces Ginevra and Eleonore, and my new brother-in-law Leo. To my co-parenting partner, Karsten Kröger, who encouraged me to write a short story and take part in a competition that was the ignition to writing again, and for all that we have shared.

And most of all, to my daughter Katrin Isabel Kröger Goded, without whom I wouldn't have found the inspiration and determination to be true to myself and pursue my dreams. For giving me each day the strength to be a better person and the joy to live a life of abundance and fulfilment. I love you!

About the Author

Born in Madrid (Spain) and trained as a scientist, Tatiana's passion for writing goes back for as long as she remembers. Writing stories has always been part of her life. Following her move to New Zealand in her mid thirties, she rediscovered her passion for writing stories, and took several courses in creative writing from the New Zealand Writers College.

Tatiana has won the second award of the "1st Letras Latinas short story competition" in 2014 organised by Alac Inc in Auckland, New Zealand, with her story "A trip to Vienna". Tatiana also had two mini short stories, "Farewell" and "If I went there for a second time", published in English and Spanish in 2018 by Letras Latinas Publishing House.

In addition to science, Tatiana has recently started a business as a life coach. In her spare time, Tatiana loves reading as much as she can, spending time with her daughter, catching up with friends, dancing, tramping and travelling.

Tatiana lives in the Wellington region with her daughter and their lovely Golden Retriever.

A Trip Towards the Sunset is her first novel.

To keep up to date with Tatiana's writing, have a look at
https://tatianagoded.com/

9 780473 734091